W9-CFH-123

SEX,
LIES,
and
ONLINE DATING

By Rachel Gibson

RACHEL GIBSON

SEX, LIES, *and* ONLINE DATING

AVON BOOKS

An Imprint of HarperCollinsPublishers

AVON BOOKS
An Imprint of HarperCollins*Publishers*
10 East 53rd Street
New York, New York 10022-5299

ISBN: 0-7394-6480-9

This book is dedicated
with much love to Cathie Wilson,
friend, writer, and quirky soul.
Critique/martini night isn't the same
without your laughter.
You will always live in my heart.

Acknowledgments

I would like to express my gratitude to Homicide Detective Danny R. Smith for his help in the writing of this book. A twenty-one-year veteran of the Los Angeles County's Sheriff's Department, Officer Smith's assistance was invaluable and went above and beyond the call of duty. Any mistakes are mine, as is any use of creative license. I would also like to thank fellow writer and friend Candis Terry for her answer to my frantic "help me" e-mail. Candis, you really came through.

Prologue

From: Lucy@mysterious.com
To: clare@finis.com; adele@biteme.com;
maddie@crimepays.com
Subject: singles.com date

Hey all,

Tonight is my last Internet coffee date. His name
is hardluvnman. I pray he has his teeth.

Wish me luck,
Lucy

From: clare@finis.com
To: Lucy@mysterious.com; adele@biteme.com;
   maddie@crimepays.com

Lucy,

Good luck with your research. Hopefully he has his own teeth *and* own hair and remembers to brush both.

Clare

From: adele@biteme.com
To: Lucy@mysterious.com; clare@finis.com;
maddie@crimepays.com

Looking forward to hearing all about Lucy's hard-luvnman.

Adele

P.S. What kind of guy calls himself hardluvnman? Is he compensating for something?

From: maddie@crimepays.com
To: adele@biteme.com; Lucy@mysterious.com;
clare@finis.com

Lucy,

For God's sakes don't do it. Serial killers lurk on those online dating sites. It's like shooting fish in a barrel for them. Next thing you know, some guy is wearing your head for a hat.

Love,
Maddie

Chapter 1

Mystrygrl: Seeks Man for Mystery . . .

Lucy Rothschild pulled her BMW into the parking slot closest to the Starbucks entrance and shoved the vehicle into park. Rain pounded the hood of her car and bounced off the asphalt as she turned off the Beemer. Her gaze slid to the front of the strip mall and sought the green-and-white Starbucks sign next to the golden glare of Blockbuster Video. Light from within the coffee shop poured out onto the wet sidewalk, while the raindrops slipping down Lucy's window smeared vivid color and inky shadows like an abstract painting.

Next thing you know, some guy is wearing your head for a hat. Lucy turned off the car and shoved her keys in the pocket of her navy blue Ralph Lauren blazer. She hated when Maddie said things like that. When she made everyone else as paranoid and freaky as she was. Maddie interviewed psychopaths for a living, but that didn't mean all men were child molesters, rapists, or serial killers. Lucy wrote about murder too, but she wrote fiction and was able to separate what she wrote from real life. Maddie seemed to have trouble with that.

Lucy grabbed her umbrella from the passenger seat and opened her car door. It wasn't as if she was going to set up a second meeting with hardluvnman or was even going to leave Starbucks with him. It wasn't even as if she was taking this coffee date any more seriously than she'd taken the others she'd had during the past few months.

She hit the button on her umbrella with her thumb, and the red canopy opened as she stepped from the car. Like the other "dates," tonight was about work. She had her small notepad and pen in her pocket, right next to her little can of mace. She'd brought the pen and paper in case she needed to write down interesting tidbits about hardluvnman after he left. She'd brought the mace in case he wanted to wear her head for a hat.

Damn that Maddie.

Lucy paused briefly to shut the door behind her, then moved across the parking lot, dodging puddles on her way. Unless hardluvnman was different, she wouldn't even use the pen and paper. Unless he was different from the others, while they waited in line for coffee he'd give her the slow up and down, as if she were an Airedale at the Westminster Kennel Club Dog Show. If she passed inspection, he'd pay for her triple grande skinny latte (hold the whip, please), ask her what she did for a living (although she'd clearly lied on her bio, stating she was a nurse), then proceed to talk about himself (what a great guy he was) and his former wife/girlfriend (and what a dumb bee-yatch she was). If Lucy didn't pass the slow up and down, she'd pay for her own coffee. Which had only happened to her once.

Bigdaddy182 had been a real cheap bastard with a silver tooth and a neck-hair ponytail. He'd taken one look at her and said, "You're skinny," as if that had been a bigger abomination than his beer belly. She'd bought her own coffee, then proceeded to listen to him talk about himself for the next hour. While he'd rambled on about his run to Sturgis and his bitch of an ex-wife, Lucy had thought about different ways to kill him off. Bad, heinous ways. In the end, she'd known she'd have to stick to her female serial killer's MO, but erotic asphyxiation had seemed too good a way for him to die.

Two steps from the sidewalk, Lucy planted her foot in a puddle. She'd almost made it. Cold water rushed over the toe of her black ankle boot and splashed the bottom of her black jeans.

"Crap-ola!" she said and stepped up on the curb. She opened the door to Starbucks and moved inside. The smell of rich, dark coffee filled her head, and the low steady hum of voices coalesced with the sound of the coffee grinder and espresso machine. No matter what city Lucy might travel to, Starbucks always looked and smelled the same. Kind of like Barnes and Noble or Border's. There was some comfort in that.

Lucy closed her umbrella, and her gaze took in the gold walls and the patrons sitting at brown tables and hard wooden chairs. No man in a red baseball hat. Hardluvnman was late.

Lucy shoved her umbrella in the stand by the door and moved to the counter. When he'd e-mailed her and asked her to meet him, he'd written that his real name was Quinn. Lucy preferred to think of him as hardluvnman. She didn't want to think of him or any of these dates as real people. It was easier to kill them off that way.

She ordered her latte, sans whip, then took a

seat at a small round table in the corner. She unbuttoned her blazer and smoothed the collar of
her navy blue turtleneck.

She supposed it was a sad commentary on
her love life that the only dates she'd had lately
hadn't even been real dates at all. The only reason she was subjecting herself to men like big-
daddy182 was that she needed research for her
new mystery novel, *dead.com*.

Lucy raised the latte to her lips and took a
cautious sip. She only needed one last victim for
her book. Even if hardluvnman turned out to be
a decent guy who didn't need to die, Lucy was
done with Internet coffee dates. She'd had
enough of men who acted like it was *her* job to
pursue *them*. Like she had to convince *them* to
ask her out again. If this last date didn't prove
fortuitous, she'd figure something else out. Like
taking all the lying, cheating, needy character-
istics of all her former boyfriends and roll them
into one. But she'd done that before, and she
was afraid her readers might catch on to the fact
that the victims in all her books were starting to
resemble the same recycled losers.

No, it was time for new losers. She'd agreed to
meet hardluvnman, as opposed to some of the
other candidates, for several intriguing reasons.
First, his photo on the dating site was so grainy
that it was hard to determine what he actually

looked like. It just gave an overall impression of
a dark, intense broodiness that she found a little
mysterious. Second, in his bio he stated he was
a plumber who owned his own business. Which
could be a lie but was probably the truth because, really, why would anyone lie about being
a plumber? Third, instead of falling into the
thirty-five-to-forty-year-old-never-been-married-
or-divorced categories, hardluvnman had stated
that he was a widower. Which could be the truth
or a sleazy way to score sympathy points and
trick women into bed. If the latter turned out to
be the case, Lucy had her last victim. Voilà!

The front door swung open, and a man with
thinning red hair stepped inside. Lucy recognized him immediately. His name was Mike,
aka klondikemike. He'd been her first coffee
date, and the first murder victim. He moved toward a blonde woman standing next to a dis-
play of mugs, and together they walked to the
counter. Mike did the up-and-down thing with
his eyes and paid for the two cups of coffee and
a bag of chocolate-covered coffee beans. As the
two made their way to a table a few feet from
Lucy, Mike's gaze met hers, then slid guiltily
away. He hadn't e-mailed her again after their
date, but she could have told him not to worry.
She had no interest in a guy who talked non-
stop while popping coffee beans like they were

cross tops, and whom she'd left with a plastic bag over his head in Chapter One.

She brushed the red lipstick on the lip of her cup and glanced about at the other tables. She was surprised the recent murders in Boise hadn't slowed down the dating scene. Surprised but relieved, as it suited her own purposes.

In the past few months, three men had been suffocated in their own homes. She'd actually met one of the victims, Lawrence Craig, aka luvstick, at Moxie Java and was still a little freaked out about it.

The police weren't releasing much information, other than saying that all three deaths had been due to suffocation. They weren't saying what *form* of suffocation, only that the perpetrator was believed to be a woman. The newspaper hadn't stated how or where the killer met her victims; Maddie had speculated that the woman probably met them in bars. Lucy figured she was probably right. The fact that Lucy was writing about erotic asphyxiation and men were being suffocated was a huge coincidence, but there were a lot of different ways to die of suffocation. As many as the human brain could conjure, and the chances of life imitating art were too huge to ponder. And besides, she refused to confuse real life with fiction and become as crazy as Maddie.

By the number of couples in Starbucks, men didn't seem worried about meeting women in coffee bars. Probably because like Lucy, they'd met these women via dating sites and had been exchanging e-mails. And out of all the places to meet, Starbucks was safe.

Before Lucy had decided to online date in the name of research, she'd always thought online dating was . . . well, desperate somehow and more than a little lazy. While Lucy could certainly understand why women sought men online, she could not understand the reverse. Why would any reasonably attractive man, who had a job, his own neatly brushed teeth, and did *not* live with his mother have to search for a date online? Wasn't picking up women in bars and restaurants or even in the vegetable aisle at Albertson's in a man's job description?

A month after her first online date, what she discovered was that the men online—like bigdaddy182 and klondikemike—expected her to pursue them. They also seemed to fall into two categories: those in want of killing, and those so boring she'd wanted to kill herself.

Oh, she was sure that out there somewhere were some great online guys. Nice men who just wanted to meet nice women and didn't meet a lot in their everyday lives, great guys who didn't hang out in bars or veggie aisles.

She just hadn't met any of them. In fact, she hadn't met any great guys, online or otherwise, in a very long time. Her last boyfriend had been a charming alcoholic who'd been off the wagon more than he'd been on. The last time she'd had to bail him out of jail, she'd finally had to admit that her friends were right. She was an issues junkie with rescue fantasies. But not anymore. She was tired of trying to rescue assorted lame asses who didn't appreciate her.

Lucy pushed back the sleeve of her jacket and looked at her watch. Ten after seven. Ten minutes late. She'd give hardluvnman another five, and then she was leaving.

She'd learned her lessons about dysfunctional men. She wanted a nice, normal guy who didn't drink too much, wasn't into extremes of any kind, and didn't have mommy/daddy issues. A man who wasn't a compulsive liar or serial cheater. Who wasn't emotionally retarded or physically repugnant. She didn't think it was too much to ask that he have sufficient verbal skills, either. A mature man who knew that grunting an answer did not pass for conversation.

Lucy took a drink of her coffee as the door to Starbucks swung open. She glanced up from the bottom of her cup to the man filling up the doorway as if he'd been blown in from a "mad, bad and dangerous to know" convention. The bill of his red ball cap was pulled low on his forehead and cast a shadow over his eyes and nose. His tanned cheeks were flushed from the cold, and the ends of his black hair curled up like fish hooks around the edge of the hat. Rain soaked the wide shoulders of his black leather bomber's jacket. The jacket's zipper lay open, and Lucy's gaze slid down a bright strip of white T-shirt to the worn waistband of faded Levi's. As he stood there, his gaze moving from table to table, he shoved his fingers into the front pockets of the worn denim, his thumbs pointing to his button fly.

Mr. hardluvnman had finally arrived.

Like his photo on the Internet site, Lucy could not see him clearly, but she knew the second his gaze focused on her. She could feel it pinning her to her chair. She slowly lowered her cup as he pulled his hands from his pockets and moved toward her. He walked from his hips, all long and lean, with a purpose to each step. He navigated his way through chairs and coffee drinkers but kept his gaze on her until he stood across the small table.

The shadow of his cap rested just above the deep bow of his top lip. He raised a hand and slowly pushed up the brim of his cap with one finger. By degrees, the shadow slid up the bridge of his nose and past thick black brows. He looked down through eyes the color of a smoldering Colombian blend.

Lucy was a writer. She worked with words. She filled each of her books with a hundred thousand of them. But only two words came to mind. *Holy crap!* Not eloquent, but fitting.

"Are you Lucy?"

"Yeah."

"Sorry I'm late," he said. His voice was deep, testosterone rough. "My dog got into the garbage just as I was leaving, and I had to clean up after her."

Which Lucy supposed could be true but, she reminded herself, probably wasn't. Not that it mattered. After tonight, she would never see this hunk of hardluvnman again. Which was kind of too bad, since he was the best-looking thing she'd seen outside of a men's magazine.

"I'm Quinn." He held his hand toward her, and the sides of his jacket fell open across his chest to reveal hard pecs and abs of steel all wrapped up in his tight T-shirt. The kind of pecs and abs that begged the question: Why did a guy like him have to go online to find a date? It didn't take her long to come up with the answer. Inside that hard body, there was something wrong with him. Had to be.

Lucy took his hand, and his warm palm

pressed into hers. Calloused. Strong. The kind that actually might belong to a plumber. She took her hand back and wrapped it around her cup. "Aren't you going to get a coffee?"

"I'm good." As he sat, his dark scrutiny touched her face, her hair, and cheeks, then slid to her mouth. His voice dropped a little lower when he asked, "Are you good?"

Was she good? She blinked several times and asked, "At what?"

He chuckled. "Do you need another coffee?"

"Oh. No. Thanks." She placed her palms flat on the table and slid them into her lap. "I've had too much caffeine." Obviously. She wasn't the sort of woman to get all rattled over a good-looking man. Usually. "That's the problem with these late-night coffee meetings."

"How many of these dates have you been on?"

Dates? "Enough." She tilted her head to the side and concentrated on finding a flaw. Just because she was a bit rattled didn't mean she'd forgotten what this meeting was all about. "How many have you been on?"

"Not many. It's been a long time since I dated, and this whole Internet, chat room, dating stuff is new to me."

There it was. He trolled the chat rooms. She'd been right. There was something wrong with him. Something that hid behind those dark eyes and long black lashes and smooth, masculine voice. "I read in your bio that your wife died. I'm sorry for your loss."

"Thank you." He took off his hat and combed his fingers through the thick black strands of his hair. The ends curled up around his knuckles. "She died six months ago."

Which seemed a relatively short time to seek a replacement, Lucy thought. It could mean he was lonely. Or a callous bastard. "How'd she die?"

"Car accident. It was our tenth wedding anniversary and she'd run to the store for a bottle of champagne. I waited at home with two dozen daisies, but she never returned."

Daisies? Was he a cheap callous bastard?

He laughed uncomfortably and pulled his hat back on his head. "Daisies were her favorite flowers."

Okay, that made her feel a little mean. It was *possible* he was telling the truth. Or it was just as possible he was a scammer. A scammer with a body that scrambled a sensible woman's brain. "You must miss her terribly."

"More than I ever thought possible. She was everything to me." He looked down at the table, and she wasn't able to see the emotion in his dark eyes for the brim of his hat. "Sometimes the pain is so bad . . ." He paused for several heartbeats before he continued, "Sometimes it's hard to breathe."

Oh my God, Lucy thought. She should write this down for Clare. Clare wrote romance novels, and this was heartbreaking stuff. Lucy had to admit that it was even working on her—a hard-core romance cynic.

"She had soft red hair, and it used to fan out across her pillow while she slept. Sometimes I stayed awake just to watch her dream."

Lucy pulled her brows together as Aerosmith played in her head. That was either the loveliest thing she'd ever heard, or he was poaching song lyrics. If the latter was the case, he was really cheesy. "What was her name?"

"Millie. We started dating our senior year in high school."

"You were high school sweethearts?"

"Yeah, but we broke up briefly once because I was a dumb ass." He shrugged his big shoulders, but he didn't look up. "I was twenty-three and thought I needed to date other women. That lasted a month before I realized Millie was everything I would ever want in a woman." He cleared his throat and said as if he were having a difficult time getting the words out, "She was the other half of my soul."

Again, that was either really romantic or really cheesy. Lucy leaned toward cheesy because there had to be something wrong with a guy who was physical perfection yet trolled the chat rooms for a date. Some hidden personality disorder. "Perhaps it's too soon for you to date?"

"No." He looked up, and his brown eyes met hers. "I have to try and get on with my life. I'm not looking to replace my wife, but some nights I just need to get out of the house. Sometimes sitting at home watching *Cold Case Files* with just a dog for company gets old."

He watched *Cold Case Files*? *Cold Case Files* was her favorite show, and if she was forced to miss an episode, she taped it. "*Cold Case Files* on CBS or A&E?"

"A&E. I like the real cases."

"Me too! Did you see it last night?"

"Where they discovered the torso in a gym bag?" He sat back, and the shoulder seams in his jacket popped as he folded his arms across his chest. "Yeah, I saw it."

"They caught some lucky breaks with that one."

Quinn slid down a little in his chair and brought his gaze level with hers. "Science finally caught up with the criminal."

"That's true. Makes you wonder how anyone can get away with anything these days." Lucy took a sip of her coffee and gave up on trying to pick him apart to discover his flaws. Since she would never see him again, it didn't matter really. "But then people do get away with crime every day. They just have to be smart about it."

His thick brows lowered in thought. "Do you think there's such a thing as the perfect crime?"

Did she? In her books, the mystery was always solved by the last page; the perpetrators brought to justice. But was that true in life? "I think if you're smart and do a little research, you could commit the perfect crime. And even if it's not so perfect, you could still get away with it."

He looked at her for several heartbeats, then asked, "How's that?"

"Most criminals are caught because they have to talk about what they've done. Except serial killers. Serial killers get away with their crimes because they don't usually talk about what they've done."

"Why do you think?" he asked.

"Probably because they don't have a conscience. Most people with a conscience tell someone about their crime. It's like a sneeze. It's got to come out to relieve the pressure."

"You don't think serial killers need to relieve the pressure?"

"Sure. But for them, the killing relieves the pressure." Talking crime was one of her favorite pastimes. When she got together with her friends and they talked about writing, it was more about the process. Each wrote in a different genre, so they didn't really get into specifics. Well, except for Maddie. She'd get into the gruesome specifics, usually over lunch, and they'd all have to tell her to stop. It was kinda nice talking murder with someone who didn't look like he was going to get excited about liver temperature.

"Did you catch the show the other night about that woman who poisoned five husbands?" Quinn asked.

"Bonnie Sweet? Yeah, I saw it." Bonnie had been the inspiration for Lucy's fourth book, *Tea By Proxy*. Like Lucy's murdering protagonist, Bonnie had boiled lilies of the valley into a toxic tea and served it in Wedgwood. "That woman just loved to garden." The fact that Lucy was having this conversation on a coffee date might seem strange, but it beat the hell out of listening to him bitch about an ex, talk about his motorcycle, or relive his hunting trip to Alaska. She was never going to see Quinn after she left Starbucks, so what did it matter what they discussed? "You gotta give Bonnie points for style."

Quinn gazed into her eyes as if he were trying to determine whether she was a psycho nutcase or spent too much time alone with her television. The truth was that she was a writer with page upon page of research in her head. Everything from lace to lividity.

He straightened and leaned forward to place his arms on the table. "It takes one coldhearted woman to slowly poison someone she supposedly loves. Or did at one time."

Which was absolutely the truth. Female serial killers were coldhearted bitches. Every last one of them. They were also neater. Smarter. Cleaner and, as far as Lucy was concerned, far more interesting than their male counterparts. "Yes, but that's what makes them ultimately fascinating."

"Fascinating?" He shook his head and laughed without humor. "Thank God there aren't many of those 'fascinating' women around."

"Maybe they are around and we just don't know it?" Lucy smiled and tilted her head to one side. "Maybe female killers are just smarter than men and don't get caught."

"Maybe." His intense gaze stared into hers, and she got the feeling that he was watching for something. For what, she had no idea. Quinn opened his mouth to say more, but a gagging sound caught his attention. Lucy looked to her left at Mike and his blonde date. Mike's hands clutched the sides of the table and his face and neck were turning a deep red.

"Oh my God!" Lucy stood so fast her chair

fell backward. "Klondikemike is choking. Somebody do something."

"Shouldn't you do something?"

She looked at Quinn as he rose also. "Me?"

"Aren't you a nurse?"

Nurse? "What?" Oh crap. That's right. She'd lied about that in her bio. Since no one else seemed to be doing anything, she quickly moved the short distance. She didn't know the Heimlich maneuver, so she did the next best thing: She thumped Mike between the shoulder blades. Nothing happened, and she thumped him harder.

Mike's date screamed. Someone across the coffee shop yelled, "Call 911! A man's choking to death."

The noise inside Starbucks went from a low steady hum to a wave of shouting and scraping chairs.

"Jesus H. Macy," Quinn swore. He grabbed Lucy by the arms, picked her up, and moved her out of the way. He hauled Mike up from behind, and with one abrupt squeeze, a coffee bean flew out and hit Mike's date between her stunned eyes. Mike took a deep, gasping breath. "Thanks," he wheezed.

Quinn nodded. "No problem."

The cacophony of raised voices grew even louder as people crowded around Mike to make sure he was all right. Quinn stood with his weight on one leg and his hands on his hips. A frown pulled at the corners of his lips as he watched the commotion in front of him. The gap between the zipper of his jacket widened across his hard chest, and Lucy thought she heard him mutter something that sounded a lot like "Nurse my ass."

Chapter 2

Dick: Seeks Jane for Fun and Games . . .

Quinn McIntyre shoved his fingers into the front pocket of his Levi's and blew the air out of his lungs. His breath hung in front of his face, and his eyes narrowed as he watched the taillights of Lucy's silver Beemer heading down Fairview. She'd taken her coffee cup with her. Short of wrestling it from her hand, there hadn't been a damn thing he'd been able to do about it, either.

The rain had stopped since he'd entered Starbucks, but inky clouds covered three-quarters of the full moon. Quinn stepped off the curb and headed across the parking lot toward a black Econoline van. Lucy was no more a nurse than he was a plumber, but he'd known that the first time he'd e-mailed her. He'd known all along that her Internet bio was complete crap, and he'd known exactly what she did for a living. By the time he'd met her tonight, he'd known a lot more about her than the color of her eyes and her blonde hair. He'd known her height was five feet seven inches, and that her weight was one thirty. He'd known she'd been born in the hospital downtown and raised in the North End, where she still lived. He'd known that her father had deserted the family when she was eleven and that that could cause a lot of resentment against men. He'd known she was educated and had sold her first mystery novel six years ago. And he'd known that in the last five years she'd received three speeding tickets and two more citations for rolling through stop signs.

What he hadn't known was that her eyes were deeper blue than they were in either her driver's license picture or in the publicity photo on the inside dust jacket of her books. Her hair had shiny streaks of gold, and her lips were much fuller. Walking into Starbucks tonight, he'd known he was going to encounter a striking woman, but he hadn't been prepared for the full feminine assault. From photos, there's no way he could have known that everything about her, from the touch of her soft hand in his to the gentle sound of her voice, was in opposition to a woman who wrote about serial killers and might be one herself.

Quinn walked beneath pools of artificial light, heedless of the puddles splashing his boots. As he approached the van, the window slowly lowered.

"Did you get all that?" he asked as he reached behind him and pulled his T-shirt from the back of his jeans.

"Yeah." Detective Kurt Weber's round face appeared in the window. "Did you get the cup?"

"She took it with her."

"Shit."

"That's what I thought."

"What was all that commotion toward the end?"

"Some guy was choking on a coffee bean." He paused to pull at the transmitter taped to the middle of his back. "I think it's pretty safe to say that Lucy Rothschild not only lied about being a nurse; she doesn't even have a passing knowledge of CPR."

"All that serial killer stuff was interesting," law enforcement technician Anita Landers commented from where she sat in the back of the van beside the receiving equipment.

Quinn had thought so, too. He wouldn't be

surprised if by morning Lucy was the prime suspect in the "Breathless" case, the name they'd given to the woman who met men online and suffocated them in their own homes. An ultrathin wire ran up his side to a tiny flat microphone taped to his right pec. "Shit," he swore as he ripped the microphone from the bare patch on his chest.

"What was your first reaction to her?" Anita asked.

Quinn handed the transmitter through the window and glanced past Kurt to Anita's dark outline in the back of the van. The second he'd spotted Lucy sitting across the crowded café, his first reaction had been purely male and purely physical. The kind of reaction a man got when he focused on a beautiful woman. The kind that reminded him how long it had been since he'd had sex. "When I first sat down with her, I thought she was picking me apart, looking for flaws."

"Maybe she was picking you for her next victim," Anita suggested.

He'd thought of that too. "Yeah, maybe." As hardluvnman, he'd been on seven online, five chat room, and three personal ad dates in the past two weeks. Kurt, aka hounddog, had been on about the same number while Quinn had sat in the Econoline, listening to every word. The two detectives' active caseloads had been shifted around so they could devote most of their time to this case.

Lucy had been Quinn's second coffee date that evening, and he was exhausted from trying to remember which lines to feed which woman. "I'll see you two tomorrow," he said as he zipped up his jacket. By morning, the Lucy Rothschild tape would be analyzed just like all the others. There was no point in standing around, freezing his ass off and talking it to death.

He moved to the silver Jeep parked a few slots from the van and opened the door.

"Hey, McIntyre," Kurt called out to him as he fired up the Econoline.

Quinn looked over the roof of the Jeep. "Yeah?"

"Is that Lucy woman as hot in person as she is in her photos?"

"She's better looking in person." Which didn't eliminate the possibility that she could be a killer, but it did bring up some interesting questions. Like why would a woman who looked like Lucy and made the kind of money she did seek men online?

"That ought to make your job easier."

Getting distracted by a pair of blue eyes and soft red lips did not make his job easier. No, it would be easier if Breathless turned out to be his first date of the night, Maureen. But even as he thought it, he recoiled. "See ya in the morning," Quinn said as he got in the Jeep and shut the door.

Maureen Dempsey, aka bignsassy, was one of the stupidest females he'd ever met. She'd rattled on about her scrapbooks and doll collection as if he'd truly given a shit. She'd kept calling him "Quint" and had topped it off by telling him that she'd read "somewhere" that aliens had landed in the Sawtooth Wilderness Area just outside of Sun Valley and were impersonating humans. Thinking she'd surely been joking, he'd made a joke and managed a laugh. She'd been serious, and he'd felt his IQ drop ten points just sitting across from her. But the truly funny thing was, Maureen worked for the state at the Idaho Industrial Commission.

He fired up the Jeep and headed out of the parking lot. A cold blast of air hit his chest from the vents. The heat hadn't kicked on yet, so he turned off the vents. His fingers fiddled with the radio, then he turned it off, too. Within two minutes of meeting Maureen, Quinn had pretty much mentally crossed her off the suspect list. It didn't matter to him that she held a regular job. Plenty of stupid people worked for the government, but a woman who was capable of killing three men without leaving a trace of herself behind wouldn't honestly believe space aliens were living in northern Idaho. Quinn tended to agree with the FBI profiler's report that Breathless was highly organized and had above average intelligence. Quinn just didn't believe Maureen's stupidity was an act. No one was that good an actress.

According to the criminal profile, Breathless was between the ages of thirty-two and forty-eight. Because of the lack of physical evidence, the profiler believed she had knowledge of forensics and police procedure. She had an interest in criminal investigations and believed she was smarter than the police. She wouldn't be caught by conventional methods and could probably pass a polygraph and withstand an interrogation without breaking down.

After reading the report, everyone in the department agreed that the best way to catch a predator like Breathless was with bait. Man bait. While Quinn could see the wisdom of the plan, he didn't like it. He had a bad feeling he was going to have to take things really far before they had enough evidence for an arrest. He wasn't afraid he'd be another victim. No, he wasn't thrilled about the thought of dangling his Schwanz in front of a psycho.

Quinn turned off Fairview and merged onto

the connector. Streetlights lit up the section of highway leading into downtown like a white ribbon. He tried the heater once more, and warm air blasted through the vents as he headed toward Broadway and home.

All of the women the detectives had set up these past two weeks had several things in common that had landed them on the suspect list. They were all dating online and had been contacted by all three of the victims within days of their deaths. They all used the same chain of dry cleaners, and they all lived alone.

All three male victims had had several things in common that had landed them on the perpetrator's list. All had been actively dating, as if they'd been on some mission from God. All had had a long list of women they'd been juggling, going on as many as five or six dates in a week—usually with different women, whom they'd met through online dating services, chat rooms, and personal ads. Judging by the number of books they'd charged at Barnes and Noble, Borders, and Hastings Books and Music, they'd been voracious readers. The first victim had been divorced, the second a widower, and the third married but posing as a widower. All three had died handcuffed to their beds.

The first victim, Charles Wilson, aka chuckles, had been found in his home off Overland, hands secured with flexi-cuffs and a Westco dry cleaner's garment bag over his head. The case had been classified a homicide, but to what degree had been uncertain. Considering the presentation of the body, it appeared the victim had been playing a fatal game of erotic asphyxiation with a rather kinky participant. The perpetrator had fled the scene leaving little evidence behind, and it was Quinn's job to determine if the kink had accidently gone bad or the death had been premeditated.

They'd interviewed Mr. Wilson's family and friends, who'd all claimed that he hadn't been seriously dating anyone for over a year. His former wife had remarried and lived out of state. Quinn had combed through his credit card receipts and his telephone records. He'd just about eliminated everyone Charles had been in contact with by phone or e-mail when the second victim had been discovered. Two bodies wasn't coincidence. The men's deaths hadn't been accidental, and by the time the third body turned up, they'd known they had a serial killer on their hands.

Charles Wilson had been murdered a month and a half ago, and if the detectives didn't move fast, there would be a fourth victim.

Soon.

Nobody wanted that. And nobody wanted

the Crimes of Violence detectives to catch a break more than Quinn did. He had no qualms about lying to women, and trapping a killer was part of his job. It had been several years since he'd worked undercover, and there had been times when he'd missed it. No, what he absolutely hated was reciting the mushy lines Kurt had written for him.

Quinn pulled his Jeep into his driveway and cut the headlights as he rolled into the garage. He parked next to his white unmarked police car and turned off the engine. Like always, Millie heard him and was waiting for him when he opened the back door. She was one female who was faithful, if a bit overly affectionate sometimes. He flipped on the light as he walked into the kitchen. Her big brown eyes looked up at him with adoration, and the light shone in her silky red hair.

"Hey girl." She licked his hand, and he went down on one knee. "You're a good dog." He scratched beneath her long ears, and her tongue flopped out of the side of her mouth in ecstasy. Her tail thumped the hardwood floor as Quinn's gaze took in the blinking light on his answering machine and the explosion of feathers scattered about the room.

A frown pulled at his mouth as he stood. Beneath the table were the shredded remains of his pillow. He hadn't been able to take Millie out for a run or to retrieve decoys in a while. She was bored, but at least she'd stayed out of the garbage this time. Not that there was anything in it now.

That was the problem with leaving a two-year-old Irish setter alone for too long a period of time. They tended to find trouble, but at least she'd only shredded his pillow.

He hung his jacket on a kitchen chair, then moved across the kitchen. The last female he'd left alone had been his fiancée, Amanda, and she'd shredded his life. While he'd been out making a living, making the world safe from bad guys, she'd been screwing Shawn, his best buddy since high school.

Quinn pulled an empty garbage can from beneath the sink and carried it across the room. As long as he lived, he didn't think he'd ever forget the afternoon he'd found them naked in his bed. He'd never forget the look on their faces or the accusations spilling from the mouth of a woman he'd loved.

"I'm always alone," Amanda had said as she'd pulled up the bedsheet to cover her bare breasts. "You're always working, and I'm always here by myself."

He'd pointed to Shawn, who'd jumped out of bed and begun pulling on his pants. "You're obviously not always alone." The handle of Quinn's H&K 9mm had pressed into his waist as rage had pounded through his chest with every beat of his heart, clawing at his stomach until he'd thought he might get sick.

"We didn't mean for this to happen," Shawn had said as he'd grabbed his shirt.

"You didn't mean to shove your dick in my fiancée?" In that moment, Quinn had understood the crime of passion; he'd understood the blind fog and consuming fury that made a man lose control and seek vengeance.

"What did you expect?" Two pretty little tears had slid from Amanda's eyes even as she'd placed the blame squarely on him. "This is your fault. You're cold and unfeeling."

He'd laughed, a raucous mix of anger and incredulity. "Get the fuck out of my house," he'd said. His hard, flat voice had filled the room as hate and anger had raced through his body. Years of experience and control had curled his hands into fists before he'd been able to do anything stupid. "Both of you." Something in his eyes, or in the tone of his voice, must have shown just how close he'd been to violence, because they'd both grabbed up their clothes and run.

Quinn didn't believe he would have used his pistol on Amanda and Shawn that night, but he couldn't say that if they'd stuck around he wouldn't have beaten Shawn to within an inch of his life just on principle. He doubted it, though, because deep down in the pit of his soul, he knew that there'd been some truth to Amanda's accusation.

He moved aside a kitchen chair and reached for the near empty remains of what had once been his pillow. Millie didn't even bother hanging her head in guilt over the destruction. Instead, she walked through the mess, scattering feathers in her wake. If it hadn't been so wet outside, he would have shut her in her kennel while he cleaned up. "Out," he commanded and pointed to the entryway leading to the living room. Her big brown eyes looked over her shoulder as she slowly left the room. Wasn't it just like a female to try and make him feel guilty for something she'd done?

Quinn tossed the pillow in the garbage, and feathers floated up and stuck to his shirt. It had been a little over a year since he'd found Amanda and Shawn together. He'd heard that the two had married and now had a kid, a mortgage, and an SUV. Living the American dream, while he was still living la vida loca. Him and Millie. And that was perfectly okay with Quinn. There had been a time when he'd thought he could have it all. When he'd thought he could have a wife, a few kids, and a minivan, but some shit just wasn't in the cards. Not for Quinn.

He picked the feathers from his shirt and dropped them into the trash. A lot of the cops he knew were on their second or third marriages, and he'd rather be alone than be part of a sad statistic. He had his job and his dog, his mother, two siblings, and seven nieces. That was enough family for anyone. And when he felt the need for female companionship, he knew where to find it. A lot of women found his badge an aphrodisiac. He wanted sex. They wanted sex with a cop. It worked out for both of them. Most of the time, it was enough.

Quinn stood and moved to a coat closet a few feet away. He pulled out a broom and dustpan and pushed Play on his answering machine. While he chased feathers around with the broom, he listened to a recording from the Sears warranty department, advising him the warranty on his refrigerator was about to expire. The second call was from his mother.

"Erin had her ultrasound today," his mother's voice informed him. Her long sigh filled the kitchen before she continued, "She's having another girl."

Quinn chuckled. Erin was married to Quinn's brother, Donny. The two already had three girls. The latest would bring the total females in

Donny's house to five. Five to one. Poor bastard. He was doomed.

Another long sigh, then, "Of course we're happy. But who will carry on the McIntyre name if Donny keeps having girls?"

Quinn was the oldest McIntyre, followed by his sister, Mary, and then Donny. Between Mary and Donny there were seven granddaughters. Quinn didn't see why he should add any more rowdy children to that mix.

"I ran into Beatrice Garner at Sunday Mass," his mother informed him as he swept feathers into the dustpan. He didn't even have to guess at his mother's point. "Her daughter Vicky works at Dillards. In the children's department. She's single and attends St. Mary's there on State Street."

"Forget it," Quinn said as he picked bits of down and feathers from the crotch and thighs of his jeans. The day he'd transferred from narcotics to violent crimes, his mother had taken a moment to thank God that Quinn had given up chasing dopers and getting shot at by crank dealers, then she'd promptly taken it as her mission in life to see him "settled." Now she was convinced that with the love of a good woman and regular trips to the confessional booth, Quinn would be happy. Whenever he pointed out that the "love of a good woman" had royally screwed him over, his mother countered that Amanda hadn't been a "good woman." Among her many sins, she'd been Presbyterian. He'd given up trying to convince his mother that he liked his life just the way it was and that he was as happy as anyone else on the planet.

Her voice rambled on for a few more moments about Father this and Deacon that before she ran out of steam and the machine clicked off. He shoved the garbage can back beneath the sink and leaned the broom against the counter. He tossed the dustpan on the stove, then grabbed a bottle of Labatt from the refrigerator. Maybe if she worried about her own love life, she wouldn't be so concerned about his. He didn't know how he felt about his mother dating again so soon after his father's death. Although, when he thought about it, it had been three years since his father had dropped dead while pruning his mother's Roses of Sharon.

He picked up his laptop and files from the table where he'd left them earlier and flipped off the lights on his way out of the kitchen. Millie rose and followed at Quinn's heels as he moved into the living room. With his free hand, he grabbed the remote and turned on the ten o'clock news. He sat on his leather couch and set his laptop and files on the glass coffee table in front of him. Millie sat on the floor next to his knee, and he reached over and scratched beneath her long red ear.

Within the dark comfort of the room, light from the television slipped across the beige carpeting and spilled over the coffee table to the toe of one boot. He watched the weather forecast, which called for more rain. So far, the press hadn't reported a lot of details concerning Breathless. All the public knew was that three men had been suffocated in their own beds. The method used to suffocate the victims hadn't been released, nor had the fact that the police believed she was meeting her victims online. The press were cooperating. For now. If one of them thought they were being scooped, that could all change.

The light flickered as the news programming switched to a commercial about insurance. Quinn raised the beer to his lips and watched a gecko dance around on the screen. He'd been a cop for sixteen of his thirty-seven years. The first six of those years he'd spent as a patrol officer before making detective and spending the next six in narcotics. He'd started out eager and naive, thinking he could save the world from drugs and related crime. He'd been raised with a strong moral compass. A clear definition of right and wrong. Good and evil. Black and white. But within a year of hanging out in dive bars and making friends with lowlives, that definition had changed. The line between good and evil had gotten blurred, and black and white had become a constant gray.

The longer he'd worked undercover, the more *he'd* changed. The more he'd changed, the more the unacceptable had become everyday life until one day he'd looked at himself in the mirror and hadn't recognized the man he'd become. What he'd seen had been a man with long hair and a beard. A man with hard and unfeeling eyes. He'd liked what he'd seen.

Narc cops had to think fast, talk smooth, and have balls of steel. They were smart and arrogant and convinced of their invincibility, and Quinn had been one of the best. For six years he'd lived in a world of drugs and violence, and he'd gotten off on the grit and spit and taste of it in his mouth. Bringing down big-time drug dealers had been a huge rush. Out-badassing the baddest badass had been an adrenalin high that had lasted for days. There had been nothing like it. His life and his job had become so intertwined that he hadn't known where one had stopped and the other had begun. The change in him had alarmed and frightened his family, so he'd rarely shown up at family functions, until one day he'd stopped going at all. He'd lived, breathed, and made love to the job. It had become his whole life, and he'd loved every minute of it.

Until it had all come apart.

Quinn took another drink, then lowered the bottle to rest on his thigh. Her name had been Merry, like she should have been happy and cheerful, but there'd never been anything in Merry's life to cheer about. She'd been a nineteen-year-old whore with a habit to support. Her drug of choice had been black tar heroin, but she'd had a falling out with her boyfriend/dealer after he'd raped and beaten the hell out of her one too many times. The first time Quinn had seen Merry, her eyes had been black and blue and swollen shut. The second time, she'd signed on to be Quinn's confidential informant and had introduced him to her dealer and supplied him with information.

For the next eight months, Quinn had done what he did the best. He'd laid on the bullshit, slowly making friends with lowlives. Then he'd gotten a phone call in the middle of the night that had blown him out of the water. Merry's body had been found in a shopping cart in the back of Winco. As he'd stood in a slow, drizzling rain, looking down at her small body and her black chipped fingernail polish, anger had clouded his head and burned a hole in his brain. Eight months of work, down the toilet.

Fuck.

He'd watched a raindrop slide down her forehead and nose. It had dropped on her chin, and something had hit the reset button on the moral compass that had gone horridly off course. A woman was dead, a girl really, and his first thought had been about the job. This time, when he'd looked in the mirror, he hadn't liked the hard, unfeeling bastard looking back at him. He hadn't liked what he'd become.

Merry had been Quinn's CI, and he'd failed her. He'd failed her as a cop, and he'd failed her as a human being. On paper, he'd done everything right. He'd gone strictly by the book, but he should have done more.

In her short life, he'd been just the last man to let her down. Her grandmother had been the only relative to claim her body, and even though he'd failed her in life, there had been something he could do for Merry in death. He'd paid for the funeral, bought the best coffin, and had been one of only a handful to attended the burial. Every year on the anniversary of her murder, he placed pink roses on her headstone. He didn't even know if she'd liked pink.

Merry had died four years ago, and he still carried the guilt of it in his chest. He figured he always would. A constant reminder to be human, and in a job where he saw the worst in people, it kept him from falling into the us-vs-them mental pit once again.

After he'd put on the suit and transferred to the Violent Crimes Division, he'd concentrated on getting pieces of himself back. Of straightening out his warped view of right and wrong. Good and evil. Black and white. He'd thought he'd succeeded. He'd started to think of maybe having a life outside of work. Of having a wife and a child and one of those kiddie backpacks. But Amanda had proved that some things just weren't meant to happen. Not for Quinn. He was resigned to it and was okay.

He raised the beer to his mouth and flipped channels on the remote. Light flashed like a strobe as he took a long drink. Quinn loved working in the violent crimes unit. He got off on collecting random clues, chasing disparate leads, and gathering seemingly unrelated evidence. He loved piecing them together until they made a complete picture and gave the investigation direction. He loved taking violent criminals off the streets. But it wasn't his whole life. He was able to keep perspective and distance. To leave it at the office—except this time. Breathless had to be stopped before she killed again.

Quinn had an inherent talent for stepping back and seeing the bigger picture, but this time there just wasn't anything to see. There were few clues, truly disparate leads, and the unrelated evidence proved to be just that. Unrelated.

This case was keeping him up at night. The who and why of it spinning around in his head without anything ever falling into place. Whoever Breathless was, she was one smart female. And if there was one thing Quinn hated above all else, he hated to be outsmarted by criminals. Female or otherwise.

Which brought his thoughts around to Lucy Rothschild. He was a cop. Trained to read deception in a person's body language—and especially the eyes. But several times during the date he'd caught himself staring at her mouth instead of her eyes. Checking out the curves of her body for reasons that had nothing to do with deception and everything to do with the way her breasts filled out her sweater. And in those moments of distraction, the overriding question in his head had been, what made a woman like Lucy date men online? He could understand why men dated online. Asking out women could be intimidating as hell for some guys. But all a woman had to do was stand around and look good. Smile once in a while to let a guy know she was interested. How hard could it be? Especially for a beautiful woman like Lucy.

There was something wrong with her. Had to be. Something hiding behind those big blue eyes. Something that might point to murder.

The only evidence linking Lucy to the Breathless case was her name on the Westco dry cleaner's customer list, one e-mail sent to her from Charles Wilson, aka chuckles, and one known coffee date with the third victim, Lawrence Craig, aka luvstick. It wasn't much, but then, the police didn't have much to go on at this point in the investigation.

The detectives were methodically eliminating suspects, and they had a lot fewer than when they'd started. Yet each begged the same question: what kind of woman would agree to meet a man who called himself luvstick? The police were betting the same kind of woman who would agree to meet someone who called himself hardluvnman or hounddog.

Chapter 3

Curious: Seeks Persistent Poet . . .

The next morning, Quinn watched his hands in the mirror above his dresser as he slid up the knot of his red-and-blue-striped tie. He lifted his freshly shaved chin and moved the knot back and forth until it fit perfectly within the closed collar of his blue dress shirt. He buttoned the points, then reached for his badge sitting on the dresser. He hooked it on his belt and shoved his pistol in the holster on his right hip. He clipped his extra ammo and cell phone on his left side and tucked a pair of handcuffs into his pants at the small of his back. A navy blue jacket lay on the foot of his bed, and he threaded his arms into the sleeves as he headed down the hallway to the kitchen. He fed Millie, made sure the dog door was unlocked, and drank the last of his coffee. On his way out the door, he grabbed his laptop and files. He jumped into his unmarked Crown Victoria and headed toward the office. As he drove across town, he checked his voice mail and jotted down notes on a pad of paper on the seat next to him. He phoned the district attorney's office regarding a pending court case, and by the time he'd pulled into his parking space, he'd crossed off a number of things on his shit-to-do list.

He made his way to the briefing room set up specifically for the Breathless case and noticed that Lucy Rothschild had been moved up to number one on the marker board, right above Maureen Dempsey. He was the first to arrive, and he set his laptop and files next to the three murder books on the table in front of him.

"We've eliminated Karla Thompson completely," Sergeant Vernon Mitchell said as he walked into the room. "We just confirmed that she was out of town when the second murder took place." A pair of reading glasses was perched on the end of the sergeant's nose, and his white crew cut was cropped so close to his head that he looked almost bald.

Quinn sat and opened one of the murder books. "There's a relief," he muttered. Karla

Thompson aka sweetpea, the woman who'd smelled like a Marlborough cigarette and sounded like the Marlborough man, had grabbed his ass as they'd stood in line for coffee.

Kurt Weber sat next to Quinn and started to laugh. "I thought I was going to have to bust in and rescue you on that one," he said, referring to Quinn's coffee date with Karla a few nights ago.

"Yeah, it was funny as hell," Quinn grumbled. There were women a guy didn't mind grabbing his ass. Then there was Karla.

"That's what you get for being a pretty boy."

"That's what I get for letting you write those stupid mushy e-mails. You made her think I wanted to get naked right then and there." Under normal circumstances, Quinn wouldn't have minded maneuvering a woman out of her clothes. In fact, getting women naked ranked high on his list, but not with some of the women he'd met lately. The thought of seeing Lucy naked held some appeal, but not when every word would be recorded. And yeah, not when she might be psychotic.

"Quinn, you're going to concentrate most of your attention on Lucy Rothschild and Maureen Dempsey until we can either clear or charge them." Sergeant Mitchell pointed to the two photos in front of Quinn.

Quinn looked at the blown-up copies of the

driver's license photos and frowned. Maureen Dempsey, possibly the stupidest woman he'd ever known, and Lucy Rothschild, the woman who wrote about serial killers. He understood why Lucy made the list. She was smart, and if anyone would know how to kill someone and get away with it, it was someone who wrote about it for a living. "I think we can eliminate Maureen. She's as dumb as a box of rocks."

"Could be an act," Kurt pointed out.

Quinn laughed and shook his head. "You heard what she said about those aliens. No one's that good an actress."

"She dated all three victims, and we can't rule her out yet." Sergeant Mitchell flipped open the top murder book to several different photos of all three victims. They all lay spread-eagle on their beds, as if they'd been posed that way, their noodles limp and pathetic, their mouths open and the dry cleaner's bag sucked down their throats. "Maybe Kurt's right. She could be acting, but after listening to the Rothschild tape, I think she's the more promising. She sounds like she might be bragging. Like she knows how to kill three men and get away with it."

Quinn flipped a few pages to pictures of sooty fingerprint dust smearing doorways, nightstands, and telephones.

"Maybe she got tired of just writing about

murder," Kurt added as Quinn flipped another page. Black powder covered three different bathroom sinks, toilets, and shower stalls.

"It's possible she wants to act out what she writes," Quinn conceded.

The technicians had lifted latent prints off the dry cleaner's bags, but all of them matched prints of Westco workers. He flipped past various crime scene photos. Three dead men and no solid physical evidence that linked any one person to all three.

"I'd like to get a look at what she might be working on now." Quinn glanced up at the sergeant. "Maybe we should just pull her in and ask her. All we have to do is catch her in a few lies."

"Not yet. We can't risk her lawyering up." Sergeant Mitchell scratched the back of his neck. "Kurt," he said and pointed a finger at the other detective. "Work on a couple more of those romantic e-mails from hardluvnman and send them to those two women."

Quinn cringed. Kurt read romance novels and watched chick flicks, and he and the sergeant thought Kurt knew what sort of mushy shit women liked to hear. He'd been married for more than twenty years, so perhaps he did. "No more shit about how hot they look in their photos," he warned. "Or that 'looking for a soul mate' crap."

The sergeant chuckled. "Set up dates for a few cocktails this time. Get those women loose. When they e-mail back, let me know." He turned to leave but said over his shoulder, "Oh, and we need to question the people at Westco again."

"Kurt and I planned to do that this afternoon," Quinn said as he watched the sergeant disappear.

An hour later, Kurt finished the "romantic" e-mail. "I just finished this," he said and handed Quinn a copy. "Sergeant Mitchell thinks it looks good. Maybe my best work yet."

Quinn glanced at what Kurt had written, and he felt his brain squeeze. "Jesus H. Macy."

Dressed for work in flannel poodle-print pajamas, Lucy grabbed a mug of coffee and headed for the office. Her slippers made scuffing sounds on the tile floor as she walked from her kitchen and moved up the curved stairs. She sat at her L-shaped desk, kicked off her slippers, and propped her feet up on the side cluttered with research books. Late morning sunlight spilled across her red toenails, a stack of magazines, and a pair of Steelhead tickets she'd been given by the Writer's League. She yawned until tears filled her eyes. After the strong coffee she'd drunk the night before, she'd come home and worked until 3:00 a.m., killing off a character she'd had to invent from past boyfriends. Using Quinn as a template hadn't worked out. Not after he'd saved klondikemike's life.

She raised the mug to her lips and leaned over the arm of her chair to turn on her computer. Not that it mattered really, but Quinn had caught her in a lie. She obviously wasn't a nurse, and she was sure she'd never hear from him again. Which was fine. Yeah, he'd been very nice looking in that dark and intense sort of way that made a girl's chest get tight and tingly, but it hadn't been a real date. She would never seriously date any man who didn't actively pursue her, and more important, she didn't have the time to date anyone. She was on page two hundred of *dead.com* and had to write another two hundred pages in the next month and a half. A demanding deadline alone was enough to drive her to drink. She did not need the distraction of a man to add to the pressure.

While Lucy's e-mail program downloaded her mail, she plugged Maroon 5 into her CD player. She grabbed the small gold-framed glasses out of the case on her desk and placed them on her face so she could see without putting her nose on the screen. The problem with getting older was that she'd inherited her mother's nearsightedness.

Her twenty-pound orange tabby, Mr. Snook-ums, whom she'd also inherited, jumped up onto the desk and scattered papers and maga-zines.

Mr. Snookums had shown up at Lucy's door five years earlier, a skinny stray that she'd nursed back to health and for whom she'd paid more than a thousand dollars in vet bills to save from certain death. Snookums repaid her by be-ing temperamental, totally passive-aggressive, and developing a raging eating disorder. But at night, when she went to bed, he curled up be-side her and purred his own brand of pure love and affection. A continuous rattling that Lucy found very comforting.

Mr. Snookums rubbed his face against her feet, then sat and curled his tail around to his front paws. He stared at her as if he could mes-merize her into adding Meow Mix to his bowl, but he was on a diet and Lucy could not be per-suaded. Instead, she checked out a Betsey John-son velvet coat at Nordstrom.com and the newest collection of handbags on the Kate Spade website. She didn't know which was hot-ter, Betsey's coat, Kate's newest leather shopper, or Adam Levine.

As she and Adam sang about being in love and standing in the pouring rain, she opened her inbox. Up popped fifty-six pieces of spam, three e-mails from her friends, and a joke of the day from her mother. While she deleted the spam, two more e-mails appeared in her reader's mail file. She thought about opening them but didn't. Ninety-nine out of a hundred e-mails she received from readers were perfectly lovely, but she never knew when she would get that one incendiary e-mail capable of ruining her day. The one that questioned her research, comma placement, and her intelligence. Opening reader mail was as risky as going to her post office box. Sometimes there was great stuff in there, and sometimes there were letters from crazy people wanting money or warning her that she was going straight to hell. Which was one of the reasons Lucy only visited her PO box once a month or so.

Just as she was about to exit her e-mail program, something popped into the account she'd set up for responding to online men. Lucy straightened and lowered her feet to the floor. Mr. Snookums jumped in her lap like a twenty-pound bowling ball, and she reached around him to open the e-mail.

From: hardluvnman@hotmail.com
To: n2u@mail.net

Lucy,

I enjoyed talking to you last night while gazing into your sparkling blue eyes. You are very different from the women I've met recently. Smart and intriguing. I have always been a sucker for brains and beauty. Meet me for dinner and let me see if I can turn that spark in your eyes into a flame.

Quinn

Lucy read the e-mail three times and didn't know whether to gag or . . . or be pleased. Which was patently ridiculous. Last night hadn't been a real date, but even if it *had* been real, it had turned into a disaster. So why was he asking her out again?

What was wrong with him?

Mr. Snookums butted his head into her jaw, and she shoved him out of her lap. The cat hit the floor with a heavy thud, and he let out an angry meow. Lucy was going to turn Quinn down, of course, but before she did, she forwarded the e-mail to her friends to get their reactions.

Typical of Clare, she thought Lucy should give Quinn points for at least trying to sound romantic. "He did get the color of your eyes right."

Adele wrote, "What kind of guy writes about sparks and flames? Is he trying too hard?"

Maddie made her opinion known with one short sentence. "Don't engage the freaks."

Lucy laughed and glanced at her calender. Next Saturday, she had to speak at the Women of Mystery readers and writers group, but other than that she was free. She talked to her friends all the time, but she hadn't been out with them for a month. "Let's get together Monday for chimichangas and margaritas," she suggested to her friends, then pushed Send. Next she brought up Quinn's e-mail and clicked Reply.

She didn't have time for a man, especially a hardluvnman who wanted to gaze into her eyes and turn her spark into a flame.

A single votive candle flickered within red jars in the center of each table inside the Red Feather restaurant and lounge. The noise level rose and fell, from the obnoxious laughter of those who'd had a few too many, to the steady murmur of those who hadn't.

Quinn sat at a table with his back to the wall, the entrance and the door to the kitchen within view. He didn't expect trouble. Not tonight, but sizing up his surroundings and zeroing in on the most advantageous spot was so ingrained that it was a part of him, like the way he tied his shoes or brushed his teeth or read a person's demeanor. Within minutes of walking into the lounge, he'd ascertained the lowlives in the place. It didn't matter that some of them wore expensive suits and drank expensive wine. He'd arrested enough of them to know that criminals crossed all social and economic bounds.

Quinn pushed the sleeves of his thick olive green sweater up his forearms and reached for the drink menu propped next to the candle. The flat transformer was once again taped to the small of Quinn's back, just above the waistband of his black trousers. Across the street, Anita sat in the van, with her receiving equipment filtering out background noises, while Kurt waited in the kitchen to snag a glass with legible fingerprints. Tomorrow night, they would repeat the same process with Maureen Dempsey.

The door to the Red Feather Lounge opened, and Quinn lifted his attention from the drink menu. Lucy Rothschild stepped inside looking even better than he remembered. It had taken Kurt two e-mails to coax her into meeting Quinn, but here she was, wrapped up in a black trench coat that tied at the waist and covered her to her knees. She wore red shoes with high heels, and for one brief second, Quinn let himself wonder if she was naked beneath that coat.

She looked right at him, and he stood and moved from behind the corner table. Subdued bar lights shone in the gold hair curling about her shoulders. She walked toward him looking like a centerfold and turning heads. Her hair bounced a little with each graceful step.

Too bad she might be psychotic.

He took the soft hand she offered him. Her fingers were chilled, and he looked down into her face, searching for signs that she was crazy. The kind of crazy that slipped a bag over a man's head while she rode him like Seabiscuit. All he saw was a hint of humor shining in her deep blue eyes.

"You're on time," she said with the same humor curving her red lips. "Your dog didn't get into the trash tonight?"

"No. I put the garbage in the garage before I left."

She let go of his hand and set a small red purse on the table. "I was a little surprised to get your e-mail." She reached for her belt, and Quinn moved behind her.

"The first e-mail? Or the second one, when I had to beg?" The tips of his fingers brushed the smooth skin of her neck as he moved her hair aside and grasped her coat by the collar. She smelled like his mother's garden in spring, and holding her hair was like holding a bit of sunshine. Like . . . he stopped. Good Lord, he was beginning to sound like those sappy e-mails

Kurt sent. Even in his own head. If he wasn't careful, before he knew it he'd be listening to Jewel and writing shitty poetry.

She looked up at him over her shoulder, and her cheek brushed the backs of his fingers. "You didn't beg. You were persistent."

"Whatever you call it, it worked." He let her hair go and held the collar as she shrugged out of the coat. He was in the Red Feather to work the Breathless case, not get sidetracked by how her hair smelled or her smooth cheek. Tonight he was going to listen and watch and seduce information out of her. If that meant he was going to have to seduce the hell out of her in the process, he was only doing his job. At some point in the investigation, he might have to slide his hand to the back of her head and bring her mouth to his. And while he did that, he was going to remember that she was the number one suspect in a criminal investigation. It wasn't personal. It was the job.

"I turned you down the first time because I'm really not dating right now."

He handed the coat to her, and she hung it over the back of a chair. "Why is that?" She wore one of those fuzzy red sweaters made of rabbit or something equally soft. It clung to the tops of her arms, defying gravity and leaving her neck and shoulders bare.

"I'm extremely busy with work," she said as his gaze slid lower, down her spine and over the curve of her behind covered in a black skirt that reached just above the backs of her knees.

He held her chair for her while she sat. "At the hospital?"

She stilled for a fraction of a second, then said, "Yeah."

"Which floor do you work on?" He moved to sit across the small table from her.

Silence as she reached for the drink menu, then, "Maternity. Hmm . . . let's see here. What should I have? Martini or mojito?"

She wasn't all that great a liar. He'd certainly been around better, but not all sociopaths were good liars. Even some of the bad ones still managed to pass a polygraph. But the one thing all of them had in common was a total lack of conscience.

A waitress who didn't even look old enough to serve drinks approached the table. Lucy ordered a mojito, Quinn, a bottle of Becks. While they waited, he sat back in his chair and tilted his head to one side. Time to get busy. "Tell me about yourself."

She leaned forward and rested her forearms on the table. "I'm so dull I'd hate to bore you to death."

"Oh, I doubt you could do that." The candle

in the center of the table flickered, scattering tiny shards of light across her clavicle and bare shoulders. "Tell me about your family."

"There's really not much to tell. My mother and father divorced when I was in the sixth grade. They fought a lot, so it wasn't a big shock when my dad left." She shrugged, and the little right sleeve of her sweater slid down her smooth arm to her elbow. "After that, my mother worked long hours, and I took care of my little brother."

"How old is your brother?"

"He's twenty-four. I'm ten years older than Matt." She raised a hand to push the sweater back up to the edge of her shoulder. "How about you? Brothers? Sisters?"

"I have a younger brother and sister," he answered truthfully. He told her about his seven nieces and how loud holidays were with all those shrieking girls running around. "My father died about three years ago, and my mother's been nagging me to produce a grandson."

"You've had a rough time in the past few years."

Quinn's gaze followed her sweater as it once again slipped down her arm. "How's that?"

"First your dad and then your wife."

Oh yeah. His wife. "Yes," he said and returned his gaze to hers. "I loved Millie very much. She was everything in the world to me, but I need to move on without her. I have to try and get my life back. She'd want that for me." He wondered if the lies about Millie sounded as lame as he thought they did. He wondered if Lucy had worn that sweater to distract him.

"She'd want you to date as many women as you can possibly meet via the Internet?"

Quinn didn't point out that Lucy was meeting men via the Internet. Possibly killing them too. Instead he said, "Millie would want me to do whatever makes me happy."

Lucy pushed her sweater back up. "I imagine a lot of women would want their husbands to pine away for them a little longer than six months."

"Millie is different from a lot of women." If Lucy continued to do battle with her clothes, it was going to be a very long night. Watching her was like watching a slow striptease.

"Don't you mean *was* different?"

"What?" He raised his gaze to hers as desire, hot and unwelcome as hell, twisted and tugged and gave a little kick to the pit of his stomach. The woman looking back at him over the flickering candle might be innocent. Might be a mystery writer and nothing more. A victim of circumstance. Or she might be responsible for the murder of three men.

"You said, 'Millie is different' as if she were still alive," Lucy said.

Shit. He'd let himself get distracted by her sweater. She was sharp, and he was going to have to be even sharper. Which meant he was going to have to pay more attention to doing his job and less attention to the smooth skin of her neck and shoulders. "I meant *was,* of course."

A tiny crease appeared between her brows. "Perhaps it's too soon for you to date."

"No." He shook his head and gave her his best "trust me" smile. One he'd used many times to put murder suspects and drug dealers at ease. "Sometimes I still refer to my father in the present tense, too," he lied as easily as he smiled. "But that doesn't mean I don't know he's gone. Just like I know Millie's gone and she's never coming back. I will always feel the loss of her, but that doesn't mean I have to stand in one place and feel the pain of it every day. For the rest of my life."

Her brow smoothed, and he knew the second she decided to believe him. Yeah, she was smart and very perceptive. If she wasn't a murder suspect, she was just the sort of woman he usually went for. But she was a suspect, and it would be a cold day in hell before a suspect outsmarted Detective Quinn McIntyre. No matter how smart and gorgeous. No matter how hot she was or how hot she made him.

Chapter 4

Skeptic: Seeks Lady in Red . . .

The cocktail waitress returned with their drinks, and Lucy sat back in her chair, the alarm bell in her head fading beneath his charming smile, which she didn't quite trust. He'd used the present tense regarding his wife. Perhaps it had been just an innocent slip as he'd explained. Or maybe he was using the whole widowed thing as a con. Yeah, maybe.

"What are your hobbies?" he asked.

"I really don't have any hobbies," she answered as she reached for her mojito. Or maybe she should believe him. Just because she was telling a few little lies about who she was didn't make him a liar, too. He could be telling the truth and really did want to move on with his life.

"Not one?" he persisted, as if he was really interested in getting to know her and not just making conversation. "There has to be something you do for fun."

Perhaps she was looking for trouble where none existed. Deflecting her guilt onto him. She decided to believe him for now. "I'm not very crafty." She took a drink and let memories of past mojitos fill her head. The sweet rum and mint drink always reminded Lucy of sitting in a cabana somewhere in Mexico. Or sitting on a beach in the Bahamas with her friends. "I can't draw or sew or glue," she added. She took another drink, then told him about the time she'd tried to make a Christmas wreath and had burned her fingers with hot glue. She talked about her experience rock climbing and the time she'd let an old boyfriend coerce her into kayaking. Both had been disasters. "Do you have hobbies?" she asked the man looking at her from across the table.

"Not really. When I have some free time, I work around my house. Hanging cabinets and refinishing floors." He raised his bottle of Becks and took a drink. He lowered the beer and said, "I take my dog out and bird hunt. That's about it."

She could picture him doing both. Tool belt hung low on his hips or wearing fatigues, shotgun in the crook of his arm, loyal dog at his heels. Looking very fine. Very studly. She wondered if he wore camo boxers or tighty whities. Maybe he went commando.

"What did you do all winter? Go on any ski trips? Take a vacation to Mexico?" he asked, breaking into her mind's libidinous wanderings.

"Last November my friends and I vacationed on Paradise Island. We drank too much. Gambled too much. And had too much fun." It really wasn't her fault her brain had gone to the sinful side. From the second she'd walked in the door, she'd felt the pull of his gaze on her, like dark, intense tractor beams. She couldn't ever recall being the sole attention of any man. Not like this. Not to the exclusion of everything and everyone else, even the young waitress in the tight shirt who'd given him a flirty smile as she'd served their drinks. "I haven't gone anywhere this year."

"Not even an overnight trip to Pocatello?" he asked, referring to a town a few hundred miles east of Boise.

"No. I've just been working." In the subdued light, his eyes looked black. A lock of thick hair fell over his forehead, while little comma curls touched the tops of his ears. It was several hours past his five o'clock shadow, and black whiskers darkened his square jaw.

"No boyfriends sweeping you off your feet for a weekend getaway?"

"No. No boyfriends for about a year now."

"You're kidding," he said as if he found it hard to believe.

Lucy stirred her mojito with the sprig of mint stuck in it. "No. I've been avoiding relationships." Her fingertips brushed the condensation on the side of the glass, and the pesky sleeve of her boat neck sweater slid down her arm again. If she'd known the sweater was going to give her so much trouble, she would have worn something else. "I've been involved with some real idiots in my life, and I've decided to take a break before I get too bitter."

"You're bitter about men?"

"Perhaps jaded is a better word." She pushed her sweater back up.

"How long have you been on break?"

She really didn't want to admit how long it had been since she'd had a real date. "A while," she answered. She didn't consider tonight a real date. Tonight was more a curiosity thing. She'd only agreed to meet with Quinn because he'd sent her those two sappy e-mails. She felt kinda sorry for him and . . . well, she'd wanted to see if he was as good looking as she remembered.

He wasn't as good. He was even better. "I prefer a good book to a bad date." Without the red ball cap to shadow the upper half of his face, she could see the fine lines at the corners of his dark brown eyes, which hinted at easy laughter.

"How many bad Internet dates have you had?"

Those hadn't been real dates either. Lord, it was getting hard to keep up the pretense. "How many have you had?"

He leaned forward and placed his forearms on the table. He reached for the candle and pushed it from one hand to the other. His silver watchband scraped the smooth surface. "Most of the women I've met have been nice ladies, just not for me. You're the only woman I've asked to meet me twice. The only woman I've thought about since I met you. The only woman I want to know better." He glanced up from the candle and looked at her as if she were the only female in the bar. He said, "Your turn."

Something in his voice spread warm, seductive tingles across her skin. She didn't even know the man. Didn't really believe what he was telling her half the time. So why was he giving her tingles? "My turn at what?"

"Tell me about your Internet dates."

Oh yeah. "Out of all the men I've met online, seventy percent were just looking for quick sex and were real losers. Twenty percent were lonely and desperate for a girlfriend, any girlfriend. The jury is still out on the last ten percent."

"Where do I fit?"

She picked up the glass and took a drink before she answered, "The jury is still out on you."

He placed his hands flat on the table and sat back in his chair. He looked at her for several heartbeats, then turned the conversation in a different direction. "What do you think about those three men who were murdered recently?"

Lucy set her drink on the table. Wow, what a way to ruin the mood. She'd only met one of the poor guys. Lawrence aka luvstick had fallen into the seventy percent looking for quick sex, and she'd killed him off in chapter three. A few weeks later she'd read in the newspaper that someone had *really* killed him. Thinking about it was freaky. A huge coincidence that she tried not to think about. She looked into Quinn's dark gaze, and she wondered if he was worried for his own safety. If she were a man, she'd be worried about it. "Are you afraid you could be next?"

He chuckled as if deeply amused and raised the Becks to his mouth. "Nah. I can take care of myself," he said before he took a drink.

That's probably what luvstick had thought. "Have you heard how the perpetrator is meeting her victims?"

He shook his head and lowered the bottle. A drop of beer clung to his top lip, and he sucked it off. "Have you?"

"No. The police must not have much evidence."

He set the bottle on the table, and he did that intense tractor beam thing with his gaze again. As if what she'd said was important. "Why do you say that?"

The way he paid attention was odd, really. Yet at the same time flattering. "They don't generally tell the press much if they don't have a lot of evidence." She'd read so many books and interviewed so many cops that she could practically predict how they'd behave. It was part of her job to know. Quinn was a plumber and wouldn't necessarily know police procedure. "They like to keep certain aspects of cases from getting out. Things that only the killer would know. If they don't have a lot, they don't leak much."

His dark brows lowered. "How does a nurse know all of that?"

Yeah, how did a nurse know all of that? She smiled. *Cold Case Files.* Remember?"

"Ah." He tilted his head back. "That's right. Did you date any of the guys who were killed?"

Lucy looked down at the table and her hand resting next to her glass. After luvstick's death, the newspaper had reported that he'd actually been married but had had a little bachelor pad/love nest set up in an apartment off State Street, where his body had been found. The report had been ugly and sordid, and his family hadn't deserved having it splashed across the news. Lucy didn't want to talk about luvstick. "No. I didn't date any of them." Which wasn't a *real* lie. She didn't consider meeting men at a coffee house a real date. Her sweater slid down her arm once more, and she decided just to leave it there. It wasn't like anything was showing, and she was tired of pushing it back up. "You should be careful, though."

Again he leaned forward to play with the candle. "Are you worried about me?"

With his wide shoulders, thick arms, and strong hands, he looked like he could sling her over his shoulder and run for a mile or two. He exuded complete confidence in himself and his abilities, but confidence didn't stop a determined killer. "Do you want me to worry about you?"

"That depends."

"On?"

He watched the flickering candle for several moments. Then he looked up, and his voice dropped to that smooth, seductive level that gave her tingles. "On what worrying about me involves."

Lucy had been around enough men in her thirty-four years to know exactly where this conversation was headed. A part of her wanted to go there, too. The part that was attracted to Quinn beyond rationality and reason. The part that felt his testosterone-laced voice slide across her flesh and felt his gaze touch her everywhere at once, even as he stared into her eyes. But she hadn't allowed that part of her to act irrationally since she'd learned the hard way that sex was much better with a man she actually knew. Sure, she'd gone to bed with her share of liars and losers, but at least she'd known the liars and losers for a while first. It seemed like a small distinction, but it was an important one. "Tell me about your plumbing business," she said, introducing a nice, safe—boring—subject.

He chuckled and told her that he mostly ran the business end of it these days, as opposed to installing toilets and running pipe. Within minutes, the subject somehow changed from plumbing to field trials. She learned he had an Irish setter that he was training to hunt, and while she didn't give a damn about bird dogs, she was a little surprised that the conversation didn't bore her. Perhaps it was because of Quinn's obvious pleasure in the subject, or maybe because he looked so good talking about it. Probably both.

The waitress approached the table just as Lucy polished off her mojito. Again the waitress gave Quinn a flirtatious smile, but he hardly spared her a glance. He asked Lucy if she'd like another drink or perhaps dinner. She declined and reached for her Dolce & Gabbana snakeskin clutch. She had to write at least ten pages tonight if she was going to meet her book deadline. She pulled out a ten-dollar bill, but Quinn insisted on settling the tab. He helped her with her coat, but this time his fingers did not brush the back of her neck as they had earlier.

She tied the belt at her waist and held out her hand. "Thank you."

Instead of taking her hand, he grasped her beneath her arm and said, "I'll walk you to your car."

"You don't have to do that."

"I know I don't have to. I want to." They moved to the entrance, and he dropped his hand from her and opened the door. "Where did you park?"

"About half a block down Bannock." Cool night air touched Lucy's face and slid down the front of her coat. She pulled the lapels close. Light from the restaurants and bars lining both sides of Eighth Street lit up patches of sidewalk as they made their way to Lucy's car. Occasional laughter from the bars leaked out into the night and drowned out the sound of Lucy's heels hitting the concrete. Quinn's arm brushed hers once, but other than that brief encounter, he didn't touch her again.

"Have dinner with me Monday," he said as they rounded the corner.

Monday. That was two days away. In the back of her brain, she knew she had plans, but at the moment she couldn't remember what they were. But even if she didn't, he was coming on so strong that Lucy didn't know whether to feel flattered or stalked. "Oh, I don't know." Perhaps because he'd been out of the dating pool for so long, he'd forgotten the rules of dating. Clearly rule number one was to pretend indifference until you could ascertain the other person's feelings. "I'm not really dating right now."

"What do you call tonight?"

"Making an exception." She was attracted to him. There was no denying it. Just as there was no denying the guy oozed a kind of brain-numbing sexual appeal. The kind that could have a girl naked before she remembered that she was supposed to "Just say no." They walked from beneath the bright light on the corner, and Lucy stopped by her car.

"Make another exception."

Feeble light from a closed printer's shop spilled across the sidewalk and onto the bottom of Quinn's pants and the toes of Lucy's shoes. She shook her head and opened her purse. "I don't know you well enough to make another exception for you."

"I can solve that problem right now." He took her purse, snapped it closed, and tossed it on the top of her car.

She looked up into the darkened shadows of his face. "What are you doing?"

He slid his hands up her arms and across her shoulders. His fingers plowed up through her hair, and he held the back of her head. "Something I've wanted to do all night," he said just above a whisper as his mouth descended toward hers. She put her hands on his chest, meaning to stop him. Then he said, "The second you walked into the bar, I wanted to kiss you," and she forgot about stopping. He gently pulled her head backward, and her lips parted. "Starting right here. With your mouth."

Lucy's hands opened and closed on his sweater, over the hard muscles of his chest. His lips pressed into hers, a warm, irresistible possession. Her palms slid to his shoulders and she held on as his slick tongue entered her mouth, teasing and coaxing a response. He tasted a little like the beer he'd drunk, but mostly like a man with sex on his mind. She should have been alarmed, and she was. But mostly because she liked the taste in her mouth. Like something hot and delicious, it poured through her and warmed the pit of her stomach. Her toes curled inside her Donald J. Pliner pumps, and her fingers dug into the weave of his sweater. His hands never left the back of her head. His mouth never left hers, yet she felt the kiss everywhere. His wet mouth ate at hers, devouring all rational thought and turning on every cell in her body. She hardly knew him, but she didn't care much as he fed her kisses that left her feeling consumed, burned alive right there on the sidewalk of downtown Boise. She moaned and leaned into him.

He lifted his face and spoke just above her moist mouth. "See me again."

It wasn't a question, and she nodded. "Okay."

"Monday."

"Okay."

He dropped his arms and took a step back. Dazed, she stared into the variegated shadows of his face and raised a hand to the tender skin below her bottom lip where his chin had abraded her. She wondered if he'd left a mark.

"Did I hurt you?"

The little patch felt raw to the touch. "I'm okay."

He placed his fingers beneath her chin and

tilted her face toward the streetlight. His thumb brushed her jaw, and he leaned forward to lightly kiss just below her bottom lip. "I'm sorry." She felt his whispered breath on her skin. The warmth of it brushed her chin and slid down the side of her throat. "I got a little carried away."

She closed her eyes and waited for the return of his mouth to hers.

"Lucy."

"Yes."

"Either you leave now, by yourself. Or you leave with me." He stepped back and cold air separated his chest from the front of her coat but did little to cool her heated cheeks. "What's it going to be?"

Lucy opened her eyes and cleared her throat. "I'm leaving." She did not believe in love at first sight. "By myself." She left that up to romantics and romance writers like Clare. But lust . . . lust was different. Lust at first sight was something that Lucy did believe in. She was staring it right in the face. It heated her blood, pooled in the pit of her stomach, and made her want to follow wherever Quinn might want to take her. Instead she turned and reached for her purse.

One kiss had sucked out her rationality and reason. She was going to see Quinn again. She hadn't meant to say yes when there were so many good reasons to say no. She didn't really know him and didn't know if she believed half of what he said. There was something about him that was just a little too intense. Something that told her he was moving too fast. There was something wrong. Something she just couldn't see, but for some inexplicable reason, none of that seemed to matter.

"Good night, Quinn," she said and moved around to the other side of her car. She glanced across the roof of her BMW at his outline against the soft glow of the printer's shop behind him. He was tall and dark and absolutely gorgeous. With one kiss, he'd turned the "curiosity thing" into a real date.

"I'll get in touch with you about Monday."

With her car separating them, her thoughts cleared a little, and she recalled her Monday night plans. She'd been given two tickets to a hockey game as a thank-you for speaking at a Writer's League meeting. She'd been meaning to ask Adele to go with her, since Adele loved hockey as much as Lucy. "I forgot that I have tickets to the Steelheads for Monday night," she said. It was a perfect excuse to get out of the date. Instead she asked, "Want to go to the game with me?"

"Dinner first?"

"Sure." She'd had the perfect out, but she hadn't taken it. She was going to see him again, and God help her if he ever touched more than the back of her head.

Chapter 5

Storyteller: Seeks Smooth Talker . . .

Monday morning, Quinn walked into the briefing room and shot the shit with a few guys from
the crime lab. While they talked about old
cases, his gaze took in the marker board. Lucy's
name was still at the top in bold red, and two
lines were drawn to the second and third murder victims.

He grabbed a cup of coffee and took a seat.
He opened his notebook on the table in front of
him to the notes he'd written about Lucy.
Everything he had was circumstantial, but
when put together, it painted a fairly damning
picture. He ran a hand down his gold-and-blue-
striped tie and wondered how long it would

take before someone mentioned the kiss he'd put on Lucy the previous Friday night.

"You sure didn't kiss Maureen like you kissed Lucy," Kurt managed through a huge grin as he entered the room and sat next to Quinn.

"Jealous?" Quinn asked through a smile as he pulled back the cuff of his dress shirt to look at his watch. One minute after eight. Kurt had waited a whole minute. If anything, Quinn was surprised that Kurt hadn't razzed him about it Saturday night when they'd met before his setup with Maureen.

"Not jealous. Impressed by how fast you work."

"I had to convince Lucy she needed to see me again. Maureen didn't need convincing." He turned a page in his notes. If his date with Lucy had been a real one, he'd have used more finesse. He would have taken his time and asked for her phone number. If he'd had time, he would have charmed her into giving him what he wanted instead of grabbing her and kissing her into submission. When given a choice, Quinn always preferred to take his time, although he had to admit that grabbing her up and getting to it hadn't been too bad. Not at all. In fact, it might have been a little too good.

"By the sound of Lucy's moan, that was some convincing."

"It's a dirty job, Weber." He hadn't expected

it to be so easy, either. He'd expected Lucy to pull back and slap him.

"But somebody's gotta do it. Right?"

"Right." Instead of slapping him, she'd done the unexpected and melted into his chest. Her response had surprised the hell out of him, and for a moment, as he'd tasted her mouth and felt the warm pull of desire, he'd forgotten who she was and exactly why he'd been standing there kissing her on a downtown street. For a few moments, she'd been just a beautiful woman and he'd been just a man. He'd let the heat of her response go straight to his head, and lower. For a few moments he'd forgotten that he'd just been doing his job.

"I don't blame you for not wanting to tongue tangle with bignsassy," Kurt said, pulling Quinn's thoughts away from kissing Lucy. "After listening to the most recent tape, I'm convinced you're right. She's as dumb as a doorknob. I don't understand how the woman can keep a job."

"Maureen works for the government," Quinn explained. There was no confusing the quick hug and kiss on the cheek he'd given Maureen for the DNA transfer he'd exchanged with Lucy. He'd always been able to tell if a woman would be any good in bed by the way she kissed. Lucy's kiss had knocked him on his ass.

Anita Landers entered the briefing room, followed by Sergeant Mitchell. They went over the latest reports from the print lab. Quinn wasn't surprised to hear that neither of the sets of prints from Lucy and Maureen matched any of the prints found at the three crime scenes. None of the prints at the scenes matched each other. Long blonde hairs found on all three victims had matched each other but were synthetic. They still had nothing solid.

The discussion moved from prints to the latest tapes. "Tell me anything new that you got the other night," the sergeant said.

Quinn flipped a few pages to the notes he'd taken while listening to the last tape. "Lucy Rothschild is still claiming to be a nurse. She admits that she hasn't been out of town in the past few months and said she quit dating because she was becoming bitter and jaded. She lied about knowing any of the murdered men, and she seems to know that we don't have a lot of evidence." Although he couldn't say why, he felt compelled to add, "All of that is completely circumstantial."

"True, but we know she met Lawrence Craig. Why would she lie about that if she didn't have something to hide?" Mitchell asked.

Quinn shrugged. She was a habitual liar, but that didn't prove she killed anyone. "We could always bring her in and question her," he reminded the sergeant.

Mitchell thought about it, then shook his head. "Not yet."

Next, they discussed Maureen Dempsey. Quinn thought they should concentrate less effort on Maureen, if not cross her off the list completely.

"She believes those stories printed in that *Weekly News of the World*," Kurt pointed out. "She's crazy as all hell."

"Crazy enough to kill three men?"

"Maybe crazy enough," Quinn pointed out. "But I doubt she's smart enough." Maureen had been so easy to lead. She'd admitted having met all three victims and that she'd been sorry to hear about their deaths. She'd told Quinn she'd prayed for their families and made donations to various religious organizations in their names. She'd said she lived in the grip of grace and danced with Jesus. Quinn had been educated in Catholic schools, but he hadn't had a real clue what she'd meant.

Mitchell scratched the top of his crew cut. "When are you seeing her again?"

"Tomorrow afternoon."

"If we can't eliminate her completely, she stays on the list." The sergeant rocked back on the heels of his wingtips and asked, "What do you have, Kurt?"

They talked about the other suspects Kurt had set up for dates and about pulling in more resources so that Quinn and Kurt could concentrate on the top four or five. After the meeting broke up, the sergeant asked, "What do you two have going today?"

"After we finish here, I'm going to follow up with the victims' families," Quinn informed him. "Later we're heading over to Barnes and Noble again. We need to talk to some of the workers who were off the last time we were there." He flipped a few pages in his notes. "Two of them will be working this afternoon."

A few minutes later, Quinn headed to his office. He had two other investigations he was working besides the Breathless case. Wednesday he had to testify in *United States v. Raymond Deluca,* an arson case involving a gasoline accelerant, resulting in the deaths of Mr. Deluca's wife and her three children from a previous marriage. The toxicology report indicated that all four victims had ingested large amounts of phenobarbital, the medication Mrs. Deluca took to control her epilepsy. Raymond claimed his wife had been depressed and must have waited for him to go out of town to kill herself and her children. He had a receipt from a Holiday Inn in Salt Lake for the night of the fire, but as Quinn had discovered, there was also a debit card transaction at 2:35 a.m. for five gallons of gas purchased at the Shell station a few minutes from the Deluca house off Maple Grove. A half hour later, a neighbor had smelled smoke and called 911.

The prosecution would present a new woman and an insurance policy as motive for the crime. Raymond Deluca's attorney would try and disprove the motive as he worked to shred Quinn's time line. Quinn needed to reread his notes before he entered the courtroom Wednesday.

Quinn spent the rest of the morning chasing down leads and searching for information about Lucy on the Internet. He visited her website again to see if it had been updated in the past few days. It hadn't. At noon, he and Kurt jumped in an unmarked car and headed to Barnes and Noble. They met with the two employees in a room filled with boxes of books.

Jan Bright was short with long, kinky eighties hair. She wore some kind of plaid dress that she'd buttoned around her throat. Cynthia Pool's platinum blonde hair was cut close to her head, and her white blouse had an embroidered Mickey Mouse climbing out of the pocket. Both women were very thin and in their mid to late forties.

Quinn pulled a piece of paper out of his notebook. On it were the photos of Charles Wilson, Dave Anderson, and Lawrence Craig. He handed it to Jan Bright. "Do you recall seeing any of these men?"

She shook her head and passed the paper to Cynthia Pool.

"Yeah, they look familiar. Especially him," Cynthia said and pointed to the second murder victim, Dave Anderson. "I think he used to come in quite a bit on Friday nights." She looked back up, and her nose scrunched. "He was one of those."

"One of those?"

"Those single guys who come in looking for single women," Cynthia explained. "Bookstores are the new singles bars. Men and women come in here on Friday and Saturday nights to hook up."

Quinn and Kurt glanced at each other. They'd known each other long enough, worked enough cases together, to know what the other was thinking. Men and women hooking up in bookstores was not only news to both of them but it was also a valuable piece of information.

Kurt asked, "Did you ever see any of these men meet with women or leave with anyone?"

"I don't recall. Do you remember, Jan?"

"No. I really don't pay attention to who's hooking up with whom in the aisles." She folded her arms across her chest and looked at a point somewhere above Quinn's left shoulder. "I think it's disturbing."

Cynthia shrugged her shoulders and handed over the paper. "So, those are the men who were murdered?"

"Yes." Quinn slid the photographs into his leather notebook. He and Kurt pulled out their business cards. "If either of you ladies remember anything else, give one of us a call." Cynthia took the cards, while they practically had to slap them in Jan's hand.

As the two detectives passed the café on their way out, they spotted a poster with Lucy's name on it. The green-and-beige sign sat on an easel beside a table stacked with her books. The sign advertised a meeting of the Women of Mystery, with guest speaker, mystery writer Lucy Rothschild.

Kurt pointed at the poster. "That's this Saturday."

"Wonder what goes on in a Women of Mystery meeting?"

"Maybe we should check it out."

"Maybe." Quinn picked up one of Lucy's books and thumbed through it. "Right now, I'm more interested in what Cynthia Pool and Jan Bright had to say about people hooking up in the aisles of bookstores."

"You think Breathless picks up men in bookstores?"

"Could be." Quinn set the book down and glanced at the café to his right. A couple sat at one of the small square tables, while a man with a laptop sat at another. Quinn imagined the place packed. The perfect hunting ground. "We need to put someone undercover in here. Not me or you. Someone the employees won't recognize." He returned his attention to the stack of Lucy's books. "Someone who's unknown to the suspects we've met or interviewed," he added as the two detectives turned and headed for the doors.

The afternoon sun hit Quinn full in the face, and he reached for the sunglasses in his breast pocket. He slid them on the bridge of his nose as they moved through the parking lot to the unmarked police cruiser. He still wasn't convinced Lucy was Breathless. Yes, she'd told some lies and could be tied to two of the victims. But she just didn't seem . . . aggressive or kinky. She'd responded to his kiss, and within his hands, she'd turned warm and willing. Not the kind of woman to go to a man's house after a few dates, cuff him to his bed, and snuff out his life. No, she seemed like the kind of woman who'd have entirely different plans for a man cuffed and at her mercy.

Of course, that could be his dick talking.

"Are you kidding?" Maddie asked as she pushed her Mexican rice to the side of her plate.

"No, he just grabbed me and planted a kiss on me."

"How was it?" Adele asked as she reached for a pitcher of blue margaritas in the center of the table.

Lucy bit her bottom lip, but the corners of her mouth turned up anyway. "Amazing." She looked across her shoulder at Clare's smile. Out of the three of them, Clare would be the only one to give her wholesale support. Clare truly did believe in what she wrote for a living. In romance and soul mates and happily ever after. Clare was also the most delusional when it came to men.

"How long have you known this Quinn guy?" Maddie wanted to know. "A week?"

"A little over a week. Tonight will be our third date," Lucy answered with a stretch of the truth. If she counted the first time they'd met at Starbucks. Which she really didn't. Nor had she considered the drink they'd had together a real date, until he'd kissed her. The kiss had been *very* real.

Adele poured margarita into her glass and set the pitcher back in the center of the table. "And you let him kiss you on your first date? That's not like you."

Let. Once his mouth had touched hers, there'd been no thought of letting. Just doing.

"You have to be careful, Lucy," Maddie said as if she were her mother when, in fact, Maddie was only a year older than Lucy.

"He's just a nice normal guy. He's a plumber and owns his own business."

"I think you should go for it." Clare paused to take a drink of her own blue margarita, then added, "I know you all don't believe in it, but there is such a thing as love at first sight. It happens all the time."

Lucy smiled to herself. Or lust at first kiss, at any rate.

A frown puckered Adele's brow. "I don't know, Lucy. I dated a plumber once. He was weird."

"Where did you meet him?" Lucy asked to take the attention off herself.

"At The Society for Creative Anachronism." Adele shrugged, then dug into her fajita salad.

Maddie's fork paused on the edge of her plate. "You're shitting me."

Adele shook her head. "No. I was writing my medieval time travel and I needed to do some research. They meet in that park off Fort, a few blocks from my house, to sword fight and all that. So I decided to watch and ask questions."

"Was your boyfriend Sir Lancelot?" Maddie asked.

"No." Lucy nudged Clare in the arm with her elbow. "Isn't it Sir Lance of Lotta Love?"

Clare smiled, her blue eyes alight with humor. "It's Sir Steely Lance of Love."

"Funny." One corner of Adele's mouth turned up as she tried to look offended. "He was Sir Richard the Resplendent."

"Not to repeat, Maddie," Lucy said as she reached for her margarita, "but you're shitting me. Right?"

Adele shook her head. "No. His real name was Dexter Potter. And he looked *good* in a pair of tights. Large codpiece, if you get my meaning."

"Oh."

"Well then."

Maddie picked at her chicken burrito and pushed the tortilla to the side with the rice. "Are we talking 'come to momma,' big? Or 'I ain't birthing no babies,' big?" Maddie held up one finger. "Because there is a difference, ladies. More than nine inches is—"

"Gee, Maddie," Clare interrupted as she glanced about. "Time and place."

"What? No one can hear me."

Lucy laughed and changed the subject again. "Are you still doing Atkins?" she asked Maddie.

"Yeah," she sighed. "And it's a bitch. I'm getting really tired of eating steak with a side of pork chops and a pound of butter for dessert."

"That doesn't sound healthy." Adele reached for the pepper and came close to dipping one large breast into her salad. "What does Mr. hardluvnman look like?" she asked Lucy.

Lucy cut into her chicken chimichanga. "He's tall, dark, and very good looking." And he could kiss all rational thought right out of her head. "He likes to bird hunt with his dog, and he watches *Cold Case Files*. His family lives here in town, and his father died a few years ago." He could put sex into his voice and take her breath away. "His wife died last year, and he's lonely."

"Uh-oh." Adele replaced the pepper and sat back.

"What uh-oh?" Lucy asked, although she knew the answer.

"You're going to try and rescue him just like all the others."

"No, I'm not."

"You always say that," Clare reminded her. "And you always get your heart broken." She cut into her enchilada and shook her head. "If you get involved with him, you make sure he treats you right. Like Lonny. He's the love of my life."

While Clare looked down at her lunch, the other three gave each other meaningful glances. Clare's boyfriend, Lonny, was a nice guy, and he did treat her well. He remembered birthdays and holidays and wasn't jealous or possessive. He would have been the perfect boyfriend if it hadn't been for the fact that he was gay. Everyone knew it. Everyone, it seemed, but Clare. Either she wasn't as smart as all of her degrees suggested, or she was in deep denial. Lucy and the others tended to believe the latter. Clare was a great person and a wonderful friend, but it was like she had a force field in front of her face and anything unpleasant bounced off. They were all secretly afraid of what might happen when she found out "the love of her life" was out loving men at the Balcony Bar behind her back.

"You're all wrong. I'm not attracted to Quinn because I feel sorry for him. Or because he needs to be rescued. I'm attracted to him because . . ." She thought of his intense brown eyes and long lashes. His square jaw covered in five o'clock shadow and the sensual curve of his mouth. "Because when he looks at me, he's looking at *me*. When he asks me about my life, I feel like he really wants to know. That he's not asking just so he can spend the rest of the time talking about himself. When I'm with him, he makes me feel like he's really into me." She took a bite of her lunch and looked at the stunned faces of her friends. "What?"

"You sound like you're falling for him," Maddie pointed out.

"Yep," Adele added.

Clare nodded. "That's what it sounds like."

"No, it doesn't. I have a book to write. I don't have time to squander on a man." Lucy reached for her drink. "And besides, I don't know him well enough to be falling for him. Half the time I don't know whether to be flattered by his attention or scared."

A crease appeared between Maddie's dark brows. "Why are you scared? Is he crazy? What did he do?"

"Nothing. Maybe scared is too strong a word." Lucy paused and tilted her head to one side. "Puzzled might be better."

"Why are you puzzled?"

"Because he wants to see more of me. He wants to call me and take me out and—"

"He's pursuing you," Clare pointed out.

"I guess." Lucy paused a moment to collect her thoughts. "It's just that I've never met a man who wanted to see so much of me right off. You know how men are, they take you out and might call you again in a week or two or not at all. Quinn doesn't seem to know that he's supposed to keep me waiting by the phone, wondering why he isn't asking me out again."

"Wait." Adele held up her fork. "You don't want to go out with him because he seems really interested in you? Now *that's* crazy."

Lucy shrugged. Maybe, but there was something about him that she just couldn't quite put her finger on. Something that told her he was too good to be true, and in her experience, if something looked too good to be true, it *was* too good to be true. "Maybe I don't trust the whole my-wife-died thing. I don't get the impression that he's lying about it—exactly. I can't put my finger on it, but I just don't trust him completely." She shook her head and cut into her chimichanga. "Maybe I'm being overly suspicious."

Adele looked up from her salad. "Get him to take you to his house. If he won't take you, then it's probably because his wife isn't really dead."

"Are you high? That's how Richard Franko got five of his victims," Maddie said, referring to the serial killer she'd written about several years ago. "He just invited them home and, like lambs to slaughter, they went. Lucy could be walking into a nightmare."

It really was no wonder Maddie didn't date.

She viewed most men she met as psychopathic killers. "He's not a killer. I just wonder if he's too good to be real."

"Adele might be on to something," Clare said. "If you see his house, you can tell right away if he's still married, or if he's set up a shag pad. If he won't take you home, he's married. If he does take you home—"

"Then he'll expect sex," Maddie interrupted.

"True." The thought of having sex with Quinn wasn't unappealing, but so soon after meeting him was out of the question.

"If you're going to be foolish enough to go to his house," Maddie said, "be sure and take the personal protection I've given you."

"I will," Lucy promised. For Christmas the previous year, Maddie had given them all pepper spray, a personal alarm, a stun pen, and a pair of brass knuckles. "And I'll make sure I have my car," she added, even though she wasn't even sure she would ever end up at Quinn's house. "So I can leave before there's any danger of getting naked."

"I don't know which is more dangerous," Adele said. "You at some guy's house you don't know, or driving your car."

"I'm an excellent driver," Lucy insisted.

"That's what Rain Man said," Clare pointed out.

Lucy knew that her friends thought she was a bad driver, but she wasn't. Sure, she drove a little fast and yelled things at other cars, but she hadn't had a wreck in five years. "How's everyone else's love life?" she asked, purposely changing the subject once again.

"Nonexistent," Maddie complained. "There aren't any men in this town."

Adele reached for her margarita. "I found an old face scrubby and a Crock-Pot on my porch yesterday."

"Dwayne," the other three said, all at the same time. A lean, mean, buff machine, Dwayne Larkin hung drywall for a living, and for two years Adele had thought he just might be Mr. Right. She'd overlooked his habit of picking his teeth at the table and smelling the armpits of his shirts before he put them on. Because he looked kind of like Viggo Mortensen, she'd put up with his beer-guzzling, belching ways, right up to the moment he'd told her she was getting a "fat ass." No one used the f-word in reference to Adele's ass, and she'd kicked him out of her life. Too bad he wouldn't go completely. Every few weeks, Adele would find one or two of the things she'd left at his house sitting on her front porch. No note. No Dwayne. Just random stuff.

"Sheesh. He just doesn't give up."

"It's like he's holding your stuff hostage,"

Lucy commented. "Doling it out like body parts or something."

"It's creepy."

"How much more does he have?"

Adele shrugged. "I don't know. We were together for two years, and I stayed at his house a lot. I'm sure there's more."

"If I hadn't already killed Dwayne off in *Shot of Love*," Lucy said, referring to her third book, "I'd kill him for you."

"Thank you."

The subject changed from men to writing, and by the time Lucy paid her portion of the check, they'd given Adele advice on what to do about her problem with Dwayne and helped Clare plot the next three chapters of her book.

Earlier, Lucy had printed out the first six chapters of her current manuscript for Maddie to look over for inconsistencies and mistakes. Maddie might be a little freaky and inappropriate sometimes, but she was brilliant and gave excellent critiques. In turn, Lucy helped Maddie out when she needed it.

Maddie followed Lucy to her car. "Promise you'll be careful about this Quinn guy."

Lucy handed over the manuscript pages and looked into Maddie's brown eyes. Sometimes Lucy got the feeling that her friend was hiding from something. Something that she hid behind her brash personality. Something she never shared with anyone. Lucy wasn't the sort of person to dig and pry, but if Maddie ever wanted to share, Lucy would be there to listen. "I promise," she said. "And you promise not to be such a hard ass."

Maddie said good-bye but didn't promise a thing.

Lucy jumped in her car. On the drive home, her thoughts returned to Quinn. Maybe Adele and Clare were right. Maybe he was just a normal man pursuing her. Maybe she was looking for trouble.

She wove in and out of traffic and blew through a yellow light on Thirteenth and Fort, telling herself that it was safer to go through a yellow than to slam on her brakes. As she drove past the junior high she'd attended as a teenager, the rational part of her brain took the opportunity to ask her if normal men trolled for women in chat rooms. No, they didn't. Not unless there was something wrong with them. Or . . . they were in it for sex.

After a few more turns, she pulled into the alley behind her house. When she was with Quinn, she didn't get the perv or creep vibe. On the contrary. More like he had a smooth sexual energy vibe. One that she had to admit was a little mesmerizing.

She hit the garage door opener pinned to the visor and waited for the old wooden door to lift. A lot of the houses in Boise's North End had been built around the turn of the twentieth century and still had carriage blocks by the curbs. But once Packards started rolling into town, Boiseans abandoned their carriages and built small detached garages in their backyards. Many of the single-car structures like Lucy's were still in use because there wasn't room for anything larger.

Lucy pulled the Beemer inside and shut the garage door. She entered the back of her house through the kitchen and tossed her purse on the tile counter. She looked out the window over the sink and into the neighbor's backyard. Mrs. Riley was out back, pulling up plastic poinsettias and replacing them with bright tulips. Plastic, of course. She would repeat the process this coming summer and fall. Lucy had asked her once why she planted plastic flowers each season, and she had answered as if it had been the most logical thing in the world, "Why, because I like pretty things." Which also explained why she'd painted her house bright yellow, blue, and green.

As Lucy watched Mrs. Riley work in the yard, her thoughts returned to Quinn and her date with him that evening. She was looking forward to seeing him more than she wanted to admit. More than was wise, since she didn't even know him.

It was possible he was a plumber trying to move on after the death of his wife, but it was just as possible that he was one of the seventy percent who were online just looking for quick sex.

Lucy supposed the bigger question, and the one more difficult to answer was, why was she picking him apart only to make excuses to put him back together again? Why was she obsessing over a guy she didn't know?

Chapter 6

Getn2knowu: Seeks Honest Mate . . .

"Get Ready for This" pounded the air inside the
Bank of America Centre as the captains for the
Idaho Steelheads and the San Diego Gulls faced
off at center ice. The music stopped, the puck
dropped, and the sound of hockey sticks hitting
the ice filled the arena.

Game on.

Quinn looked across his shoulder at Lucy
Rothschild, at her red-and-black Steelhead's jersey and the big foam finger stuck on her hand.
He'd never encountered anyone in his life who
looked *less* like a serial killer.

"That's what I'm talking about!" she yelled as
a Gull got knocked on his ass.

Okay, so she was a little bloodthirsty, but for some strange reason, that didn't shrivel his sac. Nor did the tape recorder jabbing the small of his back, reminding him that she just might be a psychopath who got off on watching men die.

Quinn leaned back in his seat, and the small black recorder pressed into his spine. Kurt was across town on a date with brneyedgrl, while Anita sat in the van recording the other detective. Quinn was on his own tonight, but he wasn't real worried, the most obvious reason being that it wasn't likely Lucy would try and kill him in an arena filled with several thousand pumped-up hockey fans. But even if they'd been alone, getting hot and sweaty in his bed, he wasn't all that convinced Lucy was a serial killer. He just didn't feel it in his gut. No, when he looked at her, he felt something entirely different in that general area. But just because he didn't feel she was a killer didn't mean he was going to rule out the possibility either.

"You suck!" a young guy a few rows up yelled as a Gull muscled the puck from a Steelhead.

Quinn didn't know much about hockey. He was more a football guy. He'd played the game from the age of ten to eighteen and knew the rules. As far as Quinn could see, hockey was chaos on ice. It looked like a bunch of guys chasing a puck and knocking the hell out of each other when the referees weren't looking.

"Ooow," Quinn winced as two players collided like freight trains but managed to stay on their skates. Beside him, Lucy laughed, and her eyes lit up like a kid on Christmas.

"Lord, I love this game," she said through a huge smile. "Especially in the play-offs when both teams are out to kill each other."

So maybe she was more than a *little* bloodthirsty, but she seemed to fit right in with the rest of the crowd.

"Do you come to a lot of games?" he asked above the sound of sticks hitting the ice and the rise and fall of shouting from the crowd.

"I try to see as many as possible. How about you?"

"I've never been before tonight."

She turned her head, and her big blue eyes met his. She blinked as if she couldn't quite figure out what she was seeing. Like maybe he was an alien. "Never? You're kidding me?"

"Nope. I'm a football guy."

"Football's okay, I guess. But hockey is more fun to watch."

"It looks chaotic."

"It's organized chaos." She returned her attention to the ice but leaned her head close to him. "The players up front are the forwards and the center." She removed her hand from the foam finger and pointed. She'd painted her fingernails red. "The guys that stay back are the defenders, and of course, the goalies." She dropped her hand to her thigh. "There are a lot of rules in hockey, and I can't keep all of them straight. And just when I think I've figured them all out, they change."

Quinn had always been a sucker for shiny red nails. He absolutely loved watching a woman slide her long fingers and red nails down his abdomen.

"See the player with the puck? He's a forward and he's about to pass it to the center." She leaned in a little closer, and her shoulder brushed his. "Just like that. Now he'll set up a shot."

Through the wafting scent of beer and concessions, he smelled her hair. He recognized it from the night of the Red Feather, when she'd reminded him of a garden and sunshine. With her head tilted toward his, her hair brushed the shoulder of her jersey and his bomber's jacket. If he leaned just a bit, he could bury his nose in the top of her head.

"Damn it!"

"What?" Quinn's gaze slid from her hair to the side of her face.

"The goalie stopped the puck." She turned to

look at him, and her nose lightly brushed his chin. If she raised her face a few inches, his lips would touch hers. A dull ache settled between his legs, which was ridiculous. He was thirty-six. He kicked ass and took names for a living. He was on a job. He didn't get sexually excited just thinking about kissing a woman.

Not usually.

Lucy lifted her gaze to Quinn's, and within her eyes he saw the same need that was twisting his insides, reflected back at him. He wondered what she'd do if he kissed her right there in front of thousands of people? If she'd kiss him back like she had on a downtown street?

She straightened and turned her attention to the game, but he hadn't imagined the desire in her eyes. Knowing she wanted him as much as he wanted her turned him from semi to stiff in seconds, no matter if he wanted to be turned or not. And he didn't. Not in the middle of a hockey game, and not with a murder suspect. If he hadn't purposely worn his jacket to conceal the recorder taped to his back, he would have slipped it off and covered his lap.

He turned his attention to the ice and sucked cool air into his lungs. He leaned forward to rest his forearms on his thighs. On the ice the referees blew their whistles, and play stopped. Chumbawamba blasted through the sound system, singing about getting knocked down, and Quinn felt the heavy beat through the soles of his boots.

He didn't know why he was getting all excited over Lucy Rothschild. Sure, she was a beautiful woman, but there were a lot of beautiful women around. She was a murder suspect, and that alone should wilt big Willie. But since the first night he'd seen her sitting in Starbucks, that fact seemed to be having the opposite effect on him. Probably because he knew he was going to have to push her for sex as hard and fast as possible. He didn't stop and wonder why the prospect didn't excite him with the other suspects. At the moment, he needed to get his mind off Lucy. Off getting hot and sweaty and freaky and back on the job.

On the ice, the puck was dropped and sticks slapped the ice. He thought he smelled flowers and sunshine again, and he purposely thought of Lawrence Craig and the others, bound to their beds, clear plastic pulled tight around their faces. Beneath his button fly, the tension in his groin eased, and Quinn relaxed.

When the first period ended, the Steelheads were up by two and the crowd buzzed with anticipation, although Quinn wasn't sure which caused the bigger buzz—the score or the Bud Lite pouring freely inside the arena.

During the second frame, Lucy and Quinn ate soft pretzels and drank beer. On the ice, the players hammered the puck and each other. The penalty boxes were put to good use, filling the Plexiglas enclosures with bloodied players and blue language.

As the game progressed, Quinn picked up the rules and began to see that hockey wasn't as chaotic as it seemed at first glance. Halfway through the third period, Lucy leaned close to Quinn and pointed to the penalty box, where a guy sat getting tampons shoved up his nose. "See number seventy-one, he still has the black eye he got four games ago."

Quinn folded his arms across his jacket and told himself not to look at her so close again. Not to get excited. To just do his damn job. "Who did you come with to that game?" He couldn't recall if any of his victims had been to hockey games.

"My friend Adele. She loves hockey, too. We spend a lot of time arguing about who's the hottest player."

Before he could stop himself, Quinn looked over his shoulder into Lucy's eyes. "So, who's the hottest player tonight?"

One corner of her mouth lifted. "Number twenty-eight on the Steelheads. He's sitting on the bench right now."

He glanced across the rink and looked at the hockey player with his helmet shoved up his forehead, chewing on his mouth guard. "You're kidding. He looks about nineteen."

"Actually, he's twenty-two."

"He's barely legal." She'd obviously read up on him.

Her eyes got all wide and innocent. "Barely legal for what?"

"You know what, and if I were looking at some twenty-two-year-old woman, you'd think I was a pervert."

"True," she said through a grin. "Aren't double standards a bitch?"

He preferred women around his own age. Mostly because women his age knew what they were doing in bed, but he knew better than to say that out loud. Women were always talk talk talking about how they wanted you to tell them the truth, but they didn't. "I like women in their thirties. There's more to talk about."

"That's probably true, but—"

Quinn slid his gaze to Lucy's. "But what?"

Her brows lowered, and she shook her head. "Who said anything about talking?"

Quinn chuckled deep in his chest. Her directness not only surprised him but it was also refreshing as hell. He appreciated a woman who was honest about sex.

Too bad she was busy lying to him about everything else. Yeah, he was lying, too. But he was trying to catch a serial killer before she struck again. Part of being a cop was being a good liar. It was his job, and he was good at it. Lucy wasn't a good liar, and if she had nothing to hide, why was she lying like it was *her* job?

The Steelheads beat the Gulls by two points and would face off with them again for a chance at the Kelly Cup title. Lucy had never been to a game with a man. She'd always gone with her friends. Tonight had been quite a different experience. Usually, the action on the ice kept her attention riveted on the men skating up and down the rink, running into each other and duking it out over six ounces of vulcanized rubber. Tonight, she'd been distracted by the man sitting next to her. The man who'd looked at her as if they'd been the only two people in an arena filled with thousands of screaming hockey fans.

After the hockey game, Quinn drove Lucy home, but he refused to come inside the house for coffee. Instead they sat on her porch swing. Lucy brought out a blanket, and they looked at the stars through the bare trees.

As the swing gently swayed back and forth, Quinn asked about her life and told her about his. He talked about the time he'd popped wheelies on his Schwinn to impress the neighbor girl only to end up in the emergency room with a broken arm. Somehow, they got on the subject of her past relationships. Lucy usually didn't talk about past boyfriends with potential future boyfriends, but for some reason, Quinn got her to talk about all the losers that littered her past.

He told her about his home off Boise Avenue that he'd bought after the death of his wife, Millie. He talked about the gazebo he and his brother had built in his backyard, and he invited her over to check out his Jacuzzi. Anytime. The skeptical part of Lucy that kept looking for problems relaxed a bit. A married man didn't invite a woman over to his house, anytime.

They talked about the latest episodes of *Cold Case Files* and *The First 48*. Once again the conversation turned to the local men who'd been killed, and they speculated about the killer. It occurred to her that every time she was with Quinn the conversation turned in that direction, but she didn't think much about it. Talking true crime was fascinating for her, and it was one thing they seemed to have in common.

"Off the top of my head, I would say that the perpetrator is an attractive woman with above average intelligence," she said, as she tried to recall all the research she'd done over the years. "She has an antisocial personality disorder, probably psychopathic rather than sociopathic. She is controlled and organized."

The swing slowly rocked, and Quinn looked at her beneath the porch light and asked, "Do you have an alibi for the nights of the murders?" He gave her one of his most charming smiles, like he'd meant it as a joke, but something within the depths of his brown eyes told her he was deadly serious.

In the distance, a back door slammed and a dog barked. She supposed that if the situation were reversed—if women were the victims—she'd want to know the same thing. "I'm not sure," she answered truthfully. "Working, I imagine."

"Diapering newborns?"

"Yeah." Lying about her job was starting to make her feel more and more guilty, but now was not the time to confess. "Are you worried I'm going to murder you?"

"Not worried." He tipped his head to the side, and this time the smile did reach his eyes. "Although it has crossed my mind that I should search your body for weapons." He stood and tossed the blanket onto the swing. "But not tonight," he said and pulled her to her feet. He placed his hands on the sides of her face and slowly lowered his head. His gaze stared into hers as his lips lightly brushed her mouth. Soft and sweet, as if he had all night and into the next morning. His breath hitched in his chest and feathered across her cheek as his tongue slid across her lower lip. The kiss teased a heated response deep in the pit of Lucy's stomach, turning her on with just the light brush of his mouth. Her hands slipped up the front of his leather jacket, and she grasped both sides of the open zipper in her fists. She raised onto the balls of her feet and parted her lips. She felt a moment of hesitation, then bam, the kiss turned hot and wet, like it slammed into him and he couldn't hold back a second more. Like he meant to eat her alive and couldn't get enough.

Beneath her porch light, his tongue touched and teased, spreading liquid heat through her. His thumbs brushed her temples and cheeks, and he moaned deep in his throat. She slipped her hands under his jacket, and she felt his hard muscles bunch as she slid her hands up and down his chest and stomach. She moved her palms around his sides to the middle of his back. Without lifting his mouth from hers, he grabbed her wrists and took a step forward. He forced her back against her front door and pinned her hands next to her head.

"You can't touch me," he said through harsh, ragged breaths.

"Why?"

He pressed his forehead into hers. "Because I like you too much."

Against her lower abdomen she could feel every inch of how much he liked her. He was long and rock hard, and he made her want to rub against him. "Are you sure you don't want to come in for coffee?"

"No, I'm not sure." He shook his head, dropped her wrists, and took a step back. "But if I come in, I'll want to make love to you. I don't think we're ready for that. Not yet."

What? He was a guy. Guys were always ready for that.

"I want more," he said and turned to leave. "I'll call you."

Lucy stood with her back against the door and watched him walk down the steps. "Good night," she whispered. The big moon shone through the naked limbs of the huge oak and walnut trees and lit Quinn in pale light as he moved down her sidewalk to his Jeep parked at the curb.

She'd never been with a man who'd left her standing on her porch, staring after him and wishing he'd come back and give her a little more right then and there. No man had ever turned down her invitation for coffee.

As the Jeep pulled away, Lucy opened her

door and entered the house. She locked the dead bolt behind her and flipped on the ceiling light in the living room. Well, she thought as she moved across the room and sank onto her burgundy silk couch, she didn't have to wonder if he'd asked her out for sex. "I want more," he'd said. To most men, sex *was* more.

She tossed her purse on her antique Chinese coffee table and stared at the brick fireplace to her left. He wasn't married, and he'd just proved he wasn't out for a quickie. He wanted more, but was that what she wanted?

Jumping into a relationship seemed a little precipitous. Rash. Crazy. She hadn't known him long enough. She didn't have time for a man. Especially a man who could be looking to replace his wife. All of those things spelled heartache for Lucy, but deep down inside, none of those very rational reasons mattered.

She wanted to see more of him. There was something about Quinn, some *thing* that made her smile and her stomach flutter a little. He intrigued her and made her want to slide her hands all over him. Yeah, she definitely wanted to see what he meant by "more."

But there was just one small problem. For any sort of relationship to survive, it had to be built on the truth. She had to be honest with him.

No more lies.

Chapter 7

Down2basix: Seeks Nontalker . . .

The last rays of the setting sun painted the valley in blue and pink as Quinn finished testifying in the Raymond Deluca case. He pushed open the glass doors of the Ada County Court House and pulled a breath of fresh air into his lungs. Outside, a chopped Nissan added its high-pitched whine to the traffic speeding past on Myrtle Street. A cool April breeze tugged at his red tie and the lapels of his navy wool blazer as he headed across the brick sidewalk toward the parking lot.

Raymond Deluca's defense lawyer had gone after Quinn as he'd expected, attacking the time line and questioning the forensic evidence, trying to make it appear as if Quinn hadn't done his job. After sixteen years of experience, Quinn had been ready for everything the lawyer had thrown at him. In the end, there had been no way the lawyer could discredit that gasoline transaction at 2:35 a.m.

Quinn moved across the parking lot and unlocked the door to his white unmarked car. Mr. Deluca was up for capital murder and would probably get the death penalty. Quinn supposed he should feel bad at the prospect. He supposed it was the compassionate, human way to feel, but he'd been at the autopsy of Mrs. Deluca and her three children. He'd seen what the fire had done to them, and he was fresh out of compassion for anyone but the victims.

He fired up his car and headed across town. He turned on Grove Street and drove past the Grove Hotel, with its infamous river sculpture on the exterior wall.

The sculpture was supposed to represent the Boise River, but it resembled quake damage more than anything else. It wasn't uncommon to see tourists standing in front of the multicolored crack, their brows scrunched as they wondered what the hell they were supposed to be looking at. To confuse them further, the crack sometimes wafted steam, which was supposed to resemble fog. It didn't.

Quinn was the first to admit that he knew zero to nothing about art. There were really cool sculptures and paintings around the city; the crack in the Grove Hotel just wasn't one of them.

He pulled to a stop at a red light and reached for his sunglasses. With the Deluca case behind him, his thoughts turned to Lucy. He was a cop, trained to pay attention to detail and have near-perfect recall, but he didn't need any tricks of the trade to recall every second of the night before when he'd stood on her front porch kissing her. He'd held her face in his hands with her smooth hair tangled in his fingers. Her mouth had tasted like warm woman, and she'd melted into him. He'd reminded himself he'd just been doing his job. That the woman running her hands up and down his chest and making him hard enough to pound nails was a murder suspect. He'd kept his hands on her face to keep them from traveling south to more interesting places. He might have given into his urge to touch her waist and hips and breasts. To drive her as crazy as she was him, but she'd slid *her* hands to his back, and he'd grabbed her wrists a split second before she'd discovered the recorder taped to his back.

He would have loved to have taken her up on her first and second invitation for coffee. He would have loved to have followed her inside and checked out her bra right before he'd have buried his face in her cleavage. He would have damn sure loved to have stripped her naked and do the hot sweaty deed, but he couldn't have followed her inside and jumped on her. Breathless did her work in the victim's bed, not her own. Sure, he probably should have followed Lucy inside and maybe gotten more information out of her, but he just wasn't into prolonged torture.

The traffic light turned green, and by the time he got to the office it was the end of his shift. He filled Sergeant Mitchell in on what had taken place in court that day. They talked about the latest developments in the Breathless case. He had a date that night with a new suspect, Carol Rey, aka sugarbaby. Carol was an Internet dater, an employee of Hastings Books and Music, and she loved animals. Once again, Quinn would buy a woman coffee and set the bait to see if he could hook a serial killer.

By the time Quinn returned home after his date that evening, he was exhausted but knew it would be hours before he slept. Hopped up on coffee and conversation, his mind went over every detail of the past several hours.

Carol had been a nice-looking woman. She'd seemed normal enough—until she'd started talking about her ex-husband. She'd torn into

the man, ripping him apart for his job performance in and out of bed. That kind of resentment
produced a lot of hatred, and Kurt would e-mail
her in the morning and set up a second date.

Quinn grabbed his laptop and files off the
counter in the kitchen and moved down the hall
to his office. He flipped on the light and walked
to his desk in the corner. Across the room he'd
set up a treadmill and weight bench. Detectives
ate on the go, in greasy spoons, or at their desks.
At the age of thirty-six, Quinn had to work out
five days a week to stay in shape and stave off
the love handles that plagued a lot of cops.

He sank into his office chair and set the laptop and files on his desk. He booted the computer and scratched Millie's head as he waited
for the program to appear.

Even after two months of online dating,
Quinn was still taken aback at the things
women confessed to virtual strangers on a first
date. If they were telling *him* about past husbands and lovers, he was sure they were telling
everyone else they dated, too. Sometimes it got
so bad that he had to fight the urge not to lean
across the table and say, "Honey, I don't want to
hear about your former husband's foot odor,
and I sure as hell don't want to know he had to
take Viagra, Cialis, or Enzyte. Some shit you
just keep to yourself."

Lucy was the only woman he'd dated that he'd actually had to ask about former boyfriends. Of course, Lucy had a bad habit of lying her ass off, so whether she'd managed the truth was open to speculation.

He reached for the phone on his desk and glanced at his watch. It was 9:30 p.m., and he flipped open his notebook and wrote down the time. On the fifth ring, she picked up.

"Hello."

"Lucy, it's Quinn." He leaned back in his chair and moved his head from side to side to work out the kinks in his neck. "I'm just calling to make sure we're still on for tomorrow night."

"Hang on." There was a pause like she put the phone down. A few drawers opened and closed, then she picked up again. "Okay. Yeah, but I was thinking you should come in for a drink first. Or we could just stay here and order takeout."

Breathless never killed and moved the body, and she probably never invited a suspect to her home. "Sounds good." The phone made a soft thud, as if she'd dropped it.

"Sorry," she said and confirmed his suspicion. "I dropped the phone."

He tapped the pen on his desk and asked, "What are you doing?"

"Right now?"

"Yeah."

"I'm standing here in my underwear getting ready to put on my pajamas."

The pen stopped. "I'll let you go," he said as a vision of her wearing licorice candy pants flashed into his head.

"It's okay. I'm going to kick my feet up and watch a little television before bed. What are you doing?"

"Nothing. Just sitting around." In his mind, he had her dressed up in an edible bra too. He wondered if she got kinky. Not the kind of kinky that killed a man, but the kind that let him eat off her undies. Quinn hadn't worked undercover in over four years now, but he still knew how it was done. When to push and how far. He set down his pen and told himself he was just doing his job. "Are they edible?" But he knew his curiosity was more than just work.

There was a pause, during which he half-expected her to tell him to go to hell. "My feet?"

"Your panties."

Another pause and then, "No. They're white satin."

He swallowed, the chair swiveled, and the arm bumped Millie's face. She looked at him like he'd done it on purpose and left the room. He didn't want to talk dirty in front of his dog and watched her go before asking, "Any lace?"

"No."

Damn, he liked lace on a woman.

She added just above a whisper. "But there's pink ribbon."

Damn. "Tell me more about the ribbon."

"It's woven around the tops of my thighs, and there's little bows."

He closed his eyes and imagined it. Imagined that pink ribbon warmed by the heat between her legs. Those panties suddenly sounded edible to him. "Are you wearing a bra?"

Her breath whispered across the line, and he could picture her pink lips. "Yes."

"Does it match your panties?"

"Yes."

He sucked a breath deep into his lungs and pressed his palm against his erection. "Where's the ribbon?"

"Woven down the front."

He could imagine that, too. "Are your nipples hard?"

Instead of answering, she asked, "Are *you* hard, Quinn?"

"Yes."

"Are you in the habit of talking dirty on the phone?" Her voice was seductive as hell.

"No." He pictured her standing right in front of him, her hair spilling across her shoulders like the sun, her feet slightly apart as he ran his hands up the backs of her thighs while he put his mouth on her flat belly. "But I'm willing to give it a try if you are, Sunshine."

Her quiet laughter reached him across the phone line. "See you tomorrow night, Quinn," she said and disconnected.

He opened his eyes and half expected to see her standing in front of him. Instead his gaze focused on the work laid out on his desk. On the mounds of folders, notes, laptop, and the photographs of Mary and Donny's kids.

The silence in the room pressed in on him. The weight of it sat on his chest and forced him to feel the loneliness deep in the black pit of his soul. For several seconds, it was stronger than him and threatened to close his throat. Then he beat it back and shoved it down once again.

He reached for a stereo remote sitting on his desk and pushed Play. The Black Crowes filled the silence with bluesy Southern rock. Chris Robinson sang about good lovin' and being hard to handle.

He was fine with his life just the way it was.

The next evening Lucy took a fortifying drink of her red wine, then set the glass on the coffee table. She didn't want to risk catching a buzz before she told Quinn the reason she'd wanted him to come over to her house instead of going out. It was time to tell him the truth, especially after the conversation they'd had on the telephone last night. She could hardly look at Quinn without her cheeks catching fire, while he didn't seem embarrassed at all.

Out of the corners of her eyes, she glanced across her shoulder at Quinn as he took a long drink of Becks. He gazed down the bottle at Mr. Snookums, who was kneading his thigh. Lucy was all too familiar with Snookums's modus operandi. If Quinn didn't return the cat's affection, he'd move his loving attention a few inches north.

"Get down, Snookie," she said and removed the heavy cat from between them on the couch.

"What did you call him?"

"Snookie. It's short for Mr. Snookums," she explained.

"Uh-huh." Quinn's eyes got kind of squinty, like his head hurt.

Lucy took a deep breath and forced herself to confess on an expelled breath. "I've been lying to you." She said it so quick that she had to wonder if he'd understood her. She hoped so, because she didn't want to have to say it again. Her stomach felt as if she'd swallowed too much air, and her mouth was dry. She was suddenly too nervous to feel any lingering embarrassment over the phone call. If he couldn't understand why she'd lied and decided he didn't want to see her anymore, then the relationship wasn't meant to last. At least that's what she'd been telling herself. But that had been before he'd walked into her living room looking good in a pair of Levi's worn in interesting places and before he'd sat so close to her on the couch that she could smell the cologne on his skin and scent of laundry soap in his clothes.

"About what?"

"I'm not a nurse."

Quinn set the green bottle on his thigh, and his dark gaze stared into hers. One brow lifted in surprise. "You're not?"

She shook her head and turned her body toward him. "No. It's this whole Internet dating thing. I just didn't want to let the world know everything about me." She pulled her knee on the couch and tucked her foot under her other leg. She picked at the seam of her khaki pants with her fingernail. "I wanted to keep some things back. Just in case." She decided not to tell him that the only reason she'd agreed to meet him that first time had been for research. That would only bring up questions about the other men she'd met and killed off. She didn't want to talk about those other men. Not tonight.

"In case what?"

"In case you were a loser or a stalker or just really insane." She pushed her hair behind her ears, then placed her hands in her lap. She lowered her gaze to the middle of his chest. His blue hooded sweatshirt was so old that the logo on the front had faded to nothing. "That night at Starbucks, I thought for sure you'd realize that I didn't have any medical training." After a few long moments filled with silence, she lifted her gaze to his face. "I guess you didn't notice that I don't know the Heimlich."

"I noticed." One corner of his mouth slid up, and a little comma creased the corner. "I just figured you sucked at being a nurse."

She let out a pent-up breath, and her nerves settled a bit. "But you asked me out again anyway?"

With his free hand, he picked up hers and brushed his thumb across the backs of her knuckles. "I figured since you're so fine, you had to be really good at other things."

Little tingles spread up her wrist to the inside of her elbow. "What things?"

"Girl things."

"Girl things?" She tried for outrage and blew it by laughing. She tried to pull her hand back, but he brought it up to his mouth. "What girl things?"

Laugh lines wrinkled the corners of his eyes

as he looked at her over her fingers. "Cooking." He pressed a kiss to the tingles on her wrist, just below the sleeve of her maroon sweater.

"I am a very good cook." When she did cook.

"Good. I like to eat." He lightly bit her palm.

The too-much-air feeling in Lucy's stomach pressed upward into her heart. "What?" she asked past the constriction in her chest.

"What do I like to eat?"

"Yeah."

"Blondes with blue eyes."

Oh God. She pulled her hand from his. "Are you hungry?"

His gaze lowered to her mouth. "I could eat."

Years of experience had taught Lucy to take it slow. Not to rush. Not to get too involved too soon. At least that's what the rational part of her brain told her. Then he raised his gaze to hers once more, and there it was. That hot, hungry something that looked out at her from the depths of his dark eyes and blew rational all to hell. "I'll order takeout," she murmured as she quickly stood and walked into the kitchen before her brain shut down and she pulled him down on top of her. "Pizza, pasta, salad?" she asked as she picked up the phone on the counter.

"Whatever." Quinn followed as far as the doorway. He leaned one shoulder into the frame and tapped the bottle against his thigh. "So, if you're not a nurse, what do you do?"

Lucy pushed number five on her speed dial. "I'm a writer."

"A writer?" His black brows lowered as if he didn't quite believe her. "What do you write?"

"Mystery novels."

He raised the bottle to his lips. "Have you sold any?" he asked before he took a drink.

"Yes. I'm writing my seventh book." A person picked up on the other end of the line. "I want to order a medium combo and two Caesar salads for delivery," she said. She gave her phone number and was told it would be half an hour to forty-five minutes.

"Under your own name?"

"Yep." She pushed End and set the phone down.

"So I can go into a bookstore and buy one of your books? Or are you a writer like you were a nurse?"

"I'll show you," she said and headed toward the stairs to her office. She stopped on the bottom step and looked back over her shoulder at him. He still stood leaning against the doorway. "Come on." She motioned to him with her hand. He pushed away, and Lucy continued upstairs to the loft.

She hadn't planned on bringing Quinn to her

office, and she wished she had dusted and maybe straightened her research books. But at least the writing hadn't gotten so crazy that she'd started piling things on the floor around her chair. Not yet. It would. It always did.

From within the confines of her seventeen-inch flat-screen monitor, hungry sharks swam the blue waters of the Great Barrier Reef. Lucy walked to her desk and reached for the mouse. The shark screen saver disappeared and revealed the scene she'd been reworking in *dead.com.* She rolled the pointer to the top right and reduced the document to an icon in the lower left of the task bar. She glanced over her shoulder at Quinn as he glanced about her office. He looked at her big L-shaped desk, which took up half the wall to her left, before he glanced about at her printer, scanner, fax, and copier, which were placed around the room according to electric outlets.

Plaques and writing awards hung on the walls and lined the numerous shelves. Her starred *Publishers Weekly* reviews sat in frames next to photos of her family and friends. The gold star trophy her mother had given her when she'd sold her first book sat on top of a stack of her books that had been translated into foreign languages.

"This is where I spend most of my life," she

said, then pointed to two closed doors. "That's a closet where I store paper, and that's a bathroom I added about two years ago so I wouldn't have to run up and down the stairs all day and night."

Quinn moved to a shelf containing a row of her published hardbacks. As he studied her books, she studied the back of his dark head. Her gaze lowered to the short black hair on the back of his neck. His wide shoulders filled out his big sweatshirt, and she lowered her attention down his back to the behind of his Levi's. He'd threaded an old brown belt through the loops low on his hips, and his wallet bulged one of the worn pockets hugging his butt. He was so tall, so completely masculine, that it was a little disconcerting to see him in her own personal space. He set his beer on a shelf, then reached for a book. He flipped it to the back and glanced at her photo on the dust cover. "This is a good picture." He raised his gaze from the photograph to her. "But you're better looking in person."

The compliment filled her with more pleasure than it should have, and she felt a little embarrassed. "Thanks." She scooted papers aside and sat on top of her desk. She folded her arms beneath her breasts and watched Quinn.

"You must be a good writer."

"What makes you say that?"

He pointed with his thumb behind him. "All those plaques on your wall. I don't imagine bad writers get plaques."

"You'd be surprised." She was surprised he'd noticed those. She'd had boyfriends whom she'd dated for years who hadn't noticed any of her accomplishments out of bed. It was silly. Nothing really, but the fact that Quinn noticed something about her after knowing her a week made her like him a whole lot more. Which was dangerous, because she already liked him a whole lot.

He slid the book back into place and turned his attention to an eight-by-ten photo of Lucy and her friends taken a few winters ago in Cancun. He leaned in to take a closer look at the four women in bikini tops and shorts, sunburned skin and drunken grins. "Those are my friends," she explained. "They're writers, too."

Quinn straightened and looked at her over his shoulder. "Mystery writers?"

"No. We all write in different genres. When we go out, it can get real interesting."

"They all live in Boise?"

"Yep."

"Wow, I didn't know so many writers lived around here."

"Well, you know what they say: Paris, London, New York, Boise."

One corner of his mouth turned downward in a dubious smile. "Who says that?" he asked as he walked toward her, his loose stride reminding her of the first time she'd seen him in Starbucks.

"The T-shirt shop at the mall."

He stopped in front of her. "Then it must be true." So close that she had to look up. So close that she thought he might touch her. Instead he reached beside her and plucked a CD from her CD rack. As if in pain, he sucked in air through his teeth. "I don't know if I can date a girl who listens to Phil Collins."

Lucy took the CD from his hands and set it on her desk. "It was a gift from an old boyfriend."

"Phil Collins sucks."

"So did the old boyfriend."

He chuckled, then of course he zeroed in on the fuzzy pink handcuffs sitting in front of a row of research books in the hutch above her monitor. He picked them up and held them with one finger. "Kinky."

"They were a gift."

"From a boyfriend?"

"No. From the Women of Mystery."

His eyelids lowered and his voice got husky. "Now that's twisted."

Lucy laughed and grabbed the cuffs dangling from his finger. She placed them next to the CD on the desk. "The Women of Mystery is a group of local writers. About once a year, they ask me to speak at one of their meetings."

"No one gets tied up?"

"No bondage of any kind."

"Damn." He shook his head. "I was hoping to hear something good." He moved between her knees. His fingers brushed her ears, and he pushed her hair out of her face. "How kinky do you get?"

She didn't. Not really. Well, not on a regular basis. After the phone call last night, she didn't expect him to believe it, though. She placed her hands behind her on the desk and leaned back. "What's your definition of kinky?"

His gaze drifted to her mouth. "Do you like to be tied up?"

She shook her head. "No, I like to be an active participant."

He leaned over her and placed his hands next to hers on the desk. A few inches from her mouth he asked, "Do you like to tie men up?"

Again she shook her head. "No, I like to be *with* an active participant. A man who isn't going to just lay there. Otherwise, what's the point of having someone else in the room?"

"Someone to talk dirty to."

"Talking dirty is overrated."

"You don't like men to talk during sex?"

For the most part, no. Nothing ruined the mood faster than "Come to daddy."

"Some talking is okay." She shrugged. "But at some point all talking dissolves to the basics anyway."

"What're the basics?"

She lowered her voice and moaned like she was in the throes of orgasm. "Harder, faster, don't stop or I'll kick your ass."

He let out a breath. "Jesus H. Macy."

Lucy laughed. "Do you like it kinky?"

"Sunshine, I'm a guy. I'll do just about anything if it means I'm going to get laid."

He'd called her Sunshine. It wasn't the first time he'd called her that, and she wondered what he called other women. She wondered what he'd called his wife. She was curious about the woman Quinn had loved and lost so tragically. The woman who'd left him so lonely that he'd turned to the Internet for companionship. "Last night you said you wanted more. What did you mean?"

"That I want to see more of you."

"Are you sure you're ready?"

He pulled back far enough to look into her eyes. "Why wouldn't I be ready?"

"Because you might still be grieving for Millie. I like you. A lot. I do, but I don't want to get involved with someone who might be looking to replace his wife." She thought he might get angry or hurt. Instead he smiled as if he found the whole idea amusing.

"I'm not looking for a woman to replace Millie." He reached for one of her hands and slid it up his chest to the back of his neck. "I want to be with you." He straightened and brought her up against his chest. "I like being with you," he continued. "When I'm not with you, I'm thinking about you. No one else. Just you."

Lucy ran her free palm up his arm to his shoulder and brought his mouth down to hers. She kissed him lightly at first. A slow brush of lips and light touch of tongues. She recognized the scent of his skin and the wet texture of his mouth. She felt his hands and fingers in her hair, and he whispered her name.

"Lucy," he said, "this is what keeps me up at night." The kiss turned hotter. Like liquid sunlight, it spread across her skin. Deeper, so deep that it touched her heart and made her feel light-headed. So light-headed that she thought she heard bells, and when Quinn lifted his mouth from hers, she realized she did hear bells.

"Pizza's here," he said as her doorbell rang once more. "We could ignore it."

Lucy dropped her hands from the back of Quinn's neck and sighed. "No. I order from them all the time. The delivery guys know to keep knocking until I answer." Occasionally, if she was really into her work, they had to call to tell her they were at her front door.

Quinn took a step back and ran his fingers through the sides of his hair. Frustration burned from his hooded gaze, and Lucy wondered how far things would have gone before one of them would have stopped. She liked to think not far, but she wouldn't have staked her life on it.

Quinn watched Lucy stand and move across her office when what he really wanted to do was put her back on that desk and crawl on top of her. His gaze moved from the top of her blonde head, down her back and narrow hips, to her round behind. He dropped his hands to his sides and let out a deep breath. He felt like a kid again, living day in and out with a constant hard-on. It was enough to drive him insane. "I'm going to use your bathroom and be right down," he told her.

She looked over her shoulder at him. "Okay," she said and walked through the doorway. Quinn listened for her footsteps descending the stairs before he turned his attention to the hutch on her desk filled with crime reference books. Homicide investigation checklists and field guides. Books on investigators' tactics, procedures, and a whole slew of books on forensics. He noticed studies of clinical disorders and criminal behavior in her shelves. Her reading covered everything from poisons and weaponry to material on the most infamous serial killers in history.

Perfectly understandable reading for a mystery writer. The more he knew Lucy, the more he was convinced she wasn't a killer. Of course, his brain reminded his groin, that could be because he was attracted to her and didn't want to believe he could get hard for a psychotic nutball.

Her cat wove itself like an orange Slinky between his feet. He didn't particularly like cats. Especially cats named Snookums. Christ, even thinking the cat's name made his sac shrivel. He reached for her mouse and enlarged the document she'd reduced when he'd first walked into her office. He didn't expect to see anything incriminating, but he placed his hands on the desk and read anyway.

Within the clear plastic, his blue eyes stared into hers, wild, pleading, filled with terror. He struggled for breath, but the more he struggled, the more thin plastic he sucked down his throat. He thrashed about on the bed, pulling and kicking. The strain of the flexi-cuffs was turning his hands white. Fighting was useless.

She sat back on her heels and waited. It wouldn't take long now. His cuffed hands curled into fists and his back arched. Then he stilled, his muscles relaxed, and she counted. Five . . .

ten . . . fifteen seconds. His body jerked and convulsed. He wet himself, then went lifeless. She leaned in close and stared into his eyes. Her blood pounded in her ears and she held her breath. She watched his blue eyes fix, his pupils enlarged. She waited . . . waited for the exact moment when life left his body. Her lungs felt like they were going to explode . . . but nothing. She leaned back and crossed her arms beneath her bare breasts. That was it? Where was his soul? She thought for sure she'd see it this time. Disappointment settled between her brows. The last guy had given her more of a glimpse into his passing from one world into the next. This one had been a dud.

She gave him a look filled with contempt and scooted across the bed. It had taken her a month to find this guy. It would probably take her a month to find the next one too. But there would be others. There were always others. It was so easy. Some men would do anything if they thought it led to sex.

She grabbed her panties off the floor. Men were so pathetic.

Quinn straightened, and everything within him got real still. He stared at the screen and the blinking cursor. Then he leaned his head back and closed his eyes.

"Fuck," he whispered to the empty room.

Chapter 8

Hugsnkisses: Seeks Hotlips . . .

Lucy stood behind the pulpit in the community room of Barnes and Noble and turned to the next page of notes she'd prepared for the Women of Mystery meeting. Cynthia Pool, Barnes and Noble employee and Women of Mystery member, handed Lucy the iced coffee she'd ordered earlier.

"Thank you," Lucy said and took a sip.

"I hope it isn't too strong. I told them a triple shot, but I think they might have gotten it too strong."

Lucy looked into Cynthia's light green eyes and smiled. She didn't know Cynthia well, only that the woman was kind of fussy. "It's perfect."

For the meeting, Lucy had decided to wear something bright and fun. She'd dressed in a cable-knit sweater the color of a tangerine, a black leather skirt, black hose, and spiky calf boots. She'd curled her hair, then pulled it up into a loose ponytail. The afternoon sunlight sliced through the windows to her left and created long rectangles on the carpet.

With the exception of a few new faces, she'd met all these ladies before. She was well acquainted with them, and she knew they were a real mix of serious writers and dabblers. Their personalities ranged from down-to-earth normal to truly bizarre, but they all had one thing in common: They loved mystery novels. They knew the genre inside and out and had great fun talking about every aspect of it.

For an hour, Lucy spoke about the importance of weaving a good, believable plot, then she opened the rest of the time up for questions. In the front row, a woman she didn't recognize raised her hand. Lucy took a drink of her coffee and pointed to the lady.

She stood, consulted her notes, then asked, "Where do you get your ideas?"

Lucy groaned silently and lowered her cup. It was the question she was asked most often, and the one she could never truly answer. "I don't know," she answered as best she could. "A snippet of conversation enters my head, or I'll get a flash of a scene, and I know that's the next book. I have to figure out what it means, but I never know where it comes from. I just thank God it keeps coming. The day it doesn't, I'm in trouble."

Next she pointed to an older woman whom she recognized from past meetings. "Yes," the older woman began as she stood. "Do you have an agent? And do you recommend getting one?"

Okay. That one is easy. "Yes I do, and yes I would."

A third woman stood. "In your talk, you mentioned the use of red herrings or false clues as important in order to keep the reader guessing. In the book I'm writing, I have one of the townspeople kill a dog. Everyone in town then thinks he must be the killer, and that's what readers are led to believe also. But he isn't. Would you say that's a good red herring?"

Lucy swallowed. The woman was serious and expected a serious answer. "Well, without reading your story and knowing the context in which the dog was killed, nor the mind-set of the townspeople, I'm not sure I can answer that for you. But I would say that you're the writer, and if you feel it works, then I'm sure it does." That answer seemed to satisfy the woman, and she sat down.

The next woman to stand was Jan Bright, president of the Women of Mystery and also a Barnes and Noble employee. "When you talked to us last year, you mentioned that the next idea you had for a book involved erotic asphyxiation and Internet dating. Is that what you're working on now?"

Lucy hadn't recalled talking about the book at a writers meeting, but she obviously had at some point. "Yes, that's the book I'm working on right now."

"Can you tell us how it's going?"

Hmm. How did one describe bouts of muse-induced euphoria sandwiched between thoughts of ramming your head through the wall? "Great." She smiled and raised her coffee. "I've killed off three men, and I'm about to kill a fourth."

The ladies laughed, and Lucy glanced up from the group seated in front of her to the store beyond. Like a magnet, her gaze was immediately drawn to a tall man leaning one hip into the "local interest" book rack a few feet beyond the last row of chairs. He had dark hair, and, like the first time she'd met him, he pinned her with his intense brown eyes. He wore a black long-sleeved Moosejaw T-shirt tucked into a pair of jeans. One corner of his mouth slid up, and her heart pinched and swelled at the same time. Quinn was the last person she'd expected to see at the Women of Mystery meeting—although technically he wasn't standing close enough to be considered in the meeting.

Lucy bit her lip to keep from smiling and answered the next question.

"How much money do you make?" someone she didn't recognize asked.

"Enough to live on, but not as much as I deserve." She didn't want to read anything into Quinn's appearance. The night before last, when she'd told him she wasn't a nurse, he'd seemed to take the news really well, but during pizza he'd become distant. It hadn't been anything tangible. Nothing that he'd said or done, but she'd felt him withdraw. She'd wondered if bringing up his dead wife had been a mistake. She'd wondered if, while he'd been in the bathroom, he'd rethought his involvement with her.

"When's your murder-on-the-Internet book going to be out?"

"May of next year."

Next question. "Can you give us four examples of books in which red herrings or false clues kept readers guessing right until the very last page?"

What? Was she back in college? Get real. Even if she hadn't been distracted by a mad, bad, and handsome-as-hell man staring at her, she'd have had a hard time with that question. She shrugged and named four of her books.

"We have time for one more question," Jan announced.

A woman with white hair and big brown glasses stood, and Lucy groaned inwardly. The woman's name was Betty, and, seeing her stand, the group as a whole gave a collective moan of agony.

"I'm writing a book that takes place in a nursing home," Betty began, although Lucy knew all about Betty's book. Betty had been writing and talking about the same scene in the same book for years. "If I wanted to kill off an old man, like my ninety-year-old father, how best should I go about doing that? I called *Ask A Nurse*, but they were no help at all."

She'd called *Ask A Nurse* for research help? Like they had nothing better to do? "I'm not sure. Perhaps if he's on heart medication, you could overdose him." Lucy straightened her papers, then shoved them into the collapsible folder in which Maddie had returned Lucy's six chapters when they'd met for lunch earlier. She was looking forward to reading Maddie's notes. Lucy placed the folder beside her briefcase and hoped Betty would get the hint.

She didn't. "I thought smothering him with a pillow might work better."

"Suffocation would be good if you want to use something that is hard to detect. There's no specific autopsy findings that can prove suffocation," she explained. "There might be bruising or abrasions if the victim struggles, but with airway constriction deaths, a coroner has to rely on physical evidence from the scene to support a diagnosis."

"Huh?"

"If you want the killer to get caught, have him or her leave something behind at the scene." She smiled. "Thank you, ladies, for inviting me here today. As always, it was my pleasure to speak to you again."

She grabbed her briefcase and shook a few hands. As she slowly made her way toward Quinn, she chatted briefly with some of the ladies who were always kind enough to attend her signings.

After Quinn had left her house the other night, a part of her had wondered if she'd see him again. When he'd left, instead of grabbing her and locking lips as he had the few times they'd been together, he'd kissed her forehead. Something had been wrong, but he'd called yesterday afternoon and asked her over to his house for dinner. She was embarrassed to admit, even to herself, how happy she'd been to hear his voice. Of course she'd agreed, but the dinner wasn't for several more hours.

"What are you doing here?" she asked as she came to stand in front of him.

He pushed away from the book rack. "You told me you were talking to these ladies today, and I wanted to hear you."

She looked down at her briefcase so he wouldn't see her smile. "That's sweet."

He chuckled, and she looked back up. "No one's ever called me sweet."

"What have they called you?"

He gazed beyond her for several seconds, then put his arm around her shoulder. "Things I can't repeat in public." Together they walked past a group of The Peacock Society lined up at the checkout. "I thought you might come over early."

"How early?"

"Now."

She really needed to work, since she doubted she'd get much work done later tonight. "I have to go home and change."

Quinn opened the doors for her. "Don't change. I like your skirt."

"Well, I still have to go home. I made dessert."

"Really?" Together they moved across the sidewalk to the curb. "What did you make?"

A chocolate torte that she worried might be too much this early in the relationship. It never paid to cook so soon. It set a bad precedent. "Something decadent."

"You wrapped up in that skirt is decadent." He slid his hand beneath her ponytail and lowered his mouth to hers. He kissed her for several heartbeats, then lifted his head. "See ya in a few."

"Yeah, see ya." She watched him move across the parking lot to his Jeep, and her gaze slid down his back to his tight behind in his jeans. He'd driven all the way across town just to hear her talk to a group of women mystery writers. It was such an incredibly sweet thing to do. She felt a scary little pinch in her heart.

She reached inside her briefcase and pulled out her sunglasses. She slipped them on the bridge of her nose, then turned to glance inside Barnes and Noble. Jan Bright and a few of the other ladies stood just inside, watching her and Quinn. Lucy waved good-bye before stepping off the curb and heading toward her car. Toward dinner and decadence with a man who seemed too good to be true. A man who made her heart pinch in her chest.

A man who, if she wasn't very careful, could make her fall in love with him.

* * *

Quinn watched Lucy raise the fork to her lips and slide the piece of chocolate torte into her mouth. She licked frosting from the corner of her lips and gave him a smooth smile. The kind of smile a woman gave a man after he'd satisfied her in bed. "Mmm," she said, her voice as deep and decadent as the cake. Her deep blue eyes shone with pure pleasure. "It's wonderful." With her hair up in soft curls, she was sexy as hell. Too bad she was a serial killer.

"Take a bite," she urged.

Breathless had never poisoned her victims. Not yet, anyway. Quinn didn't want to be the first. He waited until she took another bite before he picked up his fork and dug in. It was better than wonderful. So damn good that he leaned across the table and kissed her on the mouth, killer or not. He meant to pull back, but her lips clung to his, tasting like fine chocolate and warm woman. In spite of everything he now knew about her, the dull throb of desire tugged at his groin. He didn't want to feel anything for her. Nothing. Anger mixed with lust as he raised his mouth from hers.

"Is something wrong?" she asked.

He gave her an easy smile. "No." He knew how to play the game. To make people think he was someone he wasn't. He'd always had fun catching the bad guys. This time, he wasn't having any fun. "Nothing other than you taste good," he said and leaned back in his chair.

She took another bite, and he watched her closely. He watched her lips close over the fork tines and her eyes get dreamy like she was in the throes of afterglow. If he hadn't seen with his own eyes the book she was working on, he wouldn't have thought the woman in front of him, who was eating cake like she was having an orgasm, was capable of killing anyone. It wasn't until he'd seen the proof that he'd realized he hadn't really believed she was Breathless. Now, there was no denying it. She'd written things that only Breathless would know. The flexi-cuffs. The polyethylene bag over the victim's head. The position of the bodies. There was no longer room for denial, and everything she'd talked about at that mystery meeting earlier took on new meaning.

Before she'd arrived tonight, he'd placed two framed photos of Anita next to the clock in the living room because she had red hair like his "dead wife Millie." The props made his house seem more like the home of a widower. The real Millie was at his mother's house.

That morning a few tech guys had shown up with their equipment. They'd placed motion detecting audio and video surveillance in an air purifier in the kitchen, in a fake clock on the mantel in the living room, and in a clock radio beside his bed. The whole house was bugged for motion and sound. The only places the cameras couldn't see or hear were down the hall and in the bathrooms. Across the street from Quinn's house, Kurt and Anita sat in the Econoline, watching, listening, waiting for Lucy to cuff him to his bed and try to kill him.

"I think the Women of Mystery thought you were cute," she said through a teasing smile. "When you left they were looking out the windows at you."

Quinn doubted they thought he was cute. More likely a few of them were wondering what Lucy was doing with a cop. He'd recognized two of them, and before they'd been able to make their way toward him, he'd hustled Lucy out of the store.

She licked the back of her fork with the tip of her tongue and he felt it between his legs. "Sometimes, chocolate is better than sex," she said.

"Sunshine, nothing is better than sex."

She set the fork on her plate and pushed it aside. "I guess that would depend on your basis of comparison."

Lucy Rothschild was Breathless. What angered him most was the fact that she could make him want her. He rose from his chair and reached for her. "Come here," he said and wrapped his arms around her. It was time to turn up the heat. Add some pressure. Trigger her stress button. It had been several weeks since the last murder. She had to be feeling the compulsion to kill again. It had to be riding her like his compulsion to bury himself deep inside her was riding him. Neither would get release.

"Let's give you something good to compare." He lowered his mouth to hers and gave her a kiss filled with need and frustrated desire. He wished it were a lie. He'd give anything if he could tell himself that it was all just an act, but the ache in his crotch called him a liar. He swept his tongue into her mouth, and his hand slid down her back to her behind. Through the cool leather of her skirt, he filled his palms and pulled her up onto the balls of her feet. Against her pelvis, he let her feel his full-blown hard-on. He fed her hot, wild kisses as he rocked his hips and slowly thrust against her. Pushing her to react.

He was in hell.

She pulled her head back and sucked in a deep breath. "I need to use your restroom," she said, her eyes wide. It wasn't quite the reaction he'd wanted.

He let go and pointed behind her. "Down the hall. Second door on your right." The heels of her boots tapped across the hardwood floor as she disappeared around the corner and down the hall. As soon as Quinn heard the bathroom door close behind her, he moved into the living room and reached for her purse, which was sitting on the couch. He turned it upside down, and a big collection of crap fell out. On top was a scarf and a set of keys, three tubes of lipstick, a business card case, an address book, and Autographed by Author stickers. He pawed through the pile, pushing aside a red leather wallet, a can of pepper spray, a personal alarm, a stun pen, and a pair of brass knuckles. If he found the flexi-cuffs and a dry-cleaning bag in her purse, he could arrest her right now. Along with everything, it would be enough circumstantial evidence to take to the prosecutor. But it seemed like she'd brought everything she owned—except those two items.

He looked at the other stuff and frowned. What? Was she planning on shocking him with a stun pen? It wouldn't kill him, but it would hurt like hell. Or did she plan to hose him with her pepper spray, then coldcock him with brass knuckles?

Down the hall, the toilet flushed, and Quinn shoved everything back into her purse. She could have the cuffs on her. Probably in her bra. It was possible. He was going to have to search her underwear.

It was his job. Shit.

* * *

Lucy washed her hands, then dried them on the dark blue towel hanging by the sink. There was something different about Quinn tonight. A few days ago, he'd said he wanted to take things slow. That he wanted more than sex. Earlier, as he'd cooked steaks on his grill and as they'd eaten dinner, he'd kept the conversation light. He'd seemed relaxed and comfortable in his white dress shirt and blue jeans. He'd entertained her with funny stories about all his nieces, and they'd talked about the latest *Cold Case Files* episode—then wham. He'd hit her with that kiss, and she'd felt as if she'd been knocked in the head. In zero to fifty, he'd gone from Mr. Friendly to Mr. Man-on-a-Mission. A mission to get her naked.

She pressed a cool palm to her hot cheek and looked at herself in the mirror. She cared about him. Even more than she wanted to admit to herself, but it was too early in the relationship for a naked mission with Quinn. No matter how tempting. And she *was* tempted. She dropped her hand and opened the door. No doubt about it.

She found Quinn standing in the middle of the living room staring into the unlit fireplace. He looked up, and his dark gaze followed her as she walked across the room to the mantel.

Across the distance, she felt his desire pulling at her. Threatening to suck her under. Maybe she should leave. Grab her purse and run before she did something stupid. Like forget she didn't have sex with guys after knowing them for little over a week. No matter how much he made her ache. No matter that she was halfway in love with him, as ridiculous as that seemed.

"Who's this?" she asked as she picked up a picture frame.

"Millie."

She looked closer at the woman he'd married. Red curls framed her face, and big green eyes looked out from behind a pair of brown framed glasses. Millie had been cute in a healthy, runs-ten-miles-and-climbs-rocks sort of way. Whatever Lucy had expected his wife to look like, this wasn't it.

Quinn moved behind her and placed his hands on her shoulders. "That was taken about a year before she died," he informed her.

"How old was she then?"

He paused a moment, then said next to her left ear, "My age."

Lucy set the photo back on the mantel. "She looks younger."

"Yeah, she hated that."

"Quinn?"

"Hmm."

"I think . . . I don't think . . ." She glanced up into his image, reflected in the mirror in front of her. "I don't think we should have sex."

His dark gaze stared into hers. "I don't want to do anything you're uncomfortable with." His hands moved down her arms and came to rest on her waist. "You tell me when to stop." Slowly, he slid his palms to her stomach and pulled her back against his chest. "Are you uncomfortable when I kiss you here?" He bent his dark head and placed his mouth on the side of her throat. She watched him brush his lips across her skin, and the fine hairs on the back of her neck tingled. She shook her head.

"That's good. I like kissing you right here. Where your skin's soft and your hair smells like flowers and looks like the sun."

He hooked his thumbs inside the waistband of her skirt and slid them to her sides. The backs of his thumbs brushed her black hose.

She tilted her head to the right and he opened his hot, wet mouth and sucked her skin. The heat of his kiss spread outward, across her shoulder and down her chest. Her heart pounded and swelled, and her breasts grew heavy. She leaned back into the solid, warm comfort of his embrace and took a deep breath. The scent of him, his musky cologne and Quinn, filled her head. His gaze locked with hers as he slipped his fingers up beneath the edge of her sweater.

His heavy lids lowered to half mast, and there was no mistaking the desire burning in his eyes. No mistaking the long hard length of it pressed into her behind. He slipped his big hands beneath her sweater, and his fingers fanned across her bare stomach. She would stop him. Soon. But not when it felt so good. When everything about him, his gaze, his touch, the scent of his skin, made her want to sink back into him and stay there awhile. Her feelings for him seemed to expand beyond her control. Overpowering, like Quinn himself, and she felt as if she were in a free fall. A long, hot fall into Quinn McIntyre, and there didn't seem to be anything she could do about it.

His thumbs brushed the underwire of her bra, a lazy back and forth that drove her crazy before sliding up the swells of her breasts to press into her hard nipples. Her breath caught in her chest, and she knew that if she was going to stop him, she had to do it now. She opened her mouth, and he circled her nipples with his thumbs. She'd tell him in a minute. A heavy ache pooled between her thighs, and she instinctively squeezed her legs together. Her lids drifted shut as his hands slid up and cupped her breasts.

"Your nipples are hard," he whispered into the side of her throat. "Like a woman who wants to make love."

She looked at him in the mirror. At his gaze looking back at her with unconcealed lust burning in his eyes. He definitely looked like a man who wanted to make love, and Lucy turned and wrapped her arms around his neck. His hands slid to her back, and her breasts smashed into his chest. She kissed him full on the mouth. He slipped the fingers of one hand beneath the waistband of her skirt and pressed his warm palm into the small of her back, holding her against his rock-hard penis. His other hand moved up her spine and the kiss got hotter, turning into a maddening chase and follow, a slick advance and retreat of hot tongues and mouths.

His fingers continued to slide up and down her spine, his touch light and feathery, making her shudder and moan deep in her throat. Lust, hot and liquid, rushed through her veins, getting all mixed up and confused with the feelings deep in her soul. The last ounce of her self-control slipped away as Quinn rubbed against her and his hands slid over her body, touching everywhere, turning up the heat and taking control. Everything got hotter and dizzier, and somehow she lost her sweater. Before she knew quite how it happened, it was on the floor by her feet. Quinn took a step back, and his hooded gaze moved from her face, down her throat and shoulders, to her breasts.

His harsh breathing lifted his chest, as if he'd just jogged ten miles. Lucy knew the feeling.

"I love a woman in lace," he whispered and lifted a hand to touch the lace edge of her bra with the tips of his fingers. "You're so beautiful, you make me forget."

She licked her lips and endeavored to control her breathing before she passed out. "Forget what?"

He glanced up at her, then returned his gaze to her nipples, which were making two distinct pebbles in the white cups of her bra. "That I should take it slow. That I don't want to blow it by rushing things," he answered even as he pressed his palms into her full breasts. "But it's been so long." The heat from his palms seeped through the satin material, and he pushed her breasts together as he bent forward and kissed her deep cleavage. "Why did you have to look like this?" he asked, his warm breath brushing across her flesh. "This would be easier if you weren't so beautiful. If I didn't want you so much that I can't think of anything but getting you naked."

Lucy knew that feeling, too. He lifted his face

to hers once more and gave her a kiss that she felt clear to the soles of her feet. He ran his hands down her bottom to the backs of her thighs, and he lifted her. She didn't hesitate to wrap her legs around his waist. He walked with her from the room, and she thought he would carry her to his bed.

They made it as far as the darker shadows of the hall before he pinned her back against the wall. He unhooked her bra and fastened his hot, wet mouth on her breast. He drew on her nipple as his hands shoved her skirt up around her waist. He slid his palms over her thighs then over her ribs and around to the small of her back.

Lucy ran her hands through his hair while he kissed and sucked her breasts as if he couldn't get enough. He ground his incredibly hard penis into her through the thin fabric of her hose and panties, driving her toward the edge until she knew she'd either stop or embarrass herself.

She slid her legs from around his waist and stood. He moved his mouth to the side of her neck just above her clavicle as her fingers unbuttoned his shirt and pulled the tails from his jeans. She slid her hands over the hard muscles of his chest, abdomen, and back. Her fingers combed through the short hair on his chest, and he whispered something against her throat.

With her skirt shoved up around her waist, Quinn slid his big hand between her thighs and cupped her through her panties and hose. She thought she heard him say, "Nothing here but Lucy." That didn't make sense, so she figured she'd heard wrong. But there was no mistaking what he said next. No mistaking what he did, either. He pulled down her hose and panties and slid his fingers where she was slick with desire. "You want me, and I want to fuck you until you can't walk for a week," he said as he touched her. "Until you can't move. Can't think. Can't do anything but moan. Do you want that, Lucy?"

She swayed, and her knees got weak, and all she could manage was a breathy, "Yes." Maybe under different circumstances she might have objected to his language. The f-bomb was not her favorite word, nor was she real fond of sex talk, but at the moment she wanted what he promised. Walking was overrated. She unbuttoned his jeans and slid her hand inside the waistband and beneath the elastic of his boxers. He sucked in a deep breath.

"You don't have to do this," he whispered next to her ear even as he began to stroke her.

"I know. I want to do this." Her fingers curled around the heavy length of him. He was hard and hot against her palm, and she squeezed him tight. She could feel his pulse, and she brushed her thumb up and over the plump head of his rigid erection.

"Lucy," he forced through a heavy groan. "I'll help you, Lucy."

"Yes. Please." God, he was a talker. She could deal with that. She moved her hand down the long hard length of him, feeling his velvet-soft skin that covered every ridge and bulging vein.

"Yes, touch me there, just like that," he whispered. "You won't be alone. Oh, God that feels good. I'll get you help. I'll get you all the help you need."

He was all the help she needed. Especially when he slipped one long finger inside her and continued to stroke her with his thumb. Her whole world narrowed and centered on Quinn and the wonderful things he was doing to her with his hand. Her flesh tingled and she opened her mouth to tell him to stop, but the first scalding wave of orgasm hit her before the words left her throat. All she managed was an, "Oh no!" before the force of it knocked her head back against the wall and her knees almost buckled. She raised her hands to his shoulder to keep from falling into a hot puddle at his feet. Her heart pounded in her ears as wave after hot wave rushed through her. Over and over, it seemed to last forever and not long enough. She held onto Quinn for support as the last pulsations eased. Above the pounding in her head and the harsh breathing that filled the hall, she heard the insistent ring of the telephone.

"I'm sorry," she said through a shallow breath. "I didn't mean to do that yet."

He chuckled and lightly bit the side of her neck. "You'll make up for it." The telephone stopped, only to start ringing again. "Shit!" he said. He lifted his head and looked at Lucy through the dark shadows of the hallway. "I'll be right back." He moved into the living room and picked up the cordless phone next to the couch. "Yeah?"

Lucy pulled up her panties and hose and pushed down her skirt. She retrieved her bra from the floor, then moved a few steps down the hall to watch Quinn pace the floor in the living room.

"Because I was busy." The phone was cradled between his shoulder and the side of his face, and his hands were busy buttoning his pants. "What?" He stilled, and one hand came up to grasp the phone. "Are you fucking kidding me?" He turned to Lucy where she stood against the wall. "Tell me you're kidding me."

The look on his face was unfathomable.

Chapter 9

Serialdater: Seeks Killer Date . . .

Flashes of red, white, and blue sliced through the darkness and cut across the office windows and door of a motel known to rent by the hour. Traffic on Chinden Boulevard sped past, not slowing a click, not even to rubberneck the latest crime scene. Not at this time of night in the part of town plagued with flophouses and drug-related crimes.

Quinn fastened his identification to his belt as he moved between police cruisers parked at every angle in the small lot. He held a clipboard under one arm and his duffle bag in his hand. He glanced up at the second floor of the motel, and a frown pulled at the corners of his mouth.

The place was bound to be a nightmare of fingerprints, hairs, and body fluids.

"Is the night manager in the office?" he asked several patrol officers standing around in front of the building.

"Yeah. We got him in there cooling his heels until you want him."

While the patrol cops filled him in on what they knew, Quinn took out a pen and glanced at his watch. He wrote down the time of his arrival, the address of the crime scene, and weather conditions.

"Write down the license plate numbers of all these vehicles and run 'em." The victim's car was probably in the lot and would need to be impounded. He ducked under the yellow crime scene tape and moved up the outside stairs. He walked past three sets of windows with their curtains drawn and continued toward the patrol officers standing outside the open door of room thirty-six.

"How many other rooms are in use?" he asked.

"It's Saturday night. Just about every one."

Someone had to have seen or heard something. "Make sure no one leaves," he said and walked into the room. Kurt, Anita, and two patrol officers stood next to the bed covered with a brown floral spread and a naked dead guy. Yellow nylon rope was bound to the bed frame and tied to the flexi-cuffs around the victim's wrists. A Westco garment bag had been placed over his head and secured around his neck with silver duct tape.

Quinn took a pair of latex gloves from the duffle and moved to the head of the bed. He snapped on the gloves and looked down into a pair of brown eyes staring up at him from within the clear bag sucked tight around his face. Quinn unclenched two of the man's fingers, then watched them curl once more. He'd say death had occurred within the last two hours. Sometime after Lucy had arrived at his house carrying a chocolate torte.

"Have you identified the vic?" he asked Kurt.

"Not yet. Anita and I just got here."

Quinn glanced up at the other detective, and Kurt's gaze slid away. While Quinn had been getting Lucy naked, and Kurt had been watching and listening from across the street, the real perpetrator had been doing her work. They'd fucked up. Big time, but he couldn't think about that now. Lucy clearly wasn't Breathless, and he would deal with her later. Right now, he had work to do. He had to deal with the dead man staring up at him through the child safety warning on the polyethylene bag.

Two crime scene investigators arrived, and

Quinn had one of them snap a picture of the beige Dockers lying on the floor at the foot of the bed. Then he knelt on one knee and pulled a wallet from the back pocket. He flipped the wallet open and looked at the driver's license of Robert D. Patterson. A forty-six-year-old white male. Brown eyes and hair. Five feet nine and one hundred and eighty pounds. Quinn stayed down on one knee, studying the dirty carpet for clues. He looked under the bed, then stood and secured Mr. Patterson's driver's license to the clipboard. He checked the other pockets of the victim's pants and a light nylon jacket also thrown on the dirty carpet. Besides the wallet, he found a set of keys and a folded motel receipt. He placed the items in a paper bag and marked it.

While one investigator got to work snapping photographs from every angle, the other got busy with his bottles of latent print powder. Kurt left the room to question potential witnesses on the second floor of the motel, and Quinn tossed his gloves in the duffle and walked back outside. He shone the flashlight hooked to his belt into the garbage can at the bottom of the stairs. It was half full, and he knew there had to be a Dumpster somewhere on the property. Before the night was over, he was going to be in waders, ass deep in garbage.

He walked into the office and was assailed with the smell of nicotine, fried chicken, and cherry sanitizer. Behind the pocked counter sat Dennis Karpowich, a man in his early sixties with thinning hair the color of Grecian Formula 16. He had bad teeth and a worse smoker's hack. When Quinn showed him Mr. Patterson's license, Dennis identified him as the man who'd paid for a four-hour stay in room thirty-six.

"Did you see anyone with him?"

"A woman."

This was the first time anyone had placed a woman with any of the victims. "What did she look like?" Quinn asked as he wrote.

"I only saw her from behind as they was walking up the stairs. I remember because she didn't strike me as one of the girls."

"Girls? Do you mean hookers?" Dennis didn't answer, and Quinn glanced up from his report. "I'm not a vice cop. I don't care if you're renting to whores or to guys who like donkeys. I'm just trying to find a woman who has a nasty habit of killing the men she dates."

Dennis lit a generic cigarette and blew the smoke toward the ceiling. "She didn't look like one of the regular girls who stay here."

"What made you think that?"

" 'Cause she had on one of them long coats that looked like it cost a lot of money. Wool or something like that. The girls who come here don't wear their good clothes to work."

Quinn tried not to smile at that. Dennis made it sound as if the girls poured concrete or painted houses for a living. "Color of the coat?"

"Red."

"How tall was she?"

"I'm not good at guessing stuff like that. I think she was about as tall as his shoulder."

Quinn figured that made her around five-two. They would be able to determine better once the coroner measured the body. "Hair color?"

"She had on a hat. A turquoise hat." He circled his head with his hands. "And it had one of those wide parts to it."

"It had a wide brim?"

"Yeah, but it kind of flopped down, and it had what looked like a big peacock feather on one side."

Quinn paused in his questioning to write that all down before he asked, "Did you hear her say anything?"

"No, but she was laughing."

Quinn glanced up. "Laughing?"

"Yeah. Like he was saying something funny. You know. Like he told her a joke and she kinda hits his arm. Playful."

A laughing, playful serial killer. Now that was seriously twisted. "Did you see anything else?"

"I don't think so."

"If you remember anything, give me a call." Quinn handed him a business card. "I'm sure I'll be in touch with more questions."

As Quinn left the office, a patrol officer informed him the couple in room thirty-five might have heard something. The deceased excluded, room thirty-six looked just like thirty-five. A prostitute in a dingy white sweater sat on the bed, picking at her arms, her eyes vacant, drugged, bored. The man beside her looked up through a pair of thick glasses. His hair was slicked back and his arms were crossed over his thin chest.

"Can I smoke?" the woman asked.

"Go ahead."

Quinn wrote down their names and the time they'd checked into the motel. The man stood up and started to pace. "I gotta get out of here. I was just going out for paper towels and dog food. My wife can't know I had a date."

Quinn looked at the guy and his choice of "dates" and didn't feel a bit sorry for him. The slob's wife should know what she lay down with every night. But that wasn't Quinn's job. Not these days. "You'll leave when I'm convinced you've told me everything you heard or saw."

"I told the other cops. I heard some banging like a bed hitting the wall, but I figured . . .

someone was having wild sex." He shrugged. "I didn't see anything."

"How about you?" Quinn asked the prostitute, who was now picking at her cuticles. Lovely.

"I didn't see nothin'," she said, moving her jaw like all addicts tended to do. "They was here before us."

"How do you know?"

"I could hear 'em. Like he said." She took a drag off her cigarette, then added, "Just some banging. But you hear that a lot around here."

Quinn handed them both his card and told them to call if they remembered anything. As he left the room, the coroner arrived, and they entered the crime scene together. An investigator knelt in the doorway dusting the jamb with black powder. "There's dozens of overlapping prints here," he complained as Quinn slid past. "It's going to take months to process these."

Too bad they didn't have months.

"Another poor bastard," the coroner said as he and Quinn snapped on new pairs of gloves, "just trying to get laid." The coroner estimated time and probable cause of death, and Quinn photographed the rope tied to the bedframe.

An hour after the coroner arrived at the scene, the body was released, and Quinn filled

Kurt in on what the manager had seen. Admittedly, it wasn't much, but it was more than they'd had before. He knew better than to get real excited about a woman in a turquoise hat and red coat. What Kurt told him next had him rethinking the direction of the case.

"There's a lot of ladies with turquoise hats these days. It has something to do with that Peacock Society."

Quinn took a measuring wheel from his duffle. "Peacock Society?" He looked over at Kurt. What the hell was a Peacock Society?

"Yeah. These days, all the older ladies are in that club where they wear big hats and bright colors." Kurt placed an evidence flag on the carpet next to a black button. "I think they have meetings and stuff."

"It's on account of that book," the investigator collecting prints at the door told them. "Some lady wrote a book about women wearing peacock feathers because they don't need men."

Quinn rolled the tape wheel across the small room and wrote down the measurement. "Did you read the book?" he asked the investigator.

"No, but I saw it at Walden's in the mall," the guy answered as he placed clear tape on the black prints, then transferred them to the lift card.

Quinn didn't bother pointing out that seeing a book wasn't quite the same as reading it. Instead, he took more measurements and drew a rough sketch of the room. Tomorrow he'd track down information on a Peacock Society. If there was such a club in town, he'd check it out.

"Why did Breathless kill in a motel this time?" Kurt wondered out loud as he looked for more evidence in the dirty carpet. "Why take the risk?"

"Probably because men are scared and aren't taking women home," Quinn speculated.

"Maybe she's getting bolder."

"They usually do." Quinn glanced about the crime scene, then looked at his watch. He figured they might be done in time for breakfast.

Lucy poured herself a cup of coffee and pushed her wet hair behind her ears. She'd slept little the night before, tossing and turning and thinking about what had happened at Quinn's house, until finally she'd gotten out of bed and decided to work. The upside was that she'd written ten pages. The downside was that she was tired this morning.

She'd finally fallen asleep around three, only to be back up again at eight. It could only mean one thing. One terrifying thing.

She was in love with Quinn. She didn't know

how it had happened. One second she'd been answering questions for the Women of Mystery, and then she'd looked up and seen him watching her. Wham, she'd felt it just like that, and there had been no turning back to the second before. No turning back her feelings to when she'd been confused about how she felt.

She'd known him just over a week. People didn't fall in love in a week. It was supposed to take longer. She didn't know whether to laugh or cry or both.

Lucy took her coffee into her bedroom and slipped on a pair of pink panties and bra. Quinn hadn't called her after he'd rushed her out the door. The last she'd seen of him had been his back as he'd hurried inside his house. Something horrible had happened, but all he'd told her was that it had been related to his work. So how horrible could it have been? Yeah, stopped-up toilets and busted pipes were a drag, but not life or death.

She pulled out a pair of jeans and a woman's marathon T-shirt from the time she'd signed up to run but had accidentally on purpose slept in until after the starting gun. Maybe someone had broken into Quinn's work and stolen equipment. She'd heard on the news the other night that theft on job sites was a real problem. Although honestly, she couldn't understand the rush. He hadn't been able to get rid of her fast enough, and that worried her.

A lot.

Her feelings were so new. So scary. So sudden, and she hadn't a clue how Quinn felt about her. Well okay, there were certain times when she was sure he was attracted to her. Like when he looked at her or kissed her or touched her, but that wasn't love.

Lucy pushed her feet into a pair of slippers, then grabbed her coffee on the way out of the room. Last night when she'd decided to get out of bed and work, she'd searched her briefcase for the six chapters Maddie had returned to her yesterday. The collapsible folder hadn't been there, and she'd figured she'd left it in her car. As much as she felt safe in her home and in her neighborhood, there was no way she'd been willing to walk outside to her garage at 3:00 a.m.

The soles of her slippers slipped across the tiles in her kitchen and slapped the concrete stairs and sidewalk as she made her way outside to the garage. She searched the BMW and found a stick of gum, a pen, and a window scraper under the seats. No folder. She retraced her steps back inside, looked up the number, and called Barnes and Noble. Jan Bright hadn't seen it, but she said she would ask the employees and the Women of Mystery.

The doorbell rang as she hung up, and she moved across the living room. She looked through the peephole at Quinn, and her heart did that crazy speedup slowdown thing. He wore black-framed sunglasses to shield his eyes from the brilliant morning sun, and dark stubble covered the lower half of his face.

She opened the door as a gust of cool air ruffled his dark hair. "Good morning." He was wearing the same clothes that he'd worn the night before—a white dress shirt and jeans. He hadn't been to bed, and he should have looked a rumpled mess. He didn't. He looked like someone she'd like to reach out and touch, soothing his brow and feeling his rough cheek against her palm. He looked like someone she'd like to undress and tuck into her bed.

From behind his glasses, he gazed at her for several long moments before he asked, "May I come in?"

"Of course." She opened the door wide, and he moved past her, bringing the scent of spring on his skin. "Coffee?" she offered as she shut the door.

"Please." He pulled off his sunglasses and stuck them in his breast pocket. He had shadows beneath his brown eyes.

"Long night?" She moved past him, resisting the urge to touch him.

"Yeah." He laughed without humor and followed close behind her into the kitchen. The heels of his boots sounded unusually loud against the tile floor.

Lucy reached into a cupboard and pulled out a mug. "I worked until about three this morning." It was such a relief not to have to lie any longer. "I do that sometimes," she explained. She'd had boyfriends in the past who'd hated the often erratic hours of a writer. Now that everything was out in the open, she wanted to be up front with Quinn. "Sometimes I work for days without much sleep. One time," she confessed as she poured coffee into a mug and handed it to him, "I forgot to shave my legs for over a month. I looked like a Clydesdale." Okay, maybe she should have kept that one to herself.

"Thanks." The corner of his mouth curved up as he blew into his coffee. "Sorry about what happened last night," he said before he took a drink. She looked at her slippers and fought the blush creeping up her neck. She wondered exactly which part of the night he was sorry for. That he'd had to run out? That they'd gotten to know each other better in his hall or that they hadn't finished? She was really sorry about the latter. "Something came up and we need to talk about it."

Okay, that didn't sound good. "All right." She moved to the small table in her kitchen and took a seat. Quinn sat across from her, and the light pouring in through the windows picked out strands of his dark hair. It lit his white shirt from behind and accentuated his wide shoulders.

"Remember when you confessed to me that you're not a nurse?"

Was he mad about that after all? She hadn't figured it was still an issue. "Yeah."

"I have a confession to make, too." His dark eyes stared into hers, tired but as intense as ever. "I'm not a plumber."

She leaned forward in her chair. "What?"

"I'm a cop." He reached for something hooked to the side of his belt and slid it across the table at her. It was a police shield. Yep, he was a cop. A detective. He'd lied to her. "Why did you lie?" And why hadn't he confessed the same night she had?

"Because when I met you, I was dating on the Internet undercover." When she didn't say anything, he explained further. "I was posing as a plumber to catch Breathless."

"Who?"

"Breathless. That's the name the police have given the woman who's killing men around town. We think she's meeting them online."

Lucy took a drink of her coffee and let the information sink in. "So the police are working undercover online to catch the woman we've been hearing about on the news?"

"Yes."

Okay, so far she understood, although it seemed bizarre.

"Last night, she killed her fourth victim."

"Oh, no."

"While you were at my house, she was at a motel on Chinden suffocating Robert D. Patterson. That's why I hustled you out so fast."

That name sounded familiar. She sat back in her chair and thought of all the men who'd e-mailed her in the past few months. "Throbbinbob?"

"Did you know him?"

"Not really. He e-mailed me a few times." He'd kind of been a pest, but he hadn't deserved to die, for goodness' sake. "Did you catch this Breathless last night?"

He shook his head and leaned back in his chair. "No, but we got some good leads."

"So, you're a homicide detective," she said, testing it out loud. Now that she thought it over, it made more sense than his being a plumber. It explained his intense gaze and his attention to detail.

"Yes."

She guessed she understood why he'd lied. She didn't like it but couldn't exactly get mad about it. That would make her a hypocrite. She watched him take a drink from his mug and took a moment to process what he'd just told her. So, he'd met her while he'd been working undercover. In a sense, she'd been working undercover too. It might not have been the best way to start a relationship, but it wasn't something that was insurmountable. They could work on it. Maybe even laugh about it sometime in the future. "So, you met me at Starbucks to see if I could be a serial killer?"

He stared into her eyes and gave an abbreviated nod of his dark head.

Okay, so their meeting had been unconventional. People met under unusual circumstances all the time. Who cared about *how* and *why* they'd met. "That's kind of funny when you think about it." Only he wasn't laughing. "How long before you realized I wasn't a killer? A minute or two?"

He set the mug on the table. "A little longer than a minute or two."

Something was wrong. Something she wasn't seeing. She felt as if she was looking at the wrong side of a picture and not seeing what was in front of her face. Then everything shifted and turned and became really clear. "Wait." She held up a hand like a traffic cop. "You thought I could be Breathless?"

"Yes."

Good Lord. The guy she'd fallen in love with had thought she was a serial killer. "But you figured out right away that was ridiculous. Right?"

He shook his head slowly. "Not right away."

"Not right away? How could you possibly think I was a serial killer for one second? Do I look like a serial killer?" Before he could answer, she said, "No, I do not!"

He sighed, and his hands moved to massage the back of his neck. "You know as well as I do that serial killers look just like anyone else."

"Yeah, but you're a trained detective. Aren't you supposed to have an instinct about these things? Some sort of cop sense? Aren't you supposed—Wait. How long before you realized that I wasn't a serial killer?" He just looked at her, and she had to repeat her question. "How long?"

"Lucy, you have to understand—"

"How long, Quinn?" she interrupted him.

He dropped his hand to his side. "Last night."

She sucked a shocked breath into her lungs, and her brows rose up to her hairline. "Before or after? . . ." His silence was her answer, and her head spun. She heard herself sputtering like an idiot, but she couldn't stop. "You . . . me . . . I . . . what . . . the hell?" She stopped to take a few calming breaths, and when she was capable of speech again, she pointed across the table and asked, "Are you shitting me?" Not exactly brilliant, but an improvement over sputtering. "Don't tell me the whole time we've dated that you thought I was a serial killer? Until last night?"

"No, I'm not shitting you. And yes to your second and third questions."

The reality of what he was telling her hit her between the eyes. "And you took off my shirt and and and—" She tried for another calming breath as thoughts spun in her head. "You wanted to have sex with me even though you thought I'd kill you? You would have had sex with a serial killer?"

"No. We didn't exactly have sex."

She sucked in a hurt breath. Suddenly something that had felt pretty darn good now felt dirty.

"It's complicated."

Oh Lord. Oh Lord. That hit-he'd-given-her-between-the-eyes feeling was working its way south toward her throat. "What? Were you trying to get me to kill you?"

He frowned. "Something like that."

She swallowed hard as the pain hit her chest.

"So the whole time you were kissing me and undressing me last night, you were only doing it because you thought I was going to try and kill you?"

"I thought there was a chance." He scrubbed his face with his hands. "Lucy, you have to understand something. I didn't mean to hurt you. I never wanted to hurt anyone, but I had a job to do."

Lucy didn't think there was anything left that he could say that would hurt her more. She was wrong.

"I was just doing my job," he said, adding insult to her injured heart.

"Oh my God." She stood and placed a shaky hand on the table to keep from falling. "This past week wasn't real. Nothing about it was. I thought you wanted to be with me because you liked me. But that wasn't the case at all. You were doing your job, and I . . ." . . . *was falling in love with a lie.* "I was a complete fool."

He stood and came around the table. "You aren't a fool. You're a great girl, and if things were dif—"

Before Lucy even knew she'd done it, she hauled off and slapped him across the face. She'd never hit anyone before in her life, and he looked as stunned as she felt. Her palm stung, and she curled her hands into fists. "Get out."

He took a step back out of her reach, but he didn't leave. "I'm sorry."

Somehow, she doubted he was as sorry as she was. Anger and pain twisted in her chest, and she placed her hand over her heart, as if she could keep it from breaking. It broke anyway. A deep physical pain that shattered her into pieces. "Go. Please."

"I'll call you later."

"I won't answer."

He lifted a hand toward her, then let it fall to his side. "I know you don't believe it right now, but I am more sorry than you know."

He was right. She didn't believe it, and she didn't particularly care if he was sorry. She'd fallen in love with a man who'd only dated her because it was his job.

"Good-bye, Lucy."

She looked at the floor to keep herself from doing something stupid, like bursting into tears. For several more beats of her broken heart, he stood in her kitchen while she died a little with each passing second. Then he turned and walked from the room. She heard the front door open and lifted her gaze to see Quinn framed by the bright morning sun. He looked over his shoulder at her one last time. He opened his mouth as if he meant to say something, but in the end there was nothing to say.

He shut the door behind him and was gone without a word.

For several long moments, Lucy stared at the door, reeling, her emotions and thoughts in total ruin. Her cat wove between her legs and she bent and picked him up. She took a seat at the table and buried her face against Mr. Snookums's fur. A sob broke from her throat. How could she have fallen in love with a lie? How was that even possible? She was a smart, successful woman. She was thirty-four years old. Things like this didn't happen in real life.

She felt so stupid.

She'd known the whole time that there had been something wrong with Quinn, but she'd made excuses and told herself it was because he was a widower. That trolling chat rooms wasn't *really* weird. The signs had been there, but she'd ignored them.

Her fingers burrowed into Mr. Snookums's fur, and a loving purr rattled his chest. "At least you love me, Snookie," she cried as he licked her hand. But her cat's love was no comfort. Not today.

She raised her gaze to Quinn's coffee cup, then closed her eyes. Quinn hadn't pursued her because he'd wanted a relationship with her. He hadn't pushed to spend time with her because he'd been attracted to her. His intense gaze hadn't had anything to do with longing or lust. He'd been watching and waiting for her to do a Lizzie Borden on him.

A hiccup lifted her aching chest, and she gave up on trying to hold back the flood. She'd fallen in love so fast, so ridiculously fast, and she felt so stupid. She could only hope that her heart would mend just as quickly.

Chapter 10

Hadenuf: Seeks Girl's Best Friend . . .

"He was only dating me because he wanted me to kill him," Lucy sobbed and took a drink of her wine. Her vision blurred, and she could hardly see the faces of her friends gathered in her living room. "Remember when I told you he was pursuing me hot and heavy? He was! He thought I was a serial killer."

Her friends, being the wonderful women that they were, were shocked and outraged on her behalf. They condemned Quinn for being a jerk, a loser, and a royal a-hole.

"It all makes sense now," Lucy cried. "All the questions about those men being killed. All the interest in whether I'd dated any of them, and I just thought he was being cautious. I excused everything because I thought we liked the same television shows!"

Two hours later, they were all feeling the buzz of alcohol and condemning all men on principle.

Maddie reached for the bottle and refilled her own glass. "Men are lying bastards."

"Sneaky, lying bastards," Adele added, her eyes getting as glassy as Lucy's. "Too bad we need them."

"Why?" Lucy asked. "Sure, they come in handy when you've got fifty pounds of cat food loaded into your car and you need someone to tote and fetch, but that doesn't make up for the sheer volume of all their lies. I've had enough of men's crap."

"They cook dinner sometimes," Clare added to the conversation as she swirled the wine in her glass. "And it is nice when they make little tables out of broken tiles." She looked at her friends and was quick to add, "But you're right. Men for the most part are a pain in the keister. Vibrators are a girl's best friend."

They all fixed their attention on Clare. On the one woman in the room who believed she'd found her soul mate the moment she'd laid eyes on him. So why was a vibrator her best friend? Perhaps all was not well in romance-ville.

"Oh, don't you all look at me like that," she said. "I know you girls aren't exactly sitting around waiting for a man to give you an orgasm."

"I'm not waiting around," Maddie said. "But I thought you were."

Clare took a drink of her wine and licked her top lip. "Sometimes Lonny is tired. He works really hard."

"Making tables out of tiles?" Maddie shook her head. "Honey, if a guy is too tired to have sex, doesn't that tell you something?"

"Yes. That he's artistic."

Lucy cleared her throat and shook her head slightly. As drunk as she was, she wasn't going to let anyone tell Clare that her dream man dreamed of doing men. Clare was one of the most genuinely nice people Lucy knew. She was kind and had a huge heart, and if she wanted to pretend that Lonny wasn't gay, that was fine with Lucy. Besides, who was she to tell anyone anything about their love life? She'd fallen in love with a man who'd only dated her because he'd thought she was a serial killer. Adele had dated a guy who kept sneaking up to her house and leaving stuff on her porch like he was some sort of double-secret knot-knot spy. Maddie was so freaky that she thought every man she met was a serial something-or-another, and she hadn't even had a date in about four years.

Frankly, Lonny and his tile tables looked pretty damn good.

Adele sat on the couch next to Lucy and rubbed her arm. "Well, at least you didn't know Quinn long enough to fall in love with him."

"That would have been a disaster."

"Good thing you don't believe in love at first sight."

"Yeah. Good thing," she lied and set her glass on the table before she dropped it. A sure sign that it was time to step away from the booze.

"You know I love you," Maddie started, which always meant trouble, "but I've got to say it. This fits your typical pattern of dating guys you want to rescue."

Lucy held up one finger. "Not this time. Quinn didn't have rescue issues, and he didn't steal my money. He's normal." She frowned and felt a little confused. "Well, except that he's a lying bastard."

"Which just made Maddie's point," Adele said. "He had lying bastard issues."

Lucy felt her forehead get all wrinkled. Was there such a thing as "lying bastard issues"? "I don't want to talk about men anymore. It's just too depressing."

"I know what we can talk about." Adele sat

up a little straighter. "I need help plotting the next scene of my book."

Lucy groaned inwardly. Plotting with Adele meant that you came up with suggestions and she never used them.

"Now might not be the best time," Maddie said, bless her neurotic soul. "I'm having a really hard time concentrating." Then she turned to Lucy and asked, "Do you really buy fifty pounds of cat food at a time?"

"I think it might be more like forty."

"No wonder Snookie is so damn fat."

"He's not fat. He's husky."

Adele laughed at that. "Husky is just a nice PC way of saying he should push away from the cat dish. If he were a man, he'd have to buy his clothes at a big and tall store."

"You need to put Snookie on a diet."

"I've tried," Lucy said through a sigh. "But if I don't get up and feed him when he wants food, he bites my feet."

Clare looked up from inspecting her fingernail and sort of listed to one side. "Did you know that Costco sells coffins online?"

Obviously it was time to sober her friends up. Time for dinner. "No way," Lucy said and reached for the phone.

"You're kidding."

"Do you have to buy two at a time?"

* * *

The next afternoon, Lucy jumped in her Beemer and headed to McDonald's. Her head pounded, her stomach felt queasy, and the dark lenses of her sunglasses did little to help the pain in her eye sockets. The night before, she'd intended to stop drinking before dinner arrived, but then she'd decided a few more glasses of wine with her meal wouldn't hurt. After that, everything got really fuzzy. She recalled toasting to everyone's futures and to Quinn getting a disease, but that was about all she remembered.

She placed her order and drove forward to the pickup window. There was just nothing that cured a hangover better than a Quarter Pounder with cheese, greasy fries, and a Diet Coke. She grabbed her food and ate in her car on the way to the post office. She hadn't been to her PO box in about two months now, and it was time to check out what might be hiding for her in there.

She pulled into a parking slot and washed down the last of her burger with a swig of Diet Coke. Yeah, she knew. What was the point of a Diet Coke when she'd just scarfed about two thousand calories and one hundred grams of carbs and fat?

Who cared?

She stuck her brown Coach hat on her head

and climbed out of her car. The sun was shining, the birds were singing, spring flowers were beginning to bloom. The world was moving on, and she felt so empty inside. Even after stuffing herself with French fries. It just didn't seem right.

She moved into the post office and opened her PO box. It was crammed with mostly junk mail, which she tossed in the trash. She shoved five reader letters in her purse and headed back home. When she got there, she checked her answering machine, but her voice mail was empty.

"I'll call you," Quinn had said, proving yet again that he was a big fat liar. Not that she would actually pick up and talk to him if he did call, but he should at least grovel on her machine.

Lucy yawned and tossed her hat on the kitchen table. She knew she should march her butt upstairs and get to work, or clean her house, or do something productive. Instead she fell into bed and curled up with Mr. Snookums.

She rolled to her side and scratched her cat's belly as her thoughts inevitably turned to Quinn. Everything he'd ever said to her, everything she believed about him, was as tangible as smoke. Did he actually have a family? Had he really broken his arm showing off for the neighbor girl? Was his wife really dead? Or was Millie an ex-wife or a former girlfriend? Or,

God forbid, he was married or in a relationship. Was his name even Quinn, or was that,
too, a lie?

Just like everything he'd said, everything
he'd made her feel was a lie. It might have felt
real. Even now it felt real. It burned inside her
chest like it was real, but it wasn't. She'd kicked
men out of her life for various reasons, but at
least she'd known those men. Quinn was different. She'd fallen in love with a man she hadn't
even known. A man who'd touched and kissed
her because it had been his job. Oh, she knew
that he'd been attracted to her. She'd felt the
proof of that against her thigh and held it in her
hand, but that didn't mean he cared anything
for her. That just meant he was a man.

Mr. Snookums purred and licked her hand.
Then, in an effort to make it all better, he pulled
out all the stops and head-butted her chin. She
wished it were that easy. That a loving head-
butt from her cat could take away the pain in
her chest, but it only made things worse by reminding her that she was probably going to die
all alone with no one but her cat. Her biggest
fear was that Snookums would blow through
his cat food and turn his hungry eyes on her
corpse.

She thought about getting out of bed and getting to work. Instead she took one of the sleep-

ing pills she usually saved for stressful times in her life. Her heart ached and her head pounded and she wanted to sleep until it all went away. She promised God that if he would just help her out with the hangover, she'd never drink red wine again.

She fell asleep until the next morning, and when she woke, she instantly noticed three things. One: She was still dressed in the clothes she'd had on the day before. Two: God had been good to her and her hangover was blessedly gone. Three: Her heart still ached. She wasn't over Quinn yet. Maybe she should have asked God to heal her heart instead of her head. The only consolation, although not a big one, was the fact that she would never have to see Quinn again.

Lucy changed into her bathrobe, then padded into the kitchen and made coffee. While she waited for it to brew, she fed Mr. Snookums and grabbed the reader mail out of her purse. Three of them had the same typed address and Boise postmark. The others were from California and Michigan. The reader from California praised Lucy's talent and wrote that she was looking forward to her next book. Lucy set that letter aside to be filed with the other readers whom she planned on sending a note and a bookmark. The writer of the Michigan letter wasn't so praiseworthy. He pointed out that the trajectory of a bullet's path in her second novel was physically impossible. He'd drawn a diagram and asked if she did research. Lucy filed that letter in the trash.

She took the three remaining letters with her to the counter and poured herself a cup of coffee. She checked the date on the postmarks and opened the oldest, which had been sent mid-February.

> *I'm your biggest fan. I've read everything you have written and consider myself quite the Rothschild aficionado.*

Aficionado? That was a little over the top, Lucy thought and leaned her behind against the counter.

> *I've followed your career closely and have read all of your books. I am in awe of your talent. You've kept me sane when I thought I would lose my mind in this insane world.*
>
> *You've given me hours of nail-biting suspense, and I would like to return the favor. I would like to share with you my own little mystery.*

Lucy took a drink of her coffee. For legal reasons, she did not read people's unpublished manuscripts. She was going to have to write to this person and tell him or her not to go to the expense of sending it. She looked at the envelope sitting on the counter and noticed there wasn't a return address. Weird.

I am sure you will appreciate my little mystery as much as I've always appreciated yours. Quid pro quo, I always say.

My story begins like this. A woman tired of dating losers just out for sex decides to take care of them one by one. Kind of like a vigilante. Ridding the world of perverts and degenerates. Men who can't commit or who are whiners. Men who beat their wives or girlfriends, cheat on them and scam women out of money, to say nothing of the trail of broken hearts they leave behind. Have you ever asked yourself why nothing bad ever happens to them? Why they are allowed to go blithely on their way to the next victim? Well, something should be done about those men. They deserve to know the pain they cause as they draw their last breath.

At first I thought I would write a book about these dirty men, but I lack discipline. And re-

*ally, the odds of getting published are so slim.
So, I've decided to live it instead.*

Lucy straightened, and she felt her forehead get tight.

*Read the front page of the Statesman dated
Feb. 25th. What the paper fails to mention (because they couldn't know something the police don't even know) was that Charles Wilson
kicked so hard I thought he was going to kick
his bed apart so I had to hold his legs down.
He was frightened and pathetic. Poetic justice,
I say.*

*Do you like my work? I'd love to sit down
with you for a critique. To get your thoughts,
but of course, that is impossible.*

Well, I have to go.

So many men. So little time. So much to do.

Lucy reached for the next letter and opened it. This time she pulled out a front-page news clipping along with a letter. A photo of a house blocked off with yellow crime scene tape dominated half the page. The headline read DAVE AN-DERSON, SECOND MAN TO DIE IN HOME WITHIN THE PAST MONTH.

This letter was shorter and more vehement.

Don't you just love the incompetence of the BPD? They haven't figured out yet that the two deaths are related. Morons. Cavemen. But what can you expect? Certainly not intelligence. Not from men. Dave Anderson was a big bumbling buffoon who flattered himself that I was interested sexually in him. Dirty man.

Read the Statesman article. What a riot. The police have nothing to release to reporters because they have nothing. I leave nothing behind. Nothing can be traced to me. I'm too smart for them. I learned everything I know from reading mystery novels. Your mystery novels.

Flattered?

Lucy might be a little slow on the uptake sometimes, like when it came to realizing that everything Quinn had ever uttered had been a damn lie, but not this time. She knew what this was. She'd done too much research, delved into too many twisted minds, written too many books, not to recognize bragging when she read it.

Breathless wanted her to know exactly what she'd done. She was showing off. Like when Mr. Snookums killed a mouse and left it on the back porch for her to discover and admire. A killer wanted Lucy to see and admire her work.

Lucy took a deep breath and let it out slowly.

Her cat jumped off a kitchen chair, and she jumped out of her skin. Her heart pounded, and she raised a hand to her throat. "Holy Jesus," she whispered. She set the letter on the news clipping and stared at the third envelope. She didn't really want to open it, but she had to. This time she was more careful. She retrieved her pink Playtex gloves from beneath the sink and pulled them on. Her hands shook as she grabbed a steak knife and sliced the top of the envelope open. She tipped it upside down, and another article and letter fell into her palm. The newspaper had run a photo of the victim, as well as a picture of the crime scene. Lawrence Craig, the man Lucy knew as luvstick, looked out from the paper, a slight smile tilting up the corners of his mouth. Her scalp got tight, and tension pulled at her brows. She took a deep breath and let it out slowly.

Well, the BPD finally figured it out. Three murders in eight weeks and they finally figured that they were related. Duh! I know they're waiting for me to mess up. Make a mistake, but I won't. I'm too smart for them. I've been thinking that maybe I will write a book about what I'm doing after all. Someday when I'm more disciplined. You know what they say; write what you know.

Here's a little FYI between professionals, in case you want to use it in your book. When you suffocate someone, they make a little noise in the backs of their throats. At least that's been my experience. Maybe that doesn't happen with everyone. I'll keep you posted. Lawrence made the most noise, thrashing about like it would do any good. He liked the idea of me tying him up, but not so much at the end, I guess.

When I first started, I thought it would be difficult to find dirty men who are willing to be handcuffed to a bed. For the most part, it has been easy. Men will do just about anything if they think they might get sex. But you're an intelligent woman, and I'm sure this doesn't surprise you. I'm sure we have a lot in common and could spend hours swapping dating horror stories.

Women want love. Men don't care about love. They just want sex.

What's a girl to do with throwbacks and bottom feeders?

Lucy set the letter and news clipping with the rest and slipped the gloves from her hands. She felt like the world had fallen out from under her feet. It was as if she was being pulled down into someone else's sick reality. The telephone rang, and she nearly jumped out of her skin.

She looked at the caller ID and didn't recognize the number. No way in hell was she going to pick up. She had the sensation of being watched, and she ran around her house, room to room, shutting all the curtains and blinds.

In the living room she sank onto her couch and stared across the room at her chinoiserie entertainment armoire, at the black lacquer paint and gold pavilion scenes. Her pulse pounded in her throat and she swallowed past the dry knot of fear choking her.

Why? Why had a psycho decided to contact her? She didn't live her books. They were fiction. She wrote fictions; not road maps to murder. She didn't want to be involved in this. It was sick and twisted and made her feel as if someone with cold, evil hands was playing with her life. She wished she'd never gone to her PO box. She wished she could close her eyes and it would all just go away.

Lucy didn't know how long she sat there thinking, trying to figure out what to do, when in reality she'd known what to do the whole time.

She reached for her phone and dialed.

Chapter 11

Hungryman: Seeks Snack Tray . . .

Using a pair of tweezers, Quinn slid the third letter into a clear evidence bag and sealed it. He set it on the table beside the others and placed the tweezers in a small collection kit. If they were lucky, they'd get some good prints and DNA. If not, at least Breathless was talking. Like a lot of organized killers, she couldn't stop herself from bragging. He just wished like hell she'd chosen to talk to anyone but Lucy Rothschild.

The last time he'd been standing in this kitchen, Lucy had slapped his face, then kicked him out. Not that he blamed her. He'd figured he'd never be in her house again. Not in a million years, but then this wasn't exactly a social call.

"Are you sure you can't think of anyone who might've written those letters?" Kurt asked Lucy. He sat in front of her chair with his notebook open on his lap.

She shook her head. "It could be anyone."

Quinn tucked the ends of his blue-and-green silk tie between two buttons on the front of his green dress shirt and planted his palms next to the evidence spread out in front of him. If he had to guess, he'd say Breathless had used Microsoft Word to construct the letters; he hoped the printer was more distinctive.

Without lifting his head, he raised his gaze to Lucy. She was pale but every bit as beautiful as when he'd seen her three days ago. She wore a pink shirt that laced up the front and a pair of jeans. The second he'd entered the house, he'd recognized the look in her blue eyes. No matter how much she tried to hide it behind anger, she was scared shitless.

"Do you have any fans whose appreciation for your work seems out of proportion?"

She took a deep breath and blew it out slowly. "Well, yeah. To me it seems out of proportion much like Trekkies seem out of proportion, but nothing as crazy as this." She'd pulled her blonde hair into a ponytail high on her head, and she looked young and very vulnerable. A slight purple bruise marked her collarbone. It was hardly noticeable really, but Quinn had noticed within seconds of seeing her. Maybe because he'd put it there.

Quinn had spent the past three days interviewing Robert Patterson's friends and relatives, going over phone records and credit card receipts. He'd discovered that, like the other victims, Robert had dated heavily online. Quinn had gathered a list of names from Robert's e-mail program; many of them he'd already crossed off the suspect list. Quinn had spent a lot of time rethinking the direction of the investigation, too. Perhaps Breathless wasn't meeting men online. And he'd spent a lot of time thinking about Lucy. Maybe he could have done some things differently where she'd been concerned.

As Kurt pressed Lucy about her friends and fans, Quinn's gaze moved to her full, pink mouth. He'd been working undercover to stop a killer. He'd worked within the legal guidelines, which allowed him to do or say anything as long as it didn't taint evidence. Yeah, he'd lied, deceived, and talked dirty to Lucy. He'd kissed and touched her, and the whole time he'd stayed within the rules. He'd just been doing his job. At least that's what he told himself.

Too bad he wasn't a better liar.

"My friends wouldn't do anything like this," she told Kurt, and Quinn's gaze slid once again down the side of her throat to the little mark on her collarbone. Yeah, he could tell himself and everyone else that he'd just been doing his job, but the fact was that he'd enjoyed it a little too much. He'd enjoyed hearing her laughter and seeing her smile. He'd enjoyed the hell out of kissing and touching and hearing her little moans. He'd enjoyed looking at her in his mirror as he'd touched her breasts and played with her through the thin lace of her bra. He'd enjoyed seeing the desire reflected in her blue eyes and the soft intake of her breath.

He'd picked her up to carry her to his bedroom, but he'd only made it as far as the hall. He'd like to tell himself he'd only stopped to catch his breath, but that wasn't true. He'd stopped because he'd wanted to get her naked away from the prying eyes and ears of the audio and video equipment. Like a jealous lover, he'd wanted her all to himself.

He'd kissed her bare breasts and touched between her legs, and he couldn't remember when he'd enjoyed himself so much. He'd felt like a kid again, touching and rubbing and tearing at each other's clothes. He'd enjoyed the hell out of making her come and the touch of her soft hand inside his pants, wrapped around him. And while they'd been getting hot and sweating, he'd never forgotten his job. Not for one second. He just hadn't cared. The way she'd looked at him, touched him, whispered his name, had made him want her with a ferocity that had trumped his self-control and made her more dangerous than a pack of serial killers armed with flexi-cuffs.

"What do you know of The Peacock Society?" Kurt asked.

"Peacock Society? You mean those women who wear colorful hats with feathers sticking out?" She shrugged. "Not much, other than I think you have to be over fifty, loving life, and loving to clash."

"You've never spoken at any of their chapter meetings?"

She shook her head. "No. Why would I? I write mysteries. Not rah-rah sisterhood stuff."

There were twenty-two chapters of The Peacock Society in Boise alone, and Quinn had contacted all of them and requested member profiles and rosters. He was also waiting for a membership roster and profiles from the Women of Mystery and the latest toxicology report from the coroner's office.

"What about the Women of Mystery?" Quinn asked her.

Lucy turned her head slightly and looked at him out of the corners of her eyes. If he'd had any doubt about her feelings for him, the daggers in the depth of those dark blues would have cleared up all confusion.

Her voice was perfectly bland when she asked, "What about them?"

"They seemed to know the plot of the book you're currently working on."

"So?"

"Has it occurred to you that your book has a lot in common with the way Breathless operates?"

She turned to look at him fully. "Not really. I know she's suffocating her victims, but it could be a coincidence. If you want to control someone's breathing, there's several different ways to do it." She pointed to the evidence on the table all neatly bagged. "That person doesn't say how she's killing these men."

"No, but we know how she's doing it." He rose to his full height and kept his gaze pinned to Lucy's. She obviously didn't like him. He didn't really blame her, but it didn't matter. He had a job to do. This time he was going to do it by the book. "She's cuffing them to a bed and placing a dry-cleaning bag over their heads. Sound familiar?"

If it were possible, Lucy's face turned a shade whiter, and even though Quinn didn't want to give a damn, he felt like a real asshole for scaring her more than she was already scared.

She stared at him for several long moments, then said as if she had a choice, "I don't want to be involved in this. It's sick."

"Too late." He untucked his tie and pointed to the letters. "She's involved you. I don't want to scare you, but this is serious. A psychopath has chosen to reach out to you because she feels a connection to you through your work."

"I realize that, but can't you just take the letters and leave me out of it?"

He wished he could. More than she could know. Normally he would be ecstatic that a serial killer was finally talking, and he would be looking at every angle and planning the next move in his head. Not this time.

"We can leave you out of the investigation as much as possible," Kurt said as he played the "good cop," patting her hand and trying to pacify her nerves. "But I don't believe you've heard the last from her. She will contact you again. You were really smart to put on gloves to open the third letter."

Quinn slid the envelopes toward her. "Have you noticed the postmarks?" He didn't wait for her to answer. "She mailed the letters three to four days after each murder."

"Meaning I should get another letter today or tomorrow."

"Exactly. I take it you haven't checked your PO box today."

"No."

"If you give us the key, we can check it."

She shook her head and stood. "No, I get important business mail in that box. I'll go."

"You just said you wanted to be left out of the investigation." Which was impossible. She just didn't know it yet.

"I know, but I can't let just anyone rummage through my mail."

It was easier not to argue with her, and Quinn shoved the collection kit into his larger evidence duffle and zipped it closed. "I'll take you."

"No thank you."

"It wasn't a suggestion, Lucy." She opened her mouth to argue, and he cut her off. "Or I can get a warrant and seize everything in the box."

"But we don't want to do that," Kurt hurried to explain, trying to soothe her.

She grabbed her purse off a kitchen chair, and Quinn's gaze slid from her face, over the laces of her pink shirt, and down her jeans to her feet. She wore brown sandals that looped over her big toes. Her toenails were painted red. "Fine, but I'm driving," she said and turned to march out the back door.

"Maybe I should go," Kurt offered. "Soften

her up so she'll work with us. She's not real fond of you."

Quinn lifted his gaze to her behind. "She'll get over it," he said, then turned his attention to the other detective.

Kurt gathered the evidence sealed in clear plastic bags and slipped them into his notebook. "What happened between the two of you that I don't know about?"

"Nothing much," Quinn lied. Only he and Lucy knew what had happened between the two of them in the hallway of his house, and he sure as hell wasn't talking.

"You're looking at her like something happened."

"I'm not looking at her like anything." Quinn grabbed the small evidence collection kit back out of the duffle. He hoped Kurt would let the subject drop, but Quinn knew better.

"Yeah you are. You look like you're kinda hungry and she's a snack tray." Kurt shook his head. "Too bad she looks at you like you stomped that fat cat of hers."

Kurt was full of shit, but Quinn didn't have time to stand around and argue. "Remember to photocopy those before we turn them into the lab. See you back at the office," he said and walked outside as Lucy backed her silver BMW out of the small garage. He opened the car door and sank into red leather upholstery and palpable animosity.

"Nice car," he said as he reached over his right shoulder for his seat belt.

"I like it." She put the car in first gear and practically laid rubber in the alley.

He looked over at her and snapped the belt in place. "Where's the fire?"

"You didn't have to come along."

"Sunshine, you're wrong about that."

She stopped the car at the end of the alley, then pulled onto the street. "Don't call me Sunshine. My name is Lucy. Ms. Rothschild to you."

He chuckled. "How long are you going to be mad at me, Mizz Rothschild?"

"I'm not mad." She shifted into third gear and shot down Fifteenth Street at least ten miles over the limit. A squirrel darted into the road, skidded to a halt, then ran back to the sidewalk instead of taking his chances.

"Right." Yeah, he'd lied to her, but it wasn't as if he'd had a choice. And yeah, he'd taken things a little far, but she hadn't exactly complained. She'd gotten off. He hadn't. If anyone should be pissed off it was him. "You always this good a driver, Mario?"

"If you don't like it, get out." She stopped at a

light on Bannock and about put him through the windshield.

He smiled and reminded himself that his job would be a lot easier with her cooperation. He'd talked confessions out of hardened criminals; he could handle Lucy. "It's good that you called me about the letters."

"Don't flatter yourself," she said as she continued to look straight ahead. She refused to look at him, but that was okay with Quinn, as it gave him the chance to look at her all he wanted. Kurt was right. She did look like a snack tray. "I didn't call you. I called someone who transferred me to you."

"It doesn't matter." His gaze took in her high cheeks, straight nose, and her full mouth. The first night he'd seen her, he'd thought she had a great mouth. "The result is the same. I'm going to be in your life for a while longer."

"Lucky me." She tapped her red fingernails on the black leather steering wheel. "I guess your name really is Quinn."

"Yep." His gaze moved from her chin to the long white column of her throat. He liked her neck. It smelled great and tasted better.

"Is there really a Millie?"

"Yes."

Tap tap tap. "Your wife? Girlfriend?"

"My dog."

Her head slowly turned toward him like she was in *The Exorcist*, and her eyes got all squinty. "Your *dog*? You made me feel sorry for you because your wife died, and the whole time Millie was really your *dog*?"

"I was doing my job, Mizz Rothschild."

"Your job sucks."

"Sometimes." The light turned green, and she sped through the intersection.

"So who was the redhead in the photographs?"

"What photographs?"

"The ones on your mantel."

"Oh, that's Anita. She works in the tech department." He could practically see the mental wheels spinning in her head. "The photographs were planted there to make me think she was your dead wife Millie."

"Something like that." He hoped to God she never found out about the video and audio tape. "Listen, I'm sorry about everything. I'm sorry you got caught up in it. I'm sorry I had to lie to you."

She made a scoffing sound. "Probably not as sorry as I am."

"The others didn't take it so hard."

Her head whipped around to look at him. "*Others*? While you dated me, there were others? You told me I . . . jerk."

Maybe he should have kept that one to himself. "Watch the road."

She frowned and looked out the windshield once more. "How many others are we talking about?"

"While I dated you? Just a couple."

Lucy slowed the car and pulled into a parking place in front of the post office. *Just a couple.* He said it as if it were okay. As if it didn't completely crush her, no matter how much she didn't want to be crushed.

"Over the course of the past month," he continued as he unbuckled his belt, "about fifteen or sixteen."

Lucy opened her car door and stepped out. "Fifteen or sixteen?" She couldn't help but wonder how far he'd gone with the others. Had he kissed them like he'd kissed her? Had he shoved them against a wall and touched them all over?

He held his evidence collection equipment in one hand as they moved up the steps. "It was exhausting," he said, holding the door open for her as if he were a gentleman.

"Yeah, I'll bet." He wasn't tricking her for a second. He wasn't a gentleman. "Poor guy. You wined and dined fifteen or sixteen women and lied to us all."

"Some I just met for coffee and never saw again."

And others he'd kissed like he hadn't been able to get enough. Others like her. And though she would rather die than admit it out loud, she felt a tiny stab of jealousy for all those faceless others.

They walked into the old post office. Across from the rows of PO boxes, she set her purse on a table used for labeling. She would *not* ask how many he'd kissed and touched as he'd kissed and touched her. Not if it killed her. "And out of all those fifteen or sixteen, I'm the one you were most convinced was a serial killer." She opened her purse and set her wallet on the table. "That's brilliant police work." Next she pulled out her brass knuckles and stun pen, then dug a little deeper. The more she thought of all those other women, the angrier she got. "I knew there was something wrong with you, but did I listen? No. I did not. I even made excuses for you trolling chat rooms and for all the really crappy e-mails you sent me." She finally pulled out the special set of keys that always ended up in the bottom of her purse. "That spark to flame stuff was so lame. I mean, get a clue, Lucy." She looked up, and Quinn took several steps backward. "What are you doing?"

"What do you have in your hand?" he asked, looking at her as if she held a cobra.

"The key. What else?" His gaze moved to her stun pen, and she smiled. Oh, that was tempting. "Are you afraid I'm going to zap you?"

"No. You wouldn't get close enough."

"Mmm hmm." She held out the keys and made a little zapping sound through her teeth as she dropped them in his open palm.

"Funny. What's your number?"

She told him, then turned to stuff everything else back into her purse.

"You're the only one who's complained about the e-mails." He rocked back on his heels. "The other women liked them."

"The other women were being kind to you. Believe me, I know hyperbolic crap when I read it."

He chuckled and said over his shoulder, "That's what I told Kurt when he wrote those e-mails. Although I'm pretty sure I didn't say his crap was 'hyperbolic.'"

He hadn't even written the e-mails she'd spent so much energy trying to excuse and justify. Figured. She leaned her hip into the table and watched him move to her PO box. For some reason, the skin on the back of her neck and arms started to tingle as she waited for him to open it. A part of her wanted to tell him to stop. Not to open it. She didn't want to see what was inside. Reading the sick rambling of a killer professing admiration for her work tainted what she'd always loved. Made it feel as if she were somehow responsible, although she knew she wasn't. The thought of writing a mystery about a female serial killer no longer seemed like fiction. The lines between fact and fiction had blurred, and it was real now. She'd always loved her work, but sitting in her chair and writing seemed too horrific. The thought of never writing added a different shade of fear into the mix. She not only loved writing but it was also how she made her living. Without it, she was uniquely qualified to work in the fast-food industry.

In the span of three hours, her whole life had changed. Her emotions were raw, her mind numb with the weight of it. More than anything, she felt disoriented, as if she'd been on a five-day bender. She watched Quinn fit the key into the lock, and her hands tingled and her fingers got cold. She didn't want to look, but she couldn't look away. The small door swung open, and Lucy's heart felt as if it were going to pound right out of her chest.

The box was empty. Not even a piece of junk mail. Lucy let out a breath. She couldn't go through this every day, but she didn't see that she had a choice. Maybe she'd heard the last from a sick woman. Maybe she could get her life back.

Quinn locked the PO box and moved toward her with that long and lean purposeful stride of his. A scowl wrinkled his dark brow, and he handed her the key. "Are you going to pass out?"

He raised a hand, as if he was going to touch her, but she stepped back out of his reach. "I'm fine."

His hand fell to his side, but his scowl remained in place. "We'll check again tomorrow."

Without a word, Lucy took the key ring and dropped it into her purse. *Tomorrow.* She didn't want to see him again tomorrow. Nor did she want to stand in the post office with her heart pounding out of her chest.

Together they walked from the post office, their shoulders inches apart as they moved down the steps. Lucy felt so alone that it might as well have been miles that separated them.

On the ride to her house neither spoke. In the past week, Lucy had fallen in love with a man who didn't love her and had only dated her because he'd thought she was a serial killer. If that wasn't crazy enough, she'd been contacted by the real killer, who claimed Lucy had taught her everything she knew about committing murder. The police thought Lucy somehow knew the killer, or at least had met her. Lucy had a feeling they were right. She'd always considered herself a strong person, but with each passing hour, as bits and pieces of those letters spun around in her head and the significance sank in, she was having a harder and harder time keeping it together. She feared she was going to dive headfirst into a freak-out, and she wished she had something to hang onto before she lost it. Someone to hold her tight and make her feel safe. Someone to tell her everything was going to be okay, even if it was a lie.

There was no one. Especially not Quinn. He was the last person to make her feel safe or the last man who could fill the emptiness that he had created.

Lucy pulled the car into the garage, and Quinn followed her into her house. "We'll check again tomorrow," he said as he reached for his duffle.

She didn't want to go back to the post office. She didn't want to stand around, watching and waiting. She walked to the kitchen window and looked out at Mrs. Riley's fake tulips. Some of them were blue. She didn't recall ever seeing real blue tulips, but who was she to question someone else's reality when she felt as if she might truly lose her mind? "What's going to happen now?" she asked, although she'd written enough books to have a very good idea. She knew that the police saw her as a link between them and a serial killer. The irony didn't escape her.

"The letters get processed in the crime lab for prints and DNA. Kurt and I will pore over every word, looking for any clue or connection that will point us in the right direction. I think these letters are going to help us find her." Lucy heard him walk across the room, and she felt, rather than saw, him come to stand directly behind her. "Do you still have my home phone and cell numbers?"

"Somewhere. Probably."

"Will you call me if you need anything at all?"

"I don't need anything. I'm fine."

"You don't look fine."

"Thanks." She laughed without humor and glanced down at her white hands grasping the edge of the counter.

"I just meant that you look pretty shook up. Those letters would get to anyone."

"Do you really think she'll write again?" Lucy asked and prayed he'd say no.

"Yes. It might be better to give me your key and I'll go to your PO box. You won't even have to see the letters. Think about it."

Lucy had always thought she was so brave. So smart. At that moment, she didn't know what she was anymore. She just knew that her life no longer felt like her own.

"Okay." She still had her purse on her shoulder, and she reached inside and pulled out the key to her PO box. She took it off the ring and turned to face him. "Could you do me one favor? Would you bring the regular mail to me?"

"Sure."

She placed the key in his palm and his hand closed, trapping her fingers in his warm grasp. She glanced up to his face. His gaze touched her forehead and cheeks, then landed on her mouth. He was looking at her as he'd looked at her before. This time she knew that the desire she thought she saw there was an illusion.

She pulled her hand away before she could give in to the illusion and sink into something bigger and stronger than herself. "Do you think she knows where I live?"

He raised his gaze, and his brown eyes looked into hers. "Your phone number is unlisted and there isn't enough personal information about you on the Internet to lead anyone to your door. Since she sent the letters to your PO box instead of to your home address, my guess would be no." He shoved the key into the front pocket of his pants. "But I'm not going to take a chance with your life."

That almost sounded like he cared. She folded her arms beneath her breasts and looked down at her ring-toe sandals. Lucy would rather not take the chance either, but she wasn't quite sure why he cared. Oh yeah, she was now valuable to his case.

"We'll increase police patrol in the area, and I'll check on you as much as I can. We can install a security system and lights. And I know cops who work security when they're off duty. They can stay with you if you'd like."

She shook her head, and her gaze slid a few inches from her sandals to the toes of his brown loafers. She had enough family and friends in the area that she didn't need strange men in her house.

He placed the tips of his fingers beneath her chin and brought her gaze up to his. His light touch seeped into her, spreading warmth down her neck and into her chest. Once again she had to fight the urge not to lean into him and hang onto something stable in a life that was quickly unraveling around her.

"Tell me what you want."

So many things. None of which he could give her. Except, "The security lights sound good."

"I'll get that rolling as soon as I leave. We'll get them working on it tomorrow." He dropped his hand to his side. "What about today?"

"I'll go stay with my mother. Tomorrow I'll have one of my friends stay with me here."

"One of the writers?"

"Yeah." He'd remembered. A few days ago she would have thought that meant something. Now she knew better.

"We're going to get her, Lucy. I promise, but until then, don't go anywhere alone if you can help it."

She wanted to ask him when he thought this whole thing might be over, but she knew he couldn't give her an answer.

"Keep that stun pen and pepper spray handy." The corner of his mouth lifted, and he almost smiled.

It didn't occur to her until much later that night, when she was lying in her old bedroom at her mother's, to wonder how Quinn knew she carried pepper spray.

Chapter 12

Wazcookin: Seeks Hunk of Beef Cake . . .

"Oh my God!"

"Lucy, come look at this."

"What now?" Lucy shoved the carafe under the iced tea maker and moved to the back door. She rose on tiptoe behind her friends, who were all crammed in the doorway looking out at the electrician in her backyard.

"Not every man can make Carhartts look that good," Maddie said, her face glued to the glass.

The man in question bent at the waist and pulled something from the bed of his truck. His brown Carhartt work pants molded to his hard behind. His name was Randy, and Quinn had sent him to Lucy's house that morning.

"He must do special butt exercises," Adele speculated.

"Squats," Clare added. "I wish he'd bend over."

Maddie nodded. "Yeah, maybe I'll go throw a dollar on the ground and see if he'll pick it up."

Lucy dropped back on her heels. "You're all perverted." As one, they turned, and three pairs of eyes looked at her as if she'd just sprouted a horn in the middle of her forehead. Lucy held up her hands and backed away. "I'm just saying he's young."

"And?"

Good Lord, she was starting to sound like Quinn. "I don't know." She placed a palm on the side of her face and shook her head. "I think I'm losing my mind." She turned and walked back into the kitchen. After everything, she still preferred to look at Quinn's behind. Yeah, she was losing it, all right.

Concerned, her friends followed. "You're under a lot of stress." Clare reached into a cupboard and pulled out four glasses. "And we're supposed to be here helping you out, not eyeing the workman."

Adele placed ice cubes in the glasses, and the four friends sat with a pitcher of tea at the kitchen table and discussed Lucy's problem. Lucy had spent the night before with her mother and probably would again before the nightmare was over. But she always felt like a kid when she stayed with her mom, and she did not want to camp out there.

"I just hate being scared," she said and raised a glass of tea to her mouth. She took a drink and added, "I've always seen myself as a strong person. Someone who could take care of herself in every situation." She set the glass on the table. "Someone fearless in the face of sinking ships or shark attacks, but this psycho woman scares me." She shook her head as the sound of a power tool made its way inside. "Yet, at the same time, I don't know if I even *should* be scared. I haven't been threatened, and this woman is killing men. Not mystery writers."

"Yet." Maddie pushed her glass aside and placed her forearms on the table. "A serial killer has contacted you, and you have to take it very seriously." Maddie knew that of which she spoke. She talked to serial killers all the time.

"I am taking it seriously. It's just that I wonder if I'm being paranoid," Lucy replied.

"Not everything is a paranoid delusion." Adele stirred her ice cubes with her finger. "Sometimes freaky things do happen."

"What has Dwayne left on your porch now?" Clare asked.

"One sock and my Some Bunny Loves You coffee mug."

"What a weirdo."

"That's creepy."

"You actually have a Some Bunny Loves You coffee mug?"

By the time the pitcher of tea was finished, the four women had decided that Lucy would take turns staying in their homes or they would stay with her in her house. They assured her that it was no imposition, but she knew it was. She just hoped that Quinn caught Breathless sooner rather than later.

Adele rose from the table and grabbed the empty pitcher. "I volunteer to go first," she said as she moved toward the sink. As she passed the back door, she glanced outside. Her feet stopped, and she took a few steps back. "Whoa Nellie."

"What's Randy doing now?" Lucy asked.

"It's not Randy. Someone new has come to play."

Clare rose and joined Adele. "Now that's a gorgeous chunk of hunk."

Lucy and Maddie stood and joined their friends. "That's a cop," Maddie said. "I can tell by his bulge."

"You can see his bulge? From all the way across the yard? You're good."

"His gun. You can see the outline of his service revolver under his suit jacket."

Lucy didn't need to lower her gaze from Quinn's face to know all about his bulges, revolver or otherwise. He stood next to Randy, talking to him and pointing up to the eaves of Lucy's house. He wore a chocolate-colored suit and a beige shirt. A slight breeze messed his hair, and dark glasses covered his eyes. "That's Quinn."

"Hardluvnman?"

"Yeah."

"Wow." Clare shook her head. "I mean, what a jerk."

Quinn dropped his hand, then moved up the sidewalk to Lucy's back door. He knocked twice and opened without bothering to wait for her to answer. Seeing the four women, he stopped in his tracks and reached for his sunglasses. "Well, hello," he said, and Lucy could practically hear her friends melting. Or maybe that was her. Quinn shoved the glasses in the inside pocket of his jacket. "You ladies must be Lucy's writer buddies. I've seen your pictures in her office."

Lucy introduced her friends, who did a pretty good job remaining cucumber cool to the man who'd lied to her—until he lowered his chin and looked into Lucy's eyes. "How're you holding up, Sunshine?"

Sunshine? She was pretty sure she'd told him not to call her Sunshine. "Okay."

"I brought your mail." He reached inside his suit jacket and pulled out a restaurant flyer.

"This is it?"

"Yeah." He tilted his head to one side, and his brown eyes continued to stare into hers. "I need to talk to you."

He meant alone. She walked into the back-yard and he followed. Beneath the shade of an old oak he told her, "The Breathless letters came back negative for prints." A shadow from the limbs overhead shaded the top of his face. "The envelopes are being tested for DNA. We put a rush on it, but I don't expect the results for a few days. If we're lucky."

That was disappointing as hell, but police work was never as easy as it was in books or on television. Never nice and tidy.

"How are you really holding up?"

Scared. Disoriented. In shock. "I really am okay. My friends are going to take turns baby-sitting me."

His gaze moved over her face and settled on her mouth. A slight breeze blew strands of her hair across her lips, and Quinn lifted a hand as if he meant to brush them behind her ear. Lucy pressed her back into the uneven bark and waited for his touch.

A frown wrinkled his brow, and he took a step back. "Call me if you need anything," he said as he turned and walked away.

For the next three days, Quinn drove to Lucy's PO box, only to find it filled with junk mail. As promised, he took it to her, and with each passing day she seemed a little more on edge than the day before. She tried to hide it, but he could tell the stress was getting to her. He could see it in her eyes, and he was afraid she was going to shatter before it was over. He was afraid there wasn't anything he could do but stand back and watch it happen. She'd made her feelings for him clear. The few times he'd reached for her, she'd recoiled, as if she couldn't stand his touch.

After the episode in her backyard, when she'd tried to push herself into a tree to avoid his touch, he'd made sure to keep his hands to himself. He should give the PO box task to Kurt. Yeah, that's probably what he should do, but he wasn't going to. Lucy might not want to see his face every day, but he wanted to see hers. He couldn't explain it, even to himself. It was more than lust, although there was plenty of that. He was drawn to her in ways that had nothing to do with sex and everything to do with her. Dangerous ways that had him thinking about more than just his career and a dog to keep him company. And that kind of thinking had never given him anything but a chest full of grief.

Sergeant Mitchell and the other detectives had discussed ways of using Lucy to draw out Breathless. They'd talked about a videotaped public appearance. Quinn hadn't liked the idea, but he'd mentioned it to Lucy yesterday when he'd driven by to give her the latest junk mail. Her flat refusal had been a relief.

The only real thing he could do for Lucy now was to catch a killer. It was a little after nine on a Saturday, and he'd come into the office to do just that.

He and Kurt had interviewed half the presidents of The Peacock Society, and he'd just received the last five membership rosters from each chapter president. Unfortunately, not all of them had included membership profiles, and he'd had to phone them and make a second request. While he waited, he cross-checked the names against the Women of Mystery roster. None of the Peacock ladies belonged to the mystery writers group, but some of the chapters of the Peacocks conducted their meetings at bookstores throughout the valley. He had a feeling Breathless was on one of the lists. Quinn leaned forward in his chair and placed the Women of Mystery roster on top of a pile of paperwork sitting on his desk. He read over each of the thirty-five names. She was there; he could feel it.

He reached for the latest crime lab reports and reread them. There wasn't a lot of good news. Except for the one set of usable prints they'd lifted off the leather passenger seat in Robert Patterson's truck there wasn't any hard evidence. They'd lifted a palm and four fingers from the left edge of the seat, where a person's hand would naturally grasp. The prints didn't belong to anyone in Robert's circle of family and friends, and they didn't belong to the victim. They didn't match any of the prints lifted from the hotel room, but Quinn wasn't surprised. Just as he'd suspected, that room had been lousy with prints and DNA, and he doubted any of it would prove useful.

He held up a copy of the lift card and studied the nice ridges of the hypothenar zone and the tented arch and whorls of all four fingers. IN-DENT had fed the prints into AFIS but unfortunately hadn't received a hit. Just like it was with the list of names on the writers list, Quinn knew in his gut that he was staring at the hand of a serial killer.

The cell phone hooked to his belt rang, and he answered without reading the caller ID. "Detective McIntyre."

"Quinn. It's here."

He straightened in his chair and set the copy of prints on his desk. "Lucy?"

"Yes." There was a pause, as if she were trying to swallow. "It's here."

"What?"

"The letter. It came to my house. She knows where I live."

Shit. "Did you open it?" He gathered the papers on his desk and put them into his notebook.

"No." A sob broke in her throat.

"You're not there alone, are you?"

"Yes. Adele spent the night, but she had to leave. I thought I'd be okay here by myself. It's broad daylight and I thought—"

"Are your windows and doors locked?" He grabbed his notebook and laptop and headed for the door.

"Yes."

"I'm on my way." He walked out the front doors and headed toward his unmarked car. "I'll be there in ten minutes."

"It's a twenty-minute drive."

He unlocked the car door and set the laptop and notebook on the seat next to a dozen pink roses. "Not for me." Probably not for her either.

Quinn hung up and called Sergeant Mitchell's and Kurt's cell phones. Neither picked up, and rather than leaving a message, he decided to call back once he had more information. Breathless had sent the letter to Lucy's house, and that changed everything.

The drive took him fifteen minutes. He parked his car by the curb and grabbed his evidence collection duffle out of the trunk. With the duffle in one hand and the laptop and his files in the other, he jogged up the sidewalk. The door to the house opened as he took the steps two at a time. He stopped on the porch and looked at her standing within her dark house, the curtains and blinds drawn against the sunlight. Her white pajamas had red lips printed all over them and were a stark contrast within the gray shadows. A sob broke between the fingers she pressed against her lips, and then she was in his arms. He wasn't quite sure how it happened. One second he was standing on her porch waiting for her to invite him inside, the next he was inside with the door closed behind him and the duffle at his feet.

She buried her face in his neck. "I thought I could handle this," she cried as her hands grasped the front of his black polo shirt.

"Shh. It's okay now." He slid his free hand up and down her back, bunching the flannel shirt. "I'm here. I'll take care of it." He pressed a kiss to the side of her head as his palm slid up her spine to her shoulders. "Don't worry. I'll take care of everything." Beneath the soft flannel of her pajamas, he didn't feel bra straps. He tried not to think about what that meant.

"I always thought I could handle anything." She shook her head, and her grasp on his shirt tightened. She seemed to want to burrow under his skin. "I always thought I was one of those fearless people who could survive a tsunami and outrun a bear. One of the smart ones who jumps in the life raft and doesn't go down with the ship. But I'm so scared I can hardly think straight."

He smiled into her hair. "Honey, no one can outrun a bear."

"I know, but I always thought that if I had to, I could do it. I thought I was the smart one, the strong one, but this whole thing has just knocked me on my ass. I'm not brave or strong or in control."

His gaze fell on the stark white envelope sitting on the coffee table. There would be plenty of time to deal with that later. "I'll help you."

"How?"

Yeah, how? He pulled back far enough to see her face. Dark circles smudged the skin beneath her eyes, and she was very pale. "When was the last time you ate?"

"Last night. Adele stayed here, and we had takeout."

He brushed a tear from her cheek with his thumb. "A real meal."

Her forehead wrinkled in thought, and he fought the urge to press a kiss there. "Like in cook?"

"Yeah."

"Wednesday Maddie made lasagna, but I haven't been really hungry."

"You're going to make yourself sick." He set his laptop and files on the table, then he grabbed her hand and pulled her with him into her kitchen. He flipped the light switch on his way toward the refrigerator. He let go of her hand, then opened the door to discover several boxes of old takeout and half a bag of chick salad, the kind that looked like weeds and flowers. He also saw a half gallon of milk, three beef weenies, and a brick of cheddar. "There's not much here."

"Except for last night, I haven't been here all that much. Just a few hours during the day to try and get some writing done and to meet you with my mail."

He shut the refrigerator and moved to open a few cupboards. "Your friend shouldn't have left you alone today."

"Adele's a writer and is busy. All my friends are busy with deadlines. They can't stay with me twenty-four/seven."

His gaze skimmed over cans of soup and veg-
etables, jars of olives, and two boxes of Kraft
macaroni and cheese. "You should have called
me." He pulled out the macaroni and cheese and
turned to look at her.

She shrugged but didn't answer. He supposed she didn't need to. They both knew why
she hadn't called him. "You're going to cook?"

"Sure. I'll make you something my mom
used to make me when I stayed home from
school sick. Where are your pots and pans?"

The bottoms of her slippers made a soft
skidding sound as she moved across the tile
floor. She walked to a cupboard next to the
stove and bent over at the waist, drawing
Quinn's gaze to all those red lips on her butt.
He wondered what she'd do if he grabbed her
up and placed kisses everywhere those lips
were printed.

"This ought to work," she said as she
straightened with a pot in one hand. She
walked toward him, and his gaze lowered to the
lips printed on the pockets covering her breasts.
He thanked God she wasn't a mind reader, or
she probably would have tried to slap his head
off like she'd done the morning he'd told her he
wasn't a plumber.

She handed him the pot, and he filled it with
water. "Weenie mac and cheese is exactly what

you need." He tore the top off the blue box and dumped the noodles in the water. "Good old-fashioned comfort food."

While the noodles boiled, he shredded cheddar cheese and cut the weenies. She stood with her hip shoved into the counter next to him with her arms folded beneath her breasts. To fill the time and take Lucy's mind off the letter in the living room, Quinn talked about the Raymond Deluca case. Yesterday, Mr. Deluca had been convicted of killing his wife and her three children, and Quinn talked about the case and the evidence that had hung him.

"I remember when that happened," Lucy said, watching as he drained the macaroni. "And the faces of those little kids in the newspaper."

While Quinn mixed the cheese sauce and tossed the cheddar and weenies into the pot and turned the burner on low, Lucy set the table. She poured two glasses of milk. "This usually gets baked for a while with extra cheese and little croutons on top," Quinn said as he filled two plates, "but you look too hungry to wait."

"Maybe I am a little more hungry than I thought," Lucy confessed as he held her chair. He sat across from her, and they ate for a few moments in silence.

Lucy reached for her glass of milk. "This is better than I thought it would be."

Quinn stabbed a few noodles and a slice of weenie with his fork. "Don't tell me you've never had weenie mac? It was a lunch staple at the McIntyre house."

A little white mustache rested on Lucy's top lip when she lowered the glass. She shook her head and licked it off with the pink tip of her tongue. "I did most of the cooking in my house. My mother had to work late a lot, so I made dinner for me and my brother. I got to be a really good cook."

Quinn recalled the chocolate torte she'd made him and how she'd said chocolate was better than sex. Granted, the torte had been good, but not that good.

She yawned behind her hand until her eyes watered.

"Am I boring you?" he asked.

She shook her head. "I'm tired."

"Are you having trouble sleeping?"

"It's more like I'm staying up late trying to work. I have a book due in four weeks and I haven't written a word since I found those letters. My deadline stress is adding to my insomnia. I'm a mess."

Yeah, she was. Her hair could use a brush, but that didn't keep him from wanting her. Spiffed or messy, he didn't care. "Why don't you take a nap? I can do some work here while you sleep." They both knew what work he was talking about, but neither wanted to talk about it just yet.

"I doubt I could sleep, but I would appreciate it if you'd stay while I took a shower."

Quinn pictured her naked and wet and all soaped up. "That's fine," he uttered as he picked up his plate and walked to the sink. He didn't have to try and imagine her naked. He knew what she looked like. He'd seen her from the waist up, and what he'd seen had rocked his world. Turned it on its head until he'd lost his friggin' mind.

Quinn rinsed while Lucy loaded the dishwasher. The late morning sun streamed golden light through the window and into Lucy's hair. It got caught in her lashes and poured across her cheek and into her parted lips. He'd lived with Amanda, had thought he'd spend the rest of his life with her, but he couldn't recall if they'd ever washed dishes together.

He handed Lucy a wet plate, and a drop of water slid from the edge to slip across her palm and wrist and disappear beneath the long sleeve of her pajamas. It wasn't until the machine was loaded that he brought up the subject they'd both been avoiding.

"Do you want to know what's in the letter?" he asked as he dried his hands with a dish towel.

"I'm not sure." She took one end and dried her hands too. "A part of me does. The curious part that killed the cat, but I know I'll regret it. So, no." Her fingers brushed his, and a wrinkle appeared between her brows, as if she was confused about something. "Thanks for lunch."

"You're welcome."

"And ah . . . if Snookie meows at you, don't feed him. He's on a diet." She moved across the kitchen to the doorway leading to the bedrooms. "And if you have to leave—"

"I'm not leaving."

She looked at him one last time and disappeared.

Quinn tossed the towel on the counter and moved into the living room. Instead of turning on lamps, he opened the drapes and let the sun in. He grabbed his duffle from the floor and tossed it on the couch, then took out a pair of rubber gloves and snapped them on his hands. He picked up the letter sitting on the table and sliced open one end with the small utility knife he kept in the front pocket of his jeans. As he sat on the couch, he pulled a letter from the envelope. This time there was no newspaper clipping.

Somewhere in the house, Quinn could hear the water turn on as he unfolded the paper and read:

Well, I am so disappointed, Lucy. I saw you with him. The cop. The one with the dark hair and eyes. He looked at you as though he was picturing you naked. Dirty man.

I thought we had an understanding. I thought I could trust you. I have felt such a deep connection to you through your books. I thought you felt it too. Through your writing, I have come to understand myself. Your words speak to me and give me power. In turn, I told you some of my secrets and shared with you my deepest thoughts. Quid pro quo— remember? You betrayed me. I know you've shown him my private letters to you.

What's to be done, now? I don't know. I'll have to think about it. I'm so upset with you. You've plunged a knife into my back.

Shall I return the favor?

The hair on the back of his neck stood up, which didn't happen to him very often anymore. He slid the letter and envelope in a clear evidence bag, sealed it shut, then pulled the gloves from his hands. He tossed them on the coffee table and skimmed the letter once more. He was going to have to tell Lucy about this one. He couldn't keep it from her. She had to know that Breathless was clearly threatening her.

When Lucy had called with this last letter,

Quinn had known the stakes had changed: He just hadn't known to what degree. Now he did. Lucy was going to have to relocate for a while or agree to have two undercover cops move in for around-the-clock protection. Those were the options—he just hoped she'd agree to one of them.

He opened his notebook and booted up his laptop. Breathless had seen him and Lucy together. She knew Quinn was a cop. Either she'd seen him on the news at a press conference, or he'd interviewed her. Quinn had a gut feeling it was the latter.

First, he wrote down all the places where he and Lucy had been together. The list started with Starbucks and included restaurants and Barnes and Noble. The list ended with the last time he'd been in her house.

Next, he flipped to his notes and wrote the names of everyone he had interviewed since the first killing. He pulled the Women of Mystery writers profile and membership roster from the notebook and circled the three members who worked at Barnes and Noble and possibly could have met the victims. Then he circled the four Peacock chapters that met in bookstores and the presidents of the group he'd already interviewed. He checked the three employees and Peacock members against the victims' phone records and e-mails. He came up with a big fat zero.

Across the house, the water shut off, and he took out the xerox copies of the other letters and laid them side by side on the coffee table, checking to see if there was anything he'd missed. There wasn't, and frustration tightened his forehead. Finding a clear connection would have been too damn easy. And nothing about the case had been easy. He flipped pages in his notebook until he turned to the interviews he'd done with employees at bookstores where all four victims had purchased books.

Bookstore receipts were just one link connecting all four victims. There were others, but the receipts were looking to be a bigger piece of the puzzle than Quinn had originally thought. If Breathless wasn't communicating with men online, then she was probably meeting them in the bookstores. Trolling the aisles for victims.

Quinn didn't have all the personal profiles from the Peacock ladies, and he didn't know which, if any, worked in bookstores. A week ago he'd seen several of them in the Barnes and Noble where Lucy had been speaking to the mystery writers group. It was possible they knew he was a cop. Even if none of the Peacocks worked at bookstores, they were readers who hung out there and could not be excluded.

"Christ," he cursed and rubbed his eyes with the palms of his hands. He was going around and around in circles. Each break in the case added as many questions as it answered. Each time he crossed off one suspect, it seemed like ten more were added. Breathless was on one of those lists, though. He knew it. If he kept whittling away, he'd find her. He had leads and suspects. It would take time to get through them all. Unfortunately, time was one thing he didn't have. Once he turned over the latest letter, the sergeant would be more determined than ever to use Lucy as bait.

Hell, if this were happening to anyone but Lucy, Quinn would be the first person to want to use her to establish more communication with Breathless. Use the media to anger Breathless into doing something stupid like showing up at a staged event, or baiting her into a physical confrontation. But this wasn't happening to anyone else, and the last thing he wanted to do was place Lucy in even more danger.

The thought of something happening to her twisted his insides into knots and burned a hole in his gut. He thought of Merry and the pink roses in his car. It was the thirtieth. He always put flowers on Merry's grave on April thirtieth.

There was no way he was going to have the death of two women on his soul. No way in hell that he would let anything happen to Lucy. He didn't care if he had to hog-tie her and shove her in a closet. His closet. The one in his bedroom was big enough.

Of course that was out of the question. Mitchell would have a fit. Besides, having her in his house would drive Quinn insane. He couldn't have her, and he couldn't keep his hands off her. Oh, he would have every intention of keeping his hands to himself, but something would happen and she'd be in his arms again, pressed up against him, and he'd be feeling for bra straps. Getting all hot and bothered and thinking about all the places on her body he wanted to put his mouth. At the same time knowing her feelings for him and that it was never going to happen.

He was thirty-six. A grown man. If he really put his mind to it, he could control his hands. The bigger problem was that he couldn't seem to control his body, and the last thing he wanted was to walk around his own damn house with a constant hard-on.

Frankly, he just wasn't up for that kind of abuse.

Chapter 13

Freefallin: Seeks Solid Place to Land . . .

Lucy looked at herself in the bathroom mirror and brushed her wet hair. As much as she hated to admit it, Quinn made her feel safe. Safer than she'd felt in days. It bothered her that it took a man to make her feel safe, and not just any man. Quinn. What she'd told him earlier was the truth. She'd always thought she was strong and could cope with anything and everything head-on. Snake bite? No problem, she'd just apply a tourniquet, then suck the venom out herself. Shark attack? No sweat, she'd just punch the shark in the eye. Chased by killer bees? Too easy, jump in a lake or run indoors and get a can of Raid. Get a letter from a wack job? Cry like a baby and call a big strong man.

Lucy brushed her teeth, then tipped her head upside down and dried her hair. She wondered what Quinn was doing, and she thought of the lunch he'd cooked for her. There was no way anyone would confuse it for a culinary master-piece, but it had been just what she'd needed. Warm and filling and full-on comfort food. It also had been a very nice thing for Quinn to do.

No, she wasn't reading too much into his every gesture and action this time. She wasn't going to read anything into the way he'd held her after she'd opened her front door earlier and flown into his arms. Nor in the way he'd touched her or pressed his lips to the side of her head. And she certainly wasn't going to read anything into his offer to make her lunch or stay while she showered. He'd been doing his job, and reading more into it was a dangerous slope she wasn't about to slide down any further.

Once her hair was dry, she walked into her bedroom and pulled on her white bra and blue-and-white-polka-dot panties. She dressed in jeans and a white blouse. She shoved her feet into her penguin footies, then made her way through the kitchen to the living room. She peeked around the corner and found Quinn sitting on the couch. His forearms rested on his thighs, and his hands hung between his knees. A notebook and papers were spread out across the coffee table and couch, and he was staring into the screen of his laptop.

He should have looked out of place, a big man parked on her sofa with his crap spread out on her antique coffee table. He didn't. He looked like a secure place to land in a suddenly insecure world. Like he alone could keep her safe. Her heart swelled a little at the sight of him, letting her know that he was anything but safe. Not for her.

Quinn turned his head as if he suddenly sensed her, and his dark gaze met hers. He straightened, and a lock of his dark hair fell over his forehead. "Do you feel better?"

"Yes," she answered and moved into the room.

His gaze followed her. "You look good."

She reminded herself that Quinn had hurt and humiliated her, and if a wack job hadn't decided to send her letters, he wouldn't be sitting in her house now. Acting like he cared. He'd be off pretending interest in the next suspect. Kissing and touching her in the name of his job. She moved to the window and looked outside. On the sidewalk beyond, two girls rode past on pink bicycles with baby dolls shoved in the baskets. Today was Saturday. Her night to stay at her mother's.

"Lucy?"

She glanced over her shoulder. "What?"

Quinn looked across the room at her for several long moments before he said, "We have to talk about the letter that came today. I know you said you didn't want to read what's in it, but you need to."

She turned. "Is it bad?"

His dark gaze continued to stare into hers, and he held up a letter encased in clear plastic. "I think so."

Lucy walked across the room and took the letter from his hand. As she read, she moved around the coffee table and sat on the couch. When she finished, she was glad she'd sat down. Her stomach pitched and got light at the same time. She was afraid she might get sick.

"Who has your home address?" Quinn asked as he looked at her across his broad shoulder.

"I don't know. It's not listed anywhere." She thought for a moment and came up with several possibilities. "Maybe someone at the DMV or post office. It's printed on my checks, so . . . who knows?" Lucy set the letter on her coffee table and rubbed her temples.

"How about bookstores?"

Bookstores? "Amazon does. I have books sent here all the time."

He shook his head. "Local bookstores."

"I don't know." She thought of all the book-stores and why they might have her address. "I have a Hastings card. I had to fill out an appli-cation, so I'm sure they have my address."

He reached for a pen. "Which one?" She told him, and he wrote it down in bold capital let-ters. "Let's talk about the Women of Mystery."

"I told Detective Weber everything I know."

"You probably know more than you think." He picked up a sheet of paper and handed it to her. It was a Women of Mystery roster. "Does anyone on the roster stick out in your mind as behaving odd or perhaps being an over-the-top fan?"

"Well, several of these women are odd." She pointed to a name on the list. "Betty has been writing and rewriting the same scene about killing off her father since I've known her, but I don't think she's a killer in real life."

"Was she the woman with white hair and glasses who was at the meeting at Barnes and Noble on the twenty-third?"

Damn, the man remembered everything. Then again, he was a cop. "That was her."

"Tell me about Cynthia Pool and Jan Bright."

Lucy shrugged. "There's not much to tell. Jan's the current president of the Women of Mystery, and she's the events person at Barnes and Noble. I know Cynthia is a member of

Women of Mystery, but I don't know how serious either woman is about her writing or whether they're just dabblers. All I really know about them is that they are both very supportive of local writers."

"How supportive?"

"They make sure our books are always in stock. Stuff like that."

"What's a dabbler?"

"A person who talks about writing but never actually finishes more than a few chapters."

He turned and looked into her eyes as he said, "We know from the Breathless letters to you that she is a wannabe writer. She reads mystery novels, especially yours." He reached for the second letter and placed it on top. "What does this line mean, 'You know what they say: write what you know'? Who is 'they'?"

" 'They' could be anyone. Could be anyone in publishing, or she could have read it in a book on writing. It's just standard industry advice."

"Jan knew that you're writing about a female serial killer who finds her victims online." He flipped a few pages in his notebook and leaned forward, searching for something. The back of his shirt came untucked from his jeans and showed a glimpse of his blue-and-white-striped boxers.

Lucy leaned forward and set the paper on the table. Her shoulder accidentally brushed against Quinn's, and his hands stilled in the act of turning pages. Traitorous little tingles spread down her arm and across her chest, and for an instant, she thought of something besides the psycho sending her letters. She recognized those tingles; each held a little spark of desire and longing and a hot zap to her heart. He'd given them to her before, when they'd both been pretending to be someone they weren't. She sat back against the couch, away from the danger to her heart. "I must have mentioned what I was writing in one of their meetings. Or in a live online chat."

"What do you mean?" He continued to flip pages as if he'd felt nothing. "What kind of on-line chat?"

"Groups ask me to be their guest speaker on-line," she answered, pushing her feelings for Quinn aside, where she could deal with them later. Or not. "It's really diverse. One night it could be a group that loves mystery novels, and the next a businesswomen's group." She brushed her hair from her face and held it at the back of her neck. "I'm asked all the time what I'm working on and when it will come out. It's always one of the questions people ask. I'm sure I've mentioned erotic asphyxiation and the fact that I'm writing about a female serial killer hunting online dozens of times and just don't remember. Believe me, I wish I knew who this woman could be." She dropped her hands to her lap, and her gaze landed on the latest letter. "It's clear she's seen us together and knows who you are."

"Yeah. I've probably interviewed her."

"Or she could recognize you from a press conference."

"I thought of that, but it's less likely she would recall my face from a press conference than a one-on-one interview."

"Not if she has something invested in the press conference, which she does." Lucy took a deep breath and asked the one question she'd been dreading. "Do you think she's going to come after me?"

Quinn turned to look at her, his brown gaze direct and his mouth a grim line. "I wish I could tell you no, but I can't. I think there's a real possibility."

That's what Lucy had feared. For the past five days, she'd tried to control the fear eating at her stomach. Now there was no controlling it. It spread up into her throat and into her head, and she couldn't think past it. The backs of her eyes stung, and she had a hard time drawing air into her lungs. She stood and quickly moved from behind the coffee table to walk across the room. She stared out her big picture window at the black shadows of bare tree limbs creeping up her sidewalk. What was she going to do now? She couldn't subject her friends and family to danger that was growing worse.

"What am I going to do?" She lifted a hand to grasp her burgundy silk drapes as her mind raced with possible solutions. "I guess I can go to a hotel. I could take my laptop and try to work." She took a deep breath and let it out slowly. A hotel room sounded confining. Safe, but confining. "Or I could go get a gun. I don't know how to shoot a gun, but how hard can it be? You just point and squeeze." Her voice shook when she added, "Right? Or . . . or I can board Snookie and head for Cancun."

Quinn placed his hands on her shoulders and pulled her back against his chest. "You don't need a gun or to head off to Mexico." He felt so solid. Warm and safe, and she stood there because it was better than falling apart. "You have me."

She wished that were true. "What are you going to do?" She laughed without humor. "Move into my guest room?" She was being facetious, although she had to admit that having a big bad cop in the house sounded like heaven.

"No, I can help you relocate for a while." He slid his hands down her arms and grasped her waist.

"Where?"

"My house."

She turned and gazed into his dark brown eyes. He didn't look crazy. He looked serious. "What are you smoking?"

"I think it's the perfect solution." She tried to pull away, but he tightened his grasp. "I have an extra bedroom. You can stay in it."

"Isn't there some cop rule against that?"

"No. You're not a suspect anymore, and besides, no one has to know where you are. In fact, for your safety, it would be best if no one knew."

The offer sounded tempting, but living in the same house as Quinn was totally out of the question. Not after the last time when she'd somehow ended up naked with his hands in very interesting places. Not when, after everything, she was tempted to let him finish what he'd started that night. "I don't think it's a good idea."

"You're wrong about that."

She folded her arms beneath her breasts and didn't answer. Her silence spoke for her.

He tilted his head back and looked down at her. "Ah. You're worried about what might happen if you're alone in my house again. You don't think you'll be able to control yourself."

"You *are* high." She knocked his hands from her waist and took several steps back. "I can control myself. I can control myself just fine. You're the one who started pulling my clothes off."

"You weren't complaining."

"I couldn't. You had your tongue down my throat."

He smiled. "Before or after you shoved your hands down my pants?"

Her gaze narrowed, and she thought her head might spin around.

"I don't know why you're so mad," he added and folded his big arms across his wide chest. "It wasn't that big a deal."

She lifted her hand and stabbed the air in front of his nose with her finger. "You thought I was a serial killer!" *And you told me you wanted a relationship with me when you didn't.* Stab. Stab. "If I'd known the real you, that night never would have happened." *And you made me fall in love with you and you were just doing your job.*

He tilted his head back again and pushed her hand aside. "If that's true, now that you know the real me, you shouldn't have any problem staying at my house through the weekend until we can get security in place. Don't turn down my offer out of anger. It's the best solution all around. You'll feel safer, and I'll worry less knowing you're safe."

Lucy dropped her hand to her side. While she didn't care if he worried or not, she had to admit that he had a point. She would feel safer at his house, and she wouldn't have to endanger her friends or her poor old mother. She would probably want to kill Quinn before this was over, but anger beat scared shitless any day of the week. "Okay, I'll stay with you, but you have to keep your hands to yourself."

He laughed as if he found what she'd said really funny. "Just my hands?"

"All body parts."

"That's no fun." His mouth curved into an upside-down smile. "But I think I can control myself. Can you?"

"I can control myself." She walked around him and added, "I can control myself just fine." She moved upstairs to her office and packed up her laptop and a few things she would need. She threw some clothes into a suitcase and left Mr. Snookums a bowl of food.

When she was ready to leave, Quinn carried her things to his car and put them in the backseat. She was probably making a big mistake. One that would make it more difficult for her poor heart to mend. But Quinn made her feel safe. She didn't know why, but he did. He made her feel as if he was the only solid thing standing between her and a psychotic killer.

On the drive across town to his house, Lucy's attention was drawn to the gadgets in the car, to the siren and police radio in the control panel. She looked up at the red-and-white lights hooked to the passenger visor, and she was dying to know what everything did. She'd relentlessly researched this sort of thing, but she'd never actually been inside a cop car. Then her gaze fell on the pink roses lying on the seat next to her, and she forgot about research and gadgets.

"Hot date?" she asked as if she didn't care. As if the thought of him with someone else didn't carve at her heart.

He glanced at her, his brows drawn together as if he just realized he wasn't alone in the car. "What?"

"The flowers. Do you have a hot date tonight?"

He returned his gaze to the road and turned onto Broadway Avenue. "No date. Just you, Sunshine."

He'd lost his mind. That was the only excuse Quinn could think of for why he'd talked Lucy into staying with him. He was going to regret it. He was going to end up wanting to kick his own ass, but her eyes had teared up and she'd stood there looking frightened and alone. Before he'd known what he was doing, he'd reached for her and pulled her back against him. His body had reacted to the smell of her hair and scent of her skin, and he'd had to stand there and fight the urge to bury his face in her neck. The touch of her beneath his hands reminded him of the last time he'd touched her— all over. The desire in the pit of his stomach reminded him of how much he'd been drawn to her, even when he'd thought she might be a homicidal psycho. How much he was drawn to her still.

Afternoon sun poured through the windshield, and he flipped down the visor. What he'd told her had been the truth. He would have wasted a lot of time worrying about her. Even if he assigned a security detail, he'd still worry. He had a job to do, and he couldn't catch a killer if he was distracted.

Of course, having her in his house was trading one distraction for another, but he'd rest easier if she was with him and Millie, where he could keep a closer eye on her. Millie might be young and immature, but she was territorial and one hell of a barker.

He turned off Broadway onto his street. Once Sergeant Mitchell found out that Quinn had stashed Lucy in his house, shit would hit the fan. There wasn't a hard-and-fast rule against moving a former-suspect-turned-state's-witness in with him, but that didn't mean the sergeant was going to like it. After the latest letter, there wasn't even a possibility that the sergeant wouldn't ask where she was or what security measures were being taken, and Quinn was going to have to tell him.

He hit the garage door opener and parked the Crown Victoria next to his Jeep. The best way to handle it was to inform the sergeant as soon as possible. That way it would appear aboveboard.

He turned off his car and grabbed his notebook and laptop off the passenger seat. He carried Lucy's suitcase with his free hand, and she followed him into the house. He set his files and computer on the kitchen table and turned on the lights as they moved down the hall to the spare room. He tossed her suitcase on the queen-sized bed, made up with a red quilt he'd bought at Costco at the same time he'd bought Millie's dog bed. The quilt was soft but not fancy, probably not the sort of thing a woman who drove a BMW would buy for her home.

"I refinished the wood floors in here," he said as he moved to the doorway and leaned a shoulder into the jamb.

"They're nice," she murmured as she set her

laptop on the dresser. She moved to the window and opened the blinds. He wondered what she thought of the room, and he wondered why he cared. Then it hit him, and he was appalled. He wanted her to *like* his house. As if it mattered squat. He wanted her to *like* him. As if that would ever happen. She was only here with him because those Breathless letters scared her more than she disliked him.

"If you change your mind about staying here, I can put you somewhere safe," he felt compelled to say.

She looked over at him through blue eyes and didn't answer for several moments. Part of him wished she'd opt for somewhere safe—the reasonable part of him that knew living with her just down the hall was going to be a pure, torturous hell.

"I'll stay with you," she answered.

"I have to go pick up my dog," he said and pushed away from the door frame.

Her eyes got that squinty look he was beginning to recognize. "The infamous Millie?"

"Yeah." He'd take the squinty look any day over the fear he'd seen there earlier. "Make yourself at home."

He left the house without looking back and drove to his mother's. On the way there, he picked up the telephone and called Kurt. He told him about the letter and where he'd stashed Lucy.

"I thought she didn't like you," Kurt said.

"She doesn't, but for some reason, I think she must feel safe with me."

"The sergeant isn't going to like this. Maybe you can figure something else out in the morning." They talked about the advantage of placing undercover cops in her house with her, but the more Quinn thought about it, the more he didn't like the idea of two men living with Lucy. Before making detective, Quinn had worked undercover security a few times, and it had worked out one of two ways. Either he'd wanted to kill the witness or he'd come to like the witness very much. He didn't have to wonder how a couple of young cops would feel about Lucy.

He hung up the phone as he pulled into his mother's driveway. He knew Kurt was right, but he was going to keep Lucy with him. He was a grown man. He'd been a cop for sixteen years and had learned a thing or two about control. He could control himself around Lucy. He could keep his hands off her. No problem.

He loaded Millie into the back of his Jeep and left his mother's before she could ask too many prying questions. He had one stop to make before he headed home.

Morris Hill Cemetery sat just above Julia Davis and Katheryn Albertson parks. Ancient trees shaded the crypts and towering headstones in the older sections of the cemetery. Quinn drove through the iron gates and wove around narrow roads until he pulled to a stop in front of a simple white headstone. He placed the roses beneath Merry's name and shoved his sunglasses over his eyes. The memory of her face in life was beginning to fade, adding to his guilt over her death. He brushed twigs for the white stone and stayed by the grave until he had a picture of her in his mind. She deserved at least that much from him. Then he got in his car and drove from the girl he'd failed to save toward the woman he intended to keep safe, or die trying.

He found Lucy asleep on top of her bed. She was curled on her side, facing the doorway, and sunlight poured through the slats of the blinds, across her face and blonde hair. One of her hands lay palm up by her nose, while her other arm fell across her stomach. Her feet were bare, and a bar of light fell across her red toenails.

Millie shoved her head between Quinn and the door frame, and he grabbed her collar before she could enter the room. Together they watched Lucy sleep, watched the slight rise and fall of her chest as she breathed in air past her slightly parted lips.

"What do you think about having another female in the house?" he asked his dog.

Millie let out a loud whine, as if she had a few complaints, and tugged at her collar. Quinn knew what Millie wanted. She could probably smell Lucy's cat on her clothes, and she was dying to investigate. Quinn figured the last thing Lucy needed was to be woken from a sound sleep by an excitable dog. "You can meet her tomorrow," he promised as he pulled Millie from the doorway and continued down the hall to his bedroom. She protested with more whining when he shut her inside. "Knock it off," he ordered, then moved to the linen closet and took out an extra blanket. Several hardwood boards protested beneath Quinn's feet as he walked into the guest room. He covered Lucy's legs with the blanket, and when he pulled it over her hips, she gasped and grabbed his arm. She sat straight up and about stopped his heart.

"Jesus H. Macy. It's okay, Lucy. It's me."

"Quinn?" Strips of light slid across her mouth and cheeks. Her wide eyes stared into his.

"Yes."

"What are you doing?"

Her hair rested on her shoulders and he could see her rapid pulse beating on the side of her throat. Beneath the white fabric of her shirt, her breasts rose and fell and pushed against the thin material with each breath. "You'd fallen asleep while I was gone, and I was just covering you up."

"Oh." She let go of his wrist and pushed her hair behind her ears. "What time is it?"

He glanced at his watch. "A little after five."

A frown wrinkled her brow. "You were gone quite a while."

"I had something important I had to do."

"With the Breathless case?"

He shook his head. "After I picked up Millie, I had to run some flowers to the cemetery."

"Who died?"

"Just a girl." He rested his weight on one foot and crossed his arms over his chest. Lucy looked up at him, waiting. "She was a confidential informant and she got killed because she was working with me."

Lucy rose to her knees on the bed, and the bars of sunlight spilled across her shoulder and throat. "I'm sorry. Did you catch the killer?"

"Yeah. He's doing life."

"And you take flowers to her grave." She shook her head. "That's sweet."

"No, it's not." He lowered his gaze to the front of her white blouse. With each breath she took, the stripes of light slid across her breasts.

No, he was not a sweet guy, but he could be an honorable guy. Even if it killed him. "If I don't do it, no one else will," he explained and raised his gaze to hers. "I do it because I have a guilty conscience. Because I didn't do my job and a girl got killed. She was a druggie and a whore, but she was a pretty nice person too. When she got killed all I could think about was how it impacted my case. All I cared about was my job."

Lucy sat back on her heels. "Is that why I'm here? So you make sure I'm safe enough to keep getting those letters to you?"

He should lie and tell her yes. That he didn't care about her at all. He'd been lying to her since the first day he'd contacted her online, and perhaps that's why he couldn't lie to her now. "I want to keep you safe, but that's not the only reason you're here. In fact, I'm sure I'm going to get reamed when my sergeant finds out."

"Then why?"

He was saved from answering by a loud thumping down the hall.

"What's that?"

Quinn glanced toward the door, then back down into Lucy's face. "Millie throwing herself against my bedroom door. She knows you're here, and she's not used to having women in the house."

Lucy tilted her head back a little, and a thin

shadow slid from her nose to her mouth. "How many women have there been?"

"Here? Besides my sister and all my nieces? Only one, but Amanda left when Millie was a puppy, so I doubt she remembers her."

"Who's Amanda?"

He dropped his hands to his sides. "She was the woman I planned to marry."

"What happened?"

He shrugged. "She decided she liked my best friend more than she liked me."

Lucy winced. "Ouch."

"Yeah. I found them in bed together."

"I've dated cheaters, but at least I never had to see it with my own eyes. What a bitch. That must have been horrible."

In that moment, he could have hauled her up and planted one on her mouth. But he'd told her he'd keep his hands and all body parts to himself. He was a man of his word, and he planned to keep it, even if it meant that walking around in a constant state of arousal just might do him in. At the very least it would take years off his life. "It was. Especially when she sat there naked in my bed and blamed me for her cheating."

"Wow, that's ballsy." Lucy smiled. A slight curve of her mouth that went straight to his groin. He should leave. Just back away toward the door.

"I guess that's one way of putting it." Back away from the blonde sitting on his bed, looking all tousled and warm from sleep. "She had a point, though. Sometimes I have to work very long hours."

Lucy shook her head, and the light slid across her lips. "That's crap, Quinn. We all have to work long hours sometimes. It's not an excuse for infidelity."

Again he fought the urge to grab her up and kiss her beautiful mouth.

"I've had boyfriends who were cheaters," she continued perilously. "And they always tried to pin the blame on me, but it wasn't my fault." She placed a finger between her breasts and pointed to herself. "I gave them lots of sex. Good sex. They were just losers. And I've always figured that it's best that you find something like that out before you marry a person. Or the next thing you know, you've got three kids while your husband is out picking up skanks in bars. Bringing home God knows *what* disease."

Quinn swallowed. Hard. "Lots?"

Her hand fell to her lap. "What?"

"Lots of good sex?"

"Well, not with a lot of different people. I haven't had all that many boyfriends, but when I do . . . yeah." She shrugged one shoulder. "Or what's the point?"

He had to leave. Do the honorable thing like he intended. Just get the hell out of the room while he could still manage to walk.

"I've always figured that if I'm going to bother getting naked with someone, I'm going to have a good time."

He swallowed—hard. A picture flashed through his mind of her up against the wall, his mouth on her breast. "Jesus H.," he forced from his suddenly raspy throat. Keeping his hand and all body parts to himself was the toughest thing he'd ever done.

"What's wrong?"

"You're torturing me."

For several heartbeats he watched her mouth, then slowly a smile tilted the corners, as if she hadn't realized until that moment what he was talking about. "Do you want me to stop, Quinn?"

"Hell no," he said just above a whisper. He was a masochist. "I want you to tell me how you give good sex."

Chapter 14

Goodstuff: Seeks Man of Dishonor . . .

Lucy had let her guard down, and Quinn had snuck past. Her only excuse was that she was tired. Tired of being frightened and hurt. Too tired to fight her feelings for him anymore.

She gazed into Quinn's eyes and the dark lust staring back at her, pulling her in with the promise of hot sin. Even if she couldn't see it in his eyes, she could hear and feel it in the velvet timbre of his voice. It brushed across her skin, a warm and sensual caress that she hadn't recognized until it was too late. It curled and warmed the pit of her stomach and heated her up from the inside out. "Good sex always starts with a man who knows what he's doing. Who's as interested in pleasing me as himself. Who knows the right spot to hit, and keeps hitting it all night long." She pushed her hair behind her ears. "Now you have to answer one of my questions."

"Shoot."

Before things went any further, she had to know. "Was I just your job?"

"Sometimes." She frowned in response, and his soft laughter filled the space between them. "I think if you knew how hard you made my job, you wouldn't be frowning at me right now. The first night I met you in Starbucks, I thought you were beautiful and smart, and I kept forgetting that I wasn't there just to wonder what it would be like to kiss you."

"You're kidding?" She hadn't known that. Hadn't even suspected.

"No. Then I did kiss you, and I wondered what it would be like to kiss you all over. Working my way from your forehead to the tips of your toes. Stopping at all the interesting bits and soft parts in between."

Her stomach got squishy and her mouth got a little dry. "But you thought I might kill you."

He chuckled. "Yeah, you'd think that might make a difference, but it didn't. Even when we were pretty sure you were the killer, I still wanted you, Lucy. There came a point where I figured dying inside you just might be worth it." His dark gaze burned her alive, yet he didn't reach out. Instead he took a few steps back, away from her.

No man had ever thought she was worth risking death for. Beyond all rationale and reason, she loved him more than she could recall loving a man. Her insides got hotter and itchy, and she moved from the bed and walked toward him. She raised her hand to the side of his face, and he turned his head and kissed her palm, spreading those little tingles he always made her feel up her arm and across her chest.

He closed his eyes and took another step back. "I wanted you more than I can ever remember wanting anything in my life." Her hand fell to her side, and he opened his eyes and looked at her. "I still do."

She knew that feeling. "Then why are you moving away from me?"

"I told you that I wouldn't touch you with any of my body parts. I spent last week lying to you, and you were hurt. That was my job. This is my life, and I want you to know that I can keep my word."

Now? He was worried about that now? "That's very honorable." She bit the side of her lip to keep from smiling.

"Are you laughing at me?" he asked, sounding mildly amused.

She took a step toward him and slid her palm to the side of his neck. "I'm just wondering if I'm allowed to touch *your* body parts."

"Hell yes."

"You won't think I can't keep my word?"

"No." He shook his head, and his jaw brushed her thumb. "Touch any part you want. I have a few ideas of where you can start."

She raised onto the balls of her bare feet and brushed her lips across his jaw. "I have a few places in mind already, but I'll let you know if I need your suggestions." The scent of him filled her head and heart, and she opened her mouth and kissed the side of his throat. She heard the harsh intake of his breath next to her ear. She ran her hand across his shoulder and down his chest to feel his heart. It pounded beneath her touch, and she raised her face to his and gave him a teasing kiss that left his mouth chasing hers until he could take no more and raised a hand to the back of her head to hold her against his mouth. Then he dove in and gave her a hot, wet kiss that made her insides tumble.

She pulled back. "Quinn. You're touching me."

"What?" He took a shuttering breath and pulled her toward him, wanting more.

"You're not supposed to touch me," she said against his mouth as she gathered his shirt in her hands. She yanked it from the waistband of his jeans and pushed it up his chest. "I wouldn't want you to compromise your honor."

"Sunshine, I lost that battle at sixteen."

"That sounds like bragging." Lucy pulled the shirt over his head and tossed it behind her on the floor.

"Just stating a fact."

She lowered her heels to the ground and slid her hands over his chest, combing her fingers through the short fine hair, feeling his hard muscles beneath her palms. "How old are you?"

"Thirty-six."

"So, you've had twenty years of practice."

"More if you count the years I practiced alone."

She laughed as she kissed his neck and lightly bit his shoulder. "I'm thirty-four."

"I know how old you are," he said just above a whisper. "I know all about you." Beneath her hands he remained perfectly still, but his breathing was harsh, ragged with the effort.

She wanted to know all about him, too, and seeing him naked seemed like a good place to start. The night they'd ripped at each other's clothes, she hadn't gotten a good look at him. She looked now. She took a step back and started with his shoes. She raised her gaze to the long legs of his worn Levi's; her attention got stuck on the serious bulge in his crotch, and she forced her gaze upward to the slight curve of his waist and the happy trail that rose from the button fly and circled his navel. His stomach was as flat as a washboard, and short, dark curls covered the hard, defined muscles of his chest. She looked up past his wide shoulders and the thick column of his neck to his face. His five o'clock shadow had arrived right on time, and dark stubble covered his jaw and outlined his mouth.

Even if he didn't touch her, his eyes told her how much he wanted her. His gaze burned with his need, touching her all over. She lifted a hand to the front of her blouse, and her eyes locked with his. Slowly she unbuttoned it and let it slide from her shoulders and fall to the floor. His gaze followed her hands to the snap of her jeans. She popped the snap, then lowered the zipper tooth by tooth. Quinn's gaze turned so hot, she was surprised her pants didn't catch fire as she slid them down her legs. Her panties slipped down on one side, and she pulled them up as she kicked her pants aside.

His hands curled into fists. "You're killing me."

The frustration in his eyes told her just how

much he was fighting the urge to grab her and toss her on the bed. "Don't die yet." She lifted her hands to the center of her bra and unhooked it. "We haven't even gotten to the good stuff," she said as she held the cups in place with her palms.

"I don't know if I'll make it to the good stuff."

She smiled and dropped her hands. She pushed the white straps down her shoulders and arms, and the bra joined her shirt on the floor.

He made a sound in the back of his throat. "You have great breasts. I could look at you all day. Every day and never get tired of the view." He reached for her. "Come here, Lucy."

She shook her head. "You promised to keep your hands to yourself."

He looked at her through all that lust smoldering in his eyes and returned his hand to his side. "For now."

She moved around behind him and pressed herself against the smooth planes and hard muscles of his back. The soft fabric of his jeans brushed against her belly, while his skin warmed her naked breasts and tightened her nipples. She lay her cheek against the back of his shoulder and slid her hands around his smooth sides to his abdomen and the hair that grew in the very center. She slipped her fingers beneath the waistband of his jeans and kissed the back of his neck. He shuddered as she slipped her hand between his jeans and boxer shorts. "What's this?" she asked as she caressed his erection.

He tried to speak, but all he managed was a deep groan.

She moved around to his front and pulled on the five buttons of his Levi's. With the fly open, she took him from his pants and slid her hand up and down the long, hot length of his shaft. With her thumb, she spread the clear moisture she found within the deep cleft across the engorged head of his penis. She lifted her face and kissed him until he pulled back far enough to say against her mouth, "Be careful. That's loaded."

"Is that cop humor?"

"No. It's a warning. I might go off in your hand."

"We can't have things going off in my hand," she said and slid to her knee before him. She looked up at him as she parted her lips and took him into her mouth.

He gasped. "Lucy." He brushed her hair lightly from her face, then tilted his head back.

She stroked him with her tongue and sucked him to the back of her throat. He moaned, and she pushed his jeans and boxers down his buttocks and thighs. She grabbed his firm behind in her hands and gave him pleasure.

One second she was on her knees, and in the next she was hauled up before him. "I don't want to get off in your mouth. Not this time," he said, then he kissed her with all the passion he'd been holding back. He crushed her against his bare chest and ate at her mouth even as he fed her kisses that made her want to climb up him. The hair on his chest rasped her nipples, and his engorged penis pressed hard into her belly.

He pulled back, breathing hard as he kicked off his pants and shoes. He yanked off his socks, then bent to take his wallet from the back pocket of his pants. He tossed it on one of the pillows, then he picked her up and tossed her there too.

"What are you doing?" she laughed as she raised onto her elbows. "I thought you were going to keep your hands to yourself."

"Fuck that." He climbed on top of her with his knees on the outsides of her thighs and planted his hands on the pillow by her head. "It's my turn."

"What are you planning?"

He yanked at her panties and pulled them down her legs. He tossed them away and slid his hand between her thighs. "I'm going to make you scream like a porn star."

She might have laughed if he hadn't placed his hot, wet mouth over hers as he stroked between her legs with his fingers. He touched and teased until she felt she would die if he stopped. But she didn't want to orgasm without him. Not again.

"Stop," she said, and he rose to his knees and reached for his wallet. He pulled out a Trojan, then tossed the wallet behind him. She pushed his hands aside and took the condom from him.

"I'll do that." She pulled it from the wrapper, placed it on the head of his penis, and rolled it down to the base of his thick shaft.

He rested his weight on one forearm as he positioned himself. Then he slid into her, and she gasped at the pleasure that spread though her body. "This," she said as she sucked air into her lungs, "is the good stuff."

He withdrew, then with two strong thrusts of his powerful hips, he buried himself deep. "Lucy," he groaned next to her ear. "You feel so damn good." He pulled out, then thrust harder. "Hot. I can feel you through the condom. So good."

Lord, he was talking. How could she get there if she had to concentrate on what he said instead of . . . That was her last coherent thought before he tilted her hips up and thrust deeper. "Oh my God!" she moaned.

He pulled out and stroked her spot with the plump head of his penis. "Does that feel good?"

She wrapped one leg around his waist. "More," she panted, giving over to the feelings rushing through her. "Right there."

"There?"

"Yes."

He stroked again. "Yes?"

"Don't stop."

He chuckled next to her ear. "Stopping at this point isn't going to happen."

He placed his hands on the sides of her face and moved within her, rocking against her with a slow, steady rhythm, pacing himself. With his face just above hers, he stared into her eyes as he moved in and out. She got the feeling he was trying to be gentle or controlled or something. But that wasn't what she wanted.

"Faster," she managed and moved with him. Matching each thrust of his hips. He picked up the pace, thrusting faster and harder, pushing her closer and closer with each powerful stab. It didn't take long before he was as mindless as she, both racing toward completion. She got there first, and as intense waves of orgasm rushed across her flesh, she moaned his name. The walls of her body convulsed around his rock-hard erection as he drove into her again and again, taking her with him until he too felt the euphoric tug and overwhelming rush. He swore and groaned deep in his chest. He thrust one last time, then collapsed on top of her. For several long moments he didn't move. "Quinn?"

"Yeah?"

"Are you okay?"

"Okay?" A deep, raspy laugh rumbled his chest against hers. "That," he said, catching his breath, "was the best good stuff I think I've ever had."

She removed her leg from around his waist and slid her hands across his shoulders before her arms fell to her sides. She smiled because she couldn't help it. He was right. It had been the best good stuff.

Quinn raised his weight onto his elbow, and she lowered her gaze, fearing that what she felt in her heart could be seen through her eyes. He kissed her pleased lips and withdrew from her body. "I'll be right back. Don't go anywhere."

He left to use the bathroom in his bedroom, and Lucy rose from the bed. She grabbed her blouse and a new pair of panties out of her suitcase and took the opportunity to use the bathroom a few doors down the hall. When she was finished, she buttoned the blouse over her bare breasts and stepped into her pink silky panties. She looked at her refection in the mirror above the sink. The same mirror she'd gazed into the last time she'd been in his house. She saw a woman who looked like she'd just had sex, but beyond the obvious flushed cheeks and messed hair, she saw what she feared would be reflected there. A woman in love. Madly. Totally. Completely in love. She wondered if he'd seen it and she hoped not. The last thing she wanted was for him to know her feelings. He didn't love her, and she didn't want to scare him away.

She pushed her hair from her face and lifted her chin to study the red patch of skin on her chin where his stubble had scratched her. He wanted her. She hadn't been wrong about that. She'd never been wrong about that, but it wasn't love.

He didn't love her and that hurt. It hurt like a red-hot clinker next to her heart. He wanted to be with her. He made her laugh and made her dizzy with his touch. He made her forget about the reason she was staying with him, and for today, that was enough. She would worry about tomorrow . . . well, tomorrow.

When she opened the bathroom door, he was waiting for her, leaning his back against the wall. His chest was bare and he wore his Levi's low enough on his hips that it was obvious he wasn't wearing his boxers. An Irish setter sat at his feet, and he held the dog's collar in one hand.

"This is Millie," he said.

She was a beautiful dog, with rich auburn hair and bright brown eyes. Her tongue hung out one side of her mouth as she looked up at Lucy. "So you're the infamous Millie." Lucy bent at the waist and scratched the top of the dog's head. "At least Quinn didn't lie about the color of your hair."

"I'm afraid if I let her go, she's going to try and sniff you." Lucy held her hand in front of the dog's nose. "That's not the part she wants to sniff."

She looked up into Quinn's face. "Which is the reason I have a cat."

"Cats don't fetch sticks or jump in ponds to retrieve birds."

"Which tells you how smart they are."

He shook his head. "Come and watch this." She followed him down the hall, watching the shadows slide over the smooth skin of his back. In the kitchen, he took a dog biscuit out of the cupboard. "Sit, Millie," he commanded. Once the dog obeyed, he set the biscuit on the end of her nose. "Stay." Poor Millie stared at the treat, her eyes crossed, until Quinn said, "Okay." Then she flipped it up into the air and caught it with her mouth.

"A cat can't do that."

"If Snookie wanted to, he could."

He gave her a skeptical look and scratched

his dog's ear. "Your cat probably can't move that fast."

He was probably right. "Are you disparaging Mr. Snookums?"

"He's fat."

"Husky."

"Same thing." Millie stood and walked a tight circle around Lucy, then sniffed her knee. "No. Sit Millie," Quinn ordered, and the dog instantly obeyed.

Lucy placed her hands on her hips. "Snookie has an eating disorder. It's not his fault."

Quinn chuckled, threaded his arms around her waist, and pulled her up against his chest. "You're cute when you get all worked up over that fat bag of fur."

"Hey—" She might have defended Mr. Snookums's honor if she hadn't felt a wet nose on the inside of her thigh. "Wow." She jumped a little and rose onto her tiptoes. "Your dog just goosed me."

"I knew it was too good to last." He dropped his hands and moved to the back door. "Out," he said.

Millie walked slowly toward Quinn, then gave Lucy one last accusing look over her shoulder. "Won't she get cold?"

"No." Quinn shut the door behind his dog. "She has a house in the garage, and there's a dog door leading into the backyard. She'll be okay." The overhead kitchen light poured down his bare shoulders and back as he walked to the refrigerator. "Are you hungry?" he asked.

"Depends on the offer." She didn't think she was up for another carb overload.

He opened the freezer. "I got raspberry sherbet."

"I could always eat sherbet."

He pulled a carton from the freezer, then shut the door. "There isn't much here, so we'll share." He grabbed a bowl and a spoon and began to scoop.

There were things Lucy was dying to know about Quinn, beyond his job and how he planned to catch a psycho who was killing men and writing letters to Lucy. Important things like, "Tell me about Amanda."

He glanced up from the carton. "Why?"

"Just making conversation." She moved to the kitchen table and leaned her behind into it. "You know, I tell you stuff and you tell me stuff."

"Amanda was short and had dark hair. Green eyes and big tits . . . ah, breasts."

"Naturally," Lucy said dryly.

He laughed and dumped the last of the sherbet into the bowl. "She had an annoying habit of leaving her long hair all over the place." He moved toward Lucy and fed her a big bite.

It was cold and kind of tangy and felt good sliding down her throat. "How does a person leave her hair all over the place?"

"Beats the hell out of me." He took a bite and pulled the spoon from his mouth. "She had this massive amount of hair, and it just fell out all over the damn house."

A woman with big breasts and massive hair. Lucy hated her on principle. "Have you had a girlfriend since Amanda?"

"No."

"Hookups?"

"I don't remember."

Great. He knew about her past relationships, but he didn't seem all that willing to talk about his. "Are you going to remember me once I'm gone?" she asked.

He fed her another bite and pulled the spoon from her mouth. "You're not going anywhere." He brushed the back of the spoon against her right nipple. It puckered beneath the cold metal.

She looked down. "What are you doing?"

"Getting your nipples to poke the front of your shirt. That's really sexy."

She tried not to roll her eyes. "How long have you been thinking about that?" She raised her gaze, but his attention was on the front of her shirt.

"Since you walked out of the bathroom."

"That's pervy. This whole time when we were talking about your dog and my cat and your former fiancée?"

"Yeah, it's called multitasking." He looked up and shrugged one bare shoulder. "I can talk to you about one thing but be thinking about something totally different."

"Must be a detective thing."

He chuckled and stuck his spoon in the middle of the sherbet. "More like a guy thing. We talk about shit you want to talk about, but we're really just trying to get you in bed. Again."

"You don't care about past relationships?"

He pulled out the spoon and set the bowl behind her on the table. "I only care about you." He slid the pink-covered spoon across the tip of her left breast. "And me. And how I'm going to get you out of those panties."

She gasped. "You got sherbet on my shirt."

A purely carnal smile curved his lips. "Isn't that a shame? I guess I'll have to clean it off." He dipped his head and sucked her through her shirt. The mix of cold sherbet and hot mouth scattered tingles across her chest and down her abdomen. She arched her back and ran her fingers through the side of his dark hair as he licked her shirt clean. When he was through, he popped a few buttons and pushed the material aside to suck her bared breast. Without lifting his mouth, he placed his hands on her hips, lifted, and sat her down. Right on the bowl of ice cream. It tipped sideways and raspberry sherbet slipped between her thighs.

"Crap!" She grabbed the bowl and scooped up the sherbet. "That's cold!"

"Looks like I made another mess. This time on your panties." He took the bowl from her hands and placed it on the table by her hip. He hooked the leg of a chair with his foot and pulled it forward.

"Put your feet on my shoulders while I clean you up," he said as he sat and scooted the chair even closer.

She didn't have to be told twice.

"Umm." He licked a spot on the inside of her thigh with his wet tongue. "You taste good. Like raspberries and warm skin." He kissed a path to the edge of her panties. "When I'm finished tasting you right here, I'm going to hit that spot of yours again."

She leaned back and rested her weight on her hands behind her. "You said something about making me scream like a porn star."

He smiled and dipped his head. Being a man who could multitask, he managed both.

Chapter 15

Goodtimes: Seeks Bad Boy . . .

The next morning, Lucy woke to something wet against her cheek. She opened her eyes and gazed into a red furry face and big brown eyes looking back at her. Millie licked her cheek, and Lucy rolled onto her back to get away. "Gross," she said as she wiped dog spit from her face. She glanced at the empty pillow next to her and sat up, holding the blue-and-white-striped sheet over her bare breasts.

After she and Quinn had had sex on the kitchen table, they'd ordered takeout and watched *Cold Case Files*. She'd discovered that Quinn loved *NYPD Blue* reruns, but throughout the show, he'd point to the television and yell,

"That would never happen!" or "No one does an interview standing over a corpse."

After the ten o'clock news, they'd taken a shower. They'd soaped each other up, touched and rubbed and made love against the shower stall. Then they'd climbed into Quinn's bed and fallen into an exhausted sleep. At least she had. Around 3:00 a.m. he'd awoken her to make love again. He'd been sweet and gentle and her heart had about burst, unable to contain her feelings in such a small place. They'd had sex four times. Four amazing times, made even more amazing because she loved him.

She loved him but didn't really have much of a clue how he felt about her. Oh, she knew he was attracted to her and that he liked her well enough. She wasn't sure what that meant—in the long term. Heck, she wasn't even sure about the short term after it was safe for her to go home again. For him, last night could have been just sex.

In the distance she heard a low and steady thumping and something that sounded a little like a conveyor belt. She glanced around for her clothes and recalled she'd last seen them on the bathroom floor. She slid naked from the bed. "Don't even think about it," she warned Millie as she walked to the master bathroom. Her clothes weren't there, and she wrapped herself in a towel and moved down the hall to the guest room. She traded the towel for her pink terry-cloth robe and followed the thumping sound to a third bedroom set up with a desk, weight equipment, and the object of the noise. Quinn, wearing a pair of loose gray shorts, with an iPod strapped around his arm and headphones plugging his ears, was jogging on a treadmill. His hair clung to the back of his neck, and with each step of his running shoes, the bottom of his shorts flipped up a little.

Lucy moved into the room and sat on a work-out bench loaded with black weights resting in the bars at one end. She crossed one leg over the other and studied his smooth skin, the play of muscles, and the slight indent of his spine. Over the rasp of the treadmill, it sounded like he was talking to himself. She listened closer and smiled.

Good Lord. He was *singing.* And not well. In fact, it was quite awful. So awful that she couldn't even begin to recognize the song. Maybe he was singing about falling on something, and when he hit a particularly sour note, Lucy laughed. She couldn't help it.

The wires to his iPod swung as he looked back over his shoulder. "Christ," he swore, grasped the hand rails, and put his feet on the sides of the treadmill as it continued without him. He pulled the earphones from his ears. "How long have you been sitting there?"

"Long enough."

He turned off the treadmill and grabbed the white towel hanging on the rail. He wiped his face and said into his towel, "Well, that sucks."

She tried not to smile. She really did. "It's a good thing you're good-looking."

He ran the towel over his head, then he hung it around his neck as he moved to stand in front of her. "Are you saying I have a shitty singing voice?"

"Yeah." Her foot swung back and forth as her eyes took in the hard muscle of his chest. "What were you listening to?"

His gaze lowered from her face to the deep V where her robe had fallen open. "Velvet Revolver. They're going to play here in a few months." He looked up into her face. "Wanna go?"

Her foot stopped. "With you?"

"No." He frowned. "With Millie. Of course with me."

"Like in a real date?"

He shrugged his bare shoulders. "Yeah. Why not?"

The concert was about three months away, which meant he saw them together three months in the future. Last night hadn't been just about sex for him. "Sure. When was the last time you were on an actual date?"

He wiped his chest with the towel. "Not counting all the Internet dates, I think it was when Kurt set me up on a blind date about four months ago."

"I hate blind dates."

He hung the towel over the weight bar. "She wasn't bad. We just didn't hit it off." He unhooked the iPod and moved to the desk filled with his laptop and open files.

"I hate getting all dressed up and going on dates and all you get out of it is a waste of time."

He set down the iPod and picked up a coffee mug. "Her cat was even more annoying than yours."

Lucy opened her mouth to defend Mr. Snookums, then closed it. "How long were you in her house?"

He raised the mug to his lips. "A while."

"I thought you didn't hit it off."

He took a long drink, then said, "We didn't. When I dropped her off, she invited me in for coffee and I went in."

Lucy stood. "When I invited you into my house for coffee, you turned me down."

"That's because I wanted to do you in every documented position and a few I'd made up." He set down the mug and moved toward her.

"But I was wired for sound and couldn't even let you touch me."

"What?" Lucy held out her hand like a traffic cop. "You wore a wire? When?"

"When we were together."

"Every time?" She dropped her hand to one hip.

He stopped a few feet in front of her. "Yeah. You didn't make any embarrassing confessions if that's what you're worried about."

Her mind moved from date to date and landed on that night in the hall. Her hands had been all over him. "Where was the wire the night I was supposed to kill you?"

He folded his arms across his bare chest, and his face set in that expression she'd come to recognize. The one that told her he didn't want to answer her. She folded her arms and waited him out. Finally he said, "I wasn't wearing one that night."

"Where was it?" Lucy asked, although she had a fairly good guess. She didn't believe for a second that the police had gone to the trouble of setting her up but hadn't wired the house for sound. She didn't know why she hadn't thought about it before—it was so obvious. Maybe because she'd had other things on her mind.

"There were digital recorders hidden in the kitchen, living room, and my bedroom."

She tried to remember what she'd said that night and couldn't. She turned away and placed a hand to her forehead. Her heart sped up and her face got hot. What had the police heard? "My God, that night . . . when my shirt was off and your hand . . . what were we saying . . . what—"

"No one could hear anything." Quinn grabbed her arm and turned her around to face him. "That's why I carried you into the hall. I didn't want anyone to hear us. I wanted you all to myself without anyone watching."

Lucy felt her speeding heart stop. "Watching?"

He leaned his head back and covered his face with his hands. "Shit."

"There were video cameras?"

"Yeah." He dropped his hands to his sides.

"Oh my God!" She pulled the lapels of the robe close around her throat and tightened the belt. "Where were the cameras?"

"The audio and video surveillance were in the air purifier in the kitchen, in a fake clock on the mantel in the living room, and in a clock radio beside my bed."

She thought back on that night. They'd never made it to his bedroom. They'd eaten dinner in the kitchen, and in the living room they'd kissed and he'd taken off her sweater. She gasped and shoved at his bare chest. "How could you do that to me?"

"Lucy." He grasped the tops of her arms. "I'm sorry. We thought . . . I thought you were Breathless. We thought that if you—"

"How many people were watching?"

"Two. Kurt and Anita were in a van outside."

Lucy thought back and could recall seeing a van parked on the opposite side of the street. Two people had been in that van watching him undress her and touch her breasts. She was horrified. "Oh God. Oh God, and there's a tape?"

"Yes."

"Where?"

"Evidence room, I would imagine."

"How many people have seen it?"

He shook his head. "I don't know." She tried to pull away, but his grasp tightened. "It isn't that bad."

"Have you seen it?"

"No, but the cameras couldn't see down the hall."

This time when she pulled away, he let her go. Lucy looked into his handsome face and felt the backs of her eyes sting. She refused to cry. Inside her, anger and humiliation gave way to a deeper feeling of utter betrayal. It didn't matter that Quinn hadn't had a choice. He'd set her up, and now there was a videotape of him taking off her sweater and touching her breasts. It was out there. Somewhere. For strange men to see. "I have to get out of here," she said and walked around him. Even in her misery, she wasn't going to act recklessly. "I'll take you up on that offer to move cops into my house." In a daze, she left the room. Maybe she could get the tapes somehow. Maybe if she called a lawyer, she could make the police give them to her.

She walked into the spare bedroom and tossed her empty suitcase on the bed. She'd call first thing tomorrow morning.

"Lucy."

She turned and looked at him standing in the doorway. A dark lock of hair fell over his forehead as his dark gaze stared into her. After everything, there was a part of her that wanted to throw herself against his bare chest and forget what he'd done. He could make her forget about everything for the few moments he held her. She loved him, and she wished she'd never met him.

"Promise me you won't leave until after I get back."

Once again she felt humiliated and heartbroken and all because she'd made the mistake of loving Quinn.

"Promise me," he repeated.

She supposed he needed to get the security in

place at her house before she returned there.
"Fine."

"Promise," he insisted.

"Cross my heart." Once again she'd been a
fool where he was concerned.

Lucy turned her back on him and unzipped
the suitcase she'd unpacked the night before.
She heard him move down the hall, and a few
moments later, the water to the shower turned
on. She shut the door and sat on the bed. Her vi-
son blurred, and she wiped her eyes with the
sleeve of her robe. She did not want to cry. She
would not let Quinn see her cry.

She thought about the night before and the
way he'd touched her. She thought about the
way he'd made her feel, and the way she felt
right now. In her mind, she could not resolve
the two feelings. They didn't fit. The pleasure
and pain of loving Quinn, being thrown from
one extreme to the other, was too much.

She listened for the water, and after it shut off,
she moved across the room to the small dresser.
She opened the top drawer and discovered the
missing white blouse and pink panties she'd
lost the night before. They'd been washed and
folded and placed neatly in the drawer. She
picked up the blouse and held it to her nose. It
smelled like Quinn's shirts. Again her vision
blurred, and she wiped her eyes with the back

of her hand. Even with everything else going on in her life, Quinn and her broken heart took front and center. It was crazy, but there was no denying it.

She heard Quinn's footsteps on the other side of the closed door. They paused for several heartbeats before continuing down the hall. A few moments later, she heard the garage door open and his Jeep pull away. When he returned, she would be ready to go.

Lucy set her black bra and underwear, a khaki skirt, and a black T-shirt on top of the dresser, then dumped the rest of her clothes back into her suitcase. She opened the door, and Millie followed her into the bathroom.

"Out," she commanded. Millie lay down and looked up at Lucy through sad eyes. "Fine," Lucy muttered. She jumped into the shower and washed her hair and body. When she was through, she stepped over Millie and brushed her teeth and dried her hair. She pulled her hair into a ponytail, and by the time Quinn returned, she was sitting on his leather couch, dressed and waiting for him.

His face was set in hard lines, and his jaw looked brittle enough to break. He wore jeans and a white Guinness T-shirt. She stood, expecting him to give her the details of the new security arrangement. Instead he took her hand

and placed two small cassettes in her palm. "What's this?"

"The videotapes taken the night the house was wired."

She looked up. He had his cop face on, the blank, expressionless set to his features that made him look hard. Except for his dark eyes. He couldn't wipe the emotion from his eyes. It flickered just beneath the surface, hot and alive and something he couldn't control the way he could control the rigid set of his jaw. "How did you get these?"

"Don't ask." He dropped his hand.

"Did you check them out or something?"

He looked at her for an eternity before he said, "No."

"Quinn?" He simply stared at her, and this time she knew that he wasn't going to answer. She couldn't outwait him for an answer, but she didn't need to. His silence spoke for him. He'd stolen them out of the evidence room. For her. "But what if they're missed? Won't you get in some kind of trouble? Fired even?"

He just continued to stare at her.

"Won't someone know they're missing?"

"Probably. The less you know about it, the better."

"What am I supposed to do with these?"

"Whatever you want. But I would recommend that you destroy them and forget that you ever saw them."

"Isn't that destroying evidence?"

He shrugged one shoulder. "Technically, yes."

She looked down at the cassettes. "Are you certain these are the right tapes?"

"They were labeled, so I'm pretty sure."

"But you're not certain."

"You want to see them?"

Not really, but she wanted to make sure she had the right tapes in her possession. She handed them back. "Yes."

He pointed to the couch. "Sit tight." He walked out of the room, and when he returned, he had a video camera. He hooked it up to the television and popped one of the cassettes inside.

She wanted to know if he'd get fired. The answer was, *Hell yes*. If caught, he'd be charged with petty theft, but since the tapes were useless to the Breathless investigation, the criminal charges would probably be set aside with the agreement that he not contest his termination.

Quinn started the tape, then he moved across the room and sat on the couch next to Lucy. On the screen, their black-and-white images appeared, and Lucy leaned forward to watch as the two of them made dinner and talked about everything from the weather to local politics.

In the past, he'd bent and stretched the rules, but he'd never completely broken them. He loved his job, and if anyone had ever told him that he'd steal evidence, he would have told them they were nuts. If they'd told him he'd steal it for a woman, he would have told them they were *fucking nuts*. But then he'd messed up and told Lucy about the tapes, and she'd looked at him as if he'd just killed her cat. One minute she'd been looking at him as if she'd wanted to jump on him and continue his workout, and the next, like he'd stabbed her in the heart. He would have done anything to have her look at him as she had the minute before.

When he'd left, he'd taken the latest Breathless letter with him and dropped it off in the crime lab for the technicians to look over in the morning. He'd planned to take it in that day anyway. What he hadn't planned until he'd looked in her eyes filling up with tears was a little petty theft, but by the time he'd walked out his front door, he'd known what he would do.

He was a dumb ass. He'd put his job on the line for a woman who would never forget that he'd undressed her in front of a hidden camera. He'd risked getting terminated for a woman who sat next to him as stiff as a poker. A woman who'd made him want something he'd given up on. Something he'd convinced himself he was better off not having in his life.

Quinn watched their images on the television screen as they ate dinner together, talking as if they were just two people getting to know each other. He didn't recall the meal so much as he did her sweater and leather skirt. Then she brought out the chocolate cake, and he recalled how he'd felt watching her put the fork into her mouth.

"Sometimes, chocolate is better than sex," she spoke from the television.

"Honey, nothing is better than sex," he'd said.

She set the fork on her plate and pushed it aside. "I guess that would depend on your basis of comparison."

He rose and said in a voice so sexually charged that he hardly recognized it, "Come here." From across the room, Quinn watched the screen, where he wrapped his arms around Lucy. "Let's give you something good to compare." Then he kissed her and it was as hot as he remembered. Sexual energy rolled in waves from the television screen, scorching a path across the living room, and Quinn got a little hot watching it. He slid his gaze to Lucy to see if she felt it too. Her brows were lowered, and she appeared more pissed off than excited.

"I need to use your restroom," she said from the tape, and Quinn returned his attention to the screen. She moved out of frame and Quinn followed. The motion-sensitive tape shut off, and Quinn rose from the couch to place the second cassette into the video camera. He pushed Play and returned to his seat.

The film started to roll with him walking into the living room, reaching for her purse, and dumping the contents on the couch.

"You went through my purse?"

He slid his gaze to hers. "Yeah, and you carry a lot of crap around with you."

She folded her arms beneath her breasts. "That's how you knew about my pepper spray."

On the screen, Quinn shoved everything back into the purse, then moved to stand in the middle of the living room. He looked up when she entered the room, his dark gaze following her. Even on the black-and-white film, he could see the desire in his eyes. He'd thought she was a killer, and he'd wanted her anyway.

On the film, she looked into the camera and told him she didn't think they should have sex. From behind her, his gaze was directed at the camera too, although he knew they'd been looking into the mirror above the fireplace.

He watched his hands move down her arms and come to rest on her waist. "You tell me when to stop," he said and pulled her back against his chest. "Are you uncomfortable when I kiss you here?" He kissed the side of her throat and she shook her head.

"That's good. I like kissing you right here. Where your skin's soft and your hair smells like flowers and looks like sunshine." He shoved his fingers inside the waistband of her skirt and slid them to her sides. She tilted her head to the right, and he sucked the side of her neck. He slid his fingers up beneath the edge of her sweater to her breasts. His eyelids were heavy, and there was no mistaking the need reflected on tape.

At the moment, Quinn didn't know what he felt most, embarrassed or turned on. He was embarrassed by the things he was saying, but at the same time, watching his hands move upward and his thumbs brush her hard nipples was the most erotic thing he'd ever done. A hundred times more erotic than watching a porno flick. On the screen, her breath caught and her lids drifted shut as his hands cupped her breasts.

"Your nipples are hard," he whispered into the side of her throat. "Like a woman who wants to make love."

She turned and wrapped her arms around his neck. As they kissed, he slid the fingers of one hand beneath the waistband of her skirt and pressed his palm into her back. His other hand moved up her spine, then he gathered her sweater in his hands and pulled it over her head.

"I love a woman in lace," he whispered and lifted a hand to touch the lace edge of her bra with the tips of his fingers. "You're so beautiful, you make me forget."

"Forget what?"

"That I should take it slow. That I don't want to blow it by rushing things," he answered and pressed his palms into her breasts. "But it's been so long." He pushed her breasts together as he bent forward and kissed her deep cleavage. "Why did you have to look like this? This would be easier if you weren't so beautiful. If I didn't want you so much that I can't think of anything but getting you naked."

He kissed her and ran his hands down her bottom to the backs of her thighs. Then he lifted her and wrapped her legs around his waist. He walked with her from the frame, and the tape kept rolling, fixed on the empty room. The sound portion continued, filling the room with the sounds of soft moans, and Quinn was stunned by the clarity. "Damn. I didn't think the audio could pick up what was going on in the hall," he said.

Lucy didn't comment. Her hands fell to her lap as they listened to Quinn's voice fill the tape. "Nothing here but Lucy," he heard himself say. "You want me, and I want to fuck you until you can't walk for a week. Until you can't move. Can't think. Can't do anything but moan. Do you want that, Lucy?"

Okay, that was a little embarrassing. On the tape came a breathy, "Yes."

More silence, and then his groaned, "I'll help you, Lucy." What she said was unintelligible, and then it was Quinn again. "Yes, touch me there, just like that. You won't be alone. Oh, God that feels good. I'll get you help. I'll get you all the help you need."

Jesus H., that was more than a *little* embarrassing, and he could feel his neck start to burn. He didn't remember saying he'd get her help. He'd been so into her, so wrapped up in the moment, that he'd thought he could fix her. As if overcoming murderous impulses were curable.

On the tape, the ringing of the telephone mixed with the telling sounds coming from the hall—his deep groan and the breathy moan she made deep in her throat.

Sitting there listening, Quinn got so hard that he almost came too. He turned his head to look at Lucy, but her gaze was directed at the televison.

"I'm sorry," she said on the tape. "I didn't mean to do that yet."

"You'll make up for it." The telephone stopped, only to start ringing again. "Shit! I'll be right back." Quinn's image moved into the living room. He picked up the cordless phone next to the couch and cradled it between his shoulder and the side of his face. "Yeah?"

"Because I was busy," he barked into the phone as he buttoned his pants. "What?" His hands stilled a second before he grasped the receiver. "Are you fucking kidding me?" He turned toward the hall. "Tell me you're kidding me."

After a few moments, Quinn could be seen hustling Lucy out of the house, then the tape shut off and the television filled with static.

A furrow between her brows, Lucy turned to look at him. "Why did you do that, Quinn?"

He thought he'd made her understand. Apparently not. "There were reasons to believe that you were Breathless. And we were—"

"No," she interrupted him. "Why did you tell me you'd get me help?"

He looked away.

"There's no help for a serial killer," she said.

"Yeah. I know." He could feel his ears turning hot.

"Did you offer to help the other suspects you were dating?"

"No. Things never got that far with the others." He looked back into her face. "I didn't touch them the way I touched you." What did it matter now? Probably she wanted to humiliate the hell out of him before she kicked him the rest of the way to the curb. Then she'd turn the tapes over to Sergeant Mitchell and get him fired.

Instead, she did something that baffled the hell out of him. She climbed into his lap and sat on his erection. With her legs on the outsides of his thighs, she placed her hands on the sides of his face and said, "I think you liked me even when you thought I was going to kill you."

He looked up into her blue eyes. "A little."

She smiled and slid her hands down his chest. "I thought you weren't going to lie to me anymore."

He grasped her legs and pressed his fingers into her. He knew what she wanted to hear, but he couldn't lie to her. Not even with her crotch warming his fly. "I do like you, Lucy. I like you a lot. When I'm not with you, I think about being with you. I like having you around. We're incredible together. The sex is hot, and you make me want things I haven't thought possible."

"What things?"

"You." He looked into her eyes and confessed, "A life outside of my work."

Her hands slid up to the side of his neck.

"Why can't you have those things? Last night you said I wasn't going anywhere."

"I shouldn't have said that. And I can't believe I'm saying this now, but you're not living here with me because you have a lot of choices. I've seen relationships develop out of stressful situations and tragedies, and sometimes they don't last past the trial."

She tugged his shirt from his jeans and pushed it up his chest. "If we'd met under normal circumstances, it still might not last."

He grabbed her hands before it went too far and he knew he couldn't stop. "True, but this situation is far from normal."

"Are you trying to be honorable again?"

"Yeah."

"Don't." She pulled his shirt over his head and tossed it on the floor. "I think I like you best when you're not quite so virtuous. When you've lost control. When you're willing to risk it all for a woman you think might kill you. I like it when you can't help being bad."

He chuckled and pushed her skirt up her thighs. She liked him best when he wasn't trying to do the right thing?

Hell, being the good guy was hard. Bad came easy.

Chapter 16

Biggestfan: Seeks Object of Obsession . . .

The next morning, Quinn stood in front of his bedroom mirror dressing for work just as he had for the past four years. Only this morning, he had an audience. She sat cross-legged in the middle of his bed, drinking coffee and wearing his T-shirt. After they'd made love yesterday, she'd handed him the tapes and they'd returned them to the evidence room.

An hour ago, he'd woken with her firm little behind against his groin and his hand on her full breast. It hadn't been a bad way to wake up. Especially for a Monday morning. Particularly since he knew his day was going to go to hell once he got to work.

He shoved the tails of his blue dress shirt into his gray trousers and glanced at Lucy through the mirror. Her attention was directed on his hands as he zipped his pants. "I need to talk to you about something," he said, beginning the conversation he'd been dreading since he'd read the most recent Breathless letter Saturday.

She looked up, and her eyes met his in the mirror. "What?"

"Once Sergeant Mitchell and the other detectives read the latest letter, they're going to want to use you to draw the suspect out. I know we talked about this last week, and if you were anyone else, I'd agree with them. I'd do my best to talk you into staging something with the media or maybe a book signing. But you're not just anyone. Not to me, and I want you to know you don't have to do anything."

She unfolded her legs, and Quinn's gaze followed the progress of his T-shirt sliding up her bare thighs and behind as she scooted to the edge of the bed. She set the coffee on his dresser and came to stand in front of him. "I've actually given this some thought," she said as she reached for the front of his shirt and buttoned it. "I want to do whatever it takes to get my life back as soon as possible." She glanced up at him, then returned her gaze to the buttons. The top of her head was just beneath his chin. "As much as I like it here with you, I want my normal life back. I want you and me to be together like normal people."

"How normal?" he asked the top of her head.

"You ask me out not because it's your job but because you want to be with me. When you pick me up, I keep you waiting while I try on shoes like it's a real date." She looked up at him. "Stuff people do when they first start to go out together. We've kind of skipped all that. I know it sounds old-fashioned, especially considering how fast I ended up in bed with you, but I guess I want you to, you know, woo me."

He chuckled. "I recall wooing the hell out of you last night." She scowled as he wrapped his arms around her waist and pulled her against his chest. "Okay." He pressed his lips to the top of her hairline. "When this is all over, I'll come over and pick you up and you can keep me waiting while you change your shoes a million times. You can even torture me by trying on clothes and asking my opinion, although we both know my opinion really doesn't matter. And even though I don't need to lie to get you into bed, I'll even tell you you're a good driver."

She tried not to smile. "And you'll be nice to Snookie?"

Yesterday when they'd gone to Lucy's house to feed her cat, Quinn had stepped on the damn cat's tail. It had been an honest-to-God accident, but he wasn't quite sure Lucy believed him. "I swear that was an accident," he reminded her. "I didn't see him."

"How could you not see a twenty-pound cat sitting in the middle of the floor?"

Because he'd been watching Lucy's breasts jiggle a bit as she'd poured cat food into a dish. He pulled her tighter against his chest. "In the future, I'll watch where I'm walking."

She laid her head against his shoulder and said, "I want my life back, Quinn. I want to be normal. If that means I have to do a news conference or book signing, let's do it as soon as possible."

"You're sure?"

She nodded and took a step back. "Yes. I'm not afraid as much as I'm pissed off." Her eyes got all Linda Blair squinty and shone with that unholy gleam he hadn't seen since the day he'd sat in her car and told her Millie was his dog. He was glad to see it again. "She's going down."

He was glad that look wasn't directed at him.

Quinn arrived at work ten minutes early, prepared to inform Sergeant Mitchell of the latest developments, but was informed that the sergeant was in a meeting and wouldn't be in his office until that afternoon. Quinn felt some of the tension leave his shoulders. He had a reprieve for a few hours.

At ten after nine, a fingerprint technician walked into the briefing room, grinning from ear to ear. "We got a thumb print off the latest envelope," he said. "It matches the thumb print taken from the seat in Robert Patterson's truck."

Quinn leaned his head back and closed his eyes. "Thank you, Jesus." They finally had a strong link between Breathless and the murders. Whoever had written the letters to Lucy had been in the Patterson truck. And whoever had written that last letter had seen Quinn and Lucy together and knew he was a cop. Breathless was starting to make mistakes.

Quinn looked at Kurt, and they both knew this was big. They were finally getting the break they needed, and Quinn wasn't going to have to use Lucy. At least not yet. She could stay tucked safely in his house. Her and Millie.

"We've interviewed her, Kurt," he said, referring to Breathless.

"You're probably right," the other detective said as he looked over a copy of the last letter.

Quinn opened his notebook and flipped to the suspect list. "We've cleared half, so—Son of a bitch!" He flipped to a Xerox with the vics' photos on it, then his attention snapped to the print technician, who was still in the room, as he pointed to the page in his notebook. "I need you to process this. If our luck holds, we can get a matching print off it."

"We must have shown that to twenty or thirty people," Kurt reminded him.

"And half of those have been cleared."

The fingerprint technician pulled a handkerchief from his back pocket and removed the Xerox from Quinn's notebook. He left, and Quinn went into his office to cool his heels and wait. He called the crime lab, but there was nothing new regarding hair and fibers found at the scenes. He checked in with the victims' families and informed them of the fingerprint evidence. Then he called Lucy on his home phone.

"McIntyre residence," she said. "Home of Quinn, crack detective and sexy man."

At the sound of her voice, he felt an overwhelming potentcy squeeze his chest. "What if this call had been from my mother?"

"I looked at your caller ID before I picked up."

He didn't feel it in his whole chest, just the left side, near his heart. Like he had a blockage. "Are you bored?"

"No. I'm trying to get some work done."

"You're writing?" Last night he'd let her look over his files on the Breathless case. He hadn't known she wore gold-framed reading glasses until she'd put them on the bridge of her nose. She'd looked hot. Of course, he thought she looked hot in everything or nothing at all.

"Trying to write. It's not going well, but I'm hoping something will shake loose." In the background, Millie started barking, like someone was busting into the house.

"What's wrong with Millie?"

"Just a second." There was a pause, and then, "She sees a cat on your lawn."

"Ah, she's protecting you from the neighborhood felines."

Lucy laughed. A soft little sound that settled next to his clogged heart. "She doesn't seem to be much of a guard dog, Quinn. If a burglar breaks in, she'll show them where you keep your good stuff."

Quinn chuckled. Lucy was his good stuff. "Maybe, but she'll bark a lot while she points the way." He pulled back his cuff and looked at his watch. It had been over an hour. "We got a print off the latest envelope," he told her, but he didn't have to mention how important it was. They talked about the case, and they talked about what they were going to do that night and what to have for dinner, like an old married couple. "When I get off work," he said, "I'll go feed your bag of fur."

"His name is Mr. Snookums."

"Yeah. I know."

Her long-suffering sigh carried across the phone line. "I want to go with you because I have to look for a very important folder. I misplaced it somewhere in my house."

"I'll help you search for it," he offered as the fingerprint technician entered his office. By the guy's smile, Quinn knew they had another hit. "I need to go," he said and hung up the telephone. "Well?"

"We have a matching index finger taken off the bottom of the vic paper."

For a week Quinn had stared at the prints taken from the truck. He wanted to kick his own ass, but he didn't have time. He stood and shoved his arms into his blazer, covering the pistol hooked to his belt. The list had just been culled down to a dozen suspects, and he knew the first place to look.

Lucy stared at the blinking cursor willing the words to flow from her fingertips and onto the computer screen. When they didn't, she took off her glasses and set them on the kitchen table next to her laptop. Millie sat beside Lucy with her head on Lucy's thigh. Lucy reached down and scratched the dog beneath the ear.

She'd thought that since she was feeling

safer today, the muse fairy would tap her on the head and her writing would once again start to flow.

It wasn't happening.

She blew out a breath and leaned back in the chair. If she had the critique from Maddie, she would at least have something to do. And hopefully, reworking a few chapters would kickstart the rest. She stood and walked into the living room. Millie followed close on her heels, and Lucy picked up the television remote and turned it on. She flipped to the twenty-fourhour news stations to see what had been happening in the world since her life had gotten so out of control. There was nothing on but depressing news, and she turned it to City Confidential and vegged out on the tube. What she'd told Quinn that morning was the truth. She wasn't as scared as she was angry. She felt an impotent rage at the woman who'd pushed her into the worst writer's block of her career.

She turned off the television and tossed the remote on the coffee table. She thought about Quinn and what he'd said yesterday about their elationship starting out under stress. She had to admit that it had started out a little less than orthodox. Okay, *a lot* less than orthodox. They'd both lied to each other and dated under false pretenses. But there had been no pretending when it had come to the sexual pull that they'd both felt from that first night in Starbucks. The way he'd looked at her hadn't been a lie. Not then and not now. There was something a little overwhelming about it. Overwhelming and intoxicating at the same time.

He hadn't told her he loved her, she reminded herself. But to be fair, she hadn't told him either. He'd moved her into his house to keep her safe, and he'd taken the tapes out of the evidence room. *Taken* was a nice word for *stolen*. He'd done it for her. No, he hadn't told her he loved her, but no man had ever risked so much to be with her.

Her cell phone rang, and she jumped a little. "Hello."

"Hello. Am I speaking to Lucy Rothschild?"

"Yes."

"I found a folder that I believe belongs to you."

Quinn stood in the inventory room at Barnes and Noble with his hands in his pants pockets, looking relaxed. In another room, Kurt was talking to the manager and letting her know that all Barnes and Noble employees were going to be reinterviewed.

"Lucy Rothschild has been receiving letters," Quinn said after five minutes of small talk. Usually, he could warm up a suspect and get them to relax a little, but this one was so cold that it was as if she had an iceberg up her ass. "We believe the person sending the letters is responsible for the recent homicides we spoke to you about the last time we were here."

Jan Bright looked at Quinn, then shifted her gaze to the shelf of books over his left shoulder. She didn't speak.

"Do you know anything about those letters?"

She shook her head, and her long, wavy hair swayed across her shoulders.

"Would you be willing to come down to the station to be interviewed?"

"When?"

"Right now."

"I suppose." She glanced at Quinn, then returned her gaze somewhere behind him. "If I can help Lucy Rothschild, I'd be happy to do it. I'm very supportive of our local authors."

"I'm sure Ms. Rothschild will appreciate it."

The ride to the station took ten minutes, and once he had Jan in an interrogation room and the camera was rolling, he handed her a cup of water. Quinn smiled and once again endeavored to put her at ease. He asked her questions about the Women of Mystery and if she knew if any of them had a grudge against Lucy.

"Oh, no. They're very supportive." She polished off her water, and he offered to get her more. He picked up the cup by the handle and passed it to the fingerprint technician waiting outside the door. He left Jan alone for a few moments, and when he returned he had more water.

"Here you go," he said and set the glass on the table.

"I had a cup before." She met his gaze and held it.

"I accidentally dropped the cup."

She frowned as if she didn't believe him. Then she looked somewhere above his head. "I suppose you are having it analyzed for fingerprints."

She was smarter than he'd thought. But then, Breathless was no idiot. "Why do you say that?"

"Because I am in a police interrogation room and you just switched cups on me. I'm in a mystery writer's critique group, and I also read a lot of detective novels."

No use in bullshitting her. Her prints were either going to match or they weren't. "Where were you the night of April twenty-third?"

Her brows scrunched together. "The twenty-third?"

"During the day you were at the Women of Mystery meeting in Barnes and Noble. I saw you there. When you left, where did you go?"

"Some of the ladies and I went to Macaroni

Grill. I had a few too many glasses of wine and got a little loose. I called my oldest son, and he came and got me."

He couldn't imagine Jan Bright loose. She was so uptight she could crap diamonds. "How old is your son?"

"Sixteen."

The door opened a crack, and the lab technician stood on the other side shaking his head. *Damn.* For all her bizarre behavior, Jan Bright was not a murderer.

"Tell me about the people you work with. Any of them date customers they meet in the bookstore?"

"A few, maybe. I think it's disgusting."

"How about Cynthia Pool?"

Jan shook her head. "Oh, no. Cynthia would never date men who come into the bookstore."

Quinn looked down at the notebook on the table in front of him. His gaze skimmed the next few names on his list. "Why's that?"

"She thinks men are dirty."

Quinn looked up. " 'Dirty'? Are those your words or hers?"

"Hers."

"Do you think she hates men enough to kill them?"

"No. Cynthia is a very kind person. She had a really difficult marriage and divorce. Her husband was abusive and cheated on her, but she is not a murderess." Jan laughed, a kind of strained sound, before she added, "And I'm sure she would never write upsetting letters to Lucy Rothschild. She's her biggest fan."

Chapter 17

Hardlonman: Seeks Sunshine . . .

"I'm your biggest fan."

Lucy stood within the shade of Cynthia Pool's porch and smiled. "Thank you." Her gaze slid down Cynthia's Mickey Mouse T-shirt and black stretch pants to her empty hands. "I'm so glad you found the folder. I've been looking for it everywhere."

"Come on in and I'll get it."

Cynthia's house was near the Boise Towne Square Mall and about a mile from the police station and Quinn's office. On her drive across town, Lucy had called and left a message for him on his voice mail. She'd hoped he wouldn't be upset that she'd had to borrow his Jeep, and she hadn't wanted him to worry if he phoned home again and she wasn't there.

Lucy stepped from the bright afternoon sun and inside Cynthia's house. The curtains were all drawn, and Lucy reached for her sunglasses as she shut the door behind her. Shoving the glasses into the purse hanging from her shoulder, she glanced about the interior. A corner lamp lit the living room, and Lucy was instantly struck by the Disney knickknacks covering every conceivable space. Every character from Mickey Mouse to Cruella De Vil stared at her through thousands of painted eyes.

"Wow. I didn't know you were a collector."

"Oh yes. I've been collecting Disney memorabilia for most of my life. Ever since my father bought me my first Mickey gum ball machine. I still have it."

Lucy wasn't much of a collector and didn't know what to say except, "Wow."

Cynthia smiled and clasped her hands together. "Have a seat and I'll get that folder for you."

Lucy moved aside a pillow featuring Donald Duck in short pants and a sailor's cap and sat on the couch. She couldn't wait to get that folder and hopefully get back to work. But even more, she couldn't wait for Quinn to get home and tell her about the latest evidence.

Cynthia returned with the folder in hand, but instead of giving it to Lucy, she moved across the room and sat in a chair. "I'm so glad you're here. It will give us a chance to talk about writing."

Lucy groaned inwardly. "Can I help you with something?"

"Actually. No." She held up the folder. "I read your chapters."

Lucy felt her brows rise up her forehead. The only person she ever let read her rough drafts was Maddie. "Really?"

"Don't look so alarmed." Cynthia tilted her head to one side and smiled. "They were wonderful as always."

It was on the tip of Lucy's tongue to ask, *What the hell?* Instead she forced a smile and said, "Thank you."

"I really liked the part where the killer stalks her victims for a while after she meets them and before she kills them. It's kind of like a honeymoon period. That's a nice touch. Very thrilling."

Okay. So Cynthia had read a few rough chapters. She'd been curious and taken a peek. No big deal. Or rather, Lucy wasn't going to make a big deal out of it. "I'm glad you liked it."

"I noticed there were comments written in the margins. I hope you don't mind, but I took the liberty of adding my critique."

Oh my God. The blood drained from Lucy's head, and all she could manage was a stunned, "Oh."

"I noticed a few comma errors, and you really need to watch for run-on sentences."

Be nice, Lucy. "Well, it is a rough draft," she heard herself say. She stood. She needed to get out of there before she said something rude and condescending.

"That's why I didn't comment on your over-use of -ly adverbs. In the future, that might be something you should watch for, too."

Lucy moved across the room and stopped in front of the chair. "I'll remember to do that."

Cynthia remained seated, looking up at Lucy through light green eyes. "And whoever wrote on your manuscript doesn't know what she's talking about."

Now that took cojones. Cojones Lucy would never have thought Cynthia possessed. "I'll let Madeline Dupree know you think so."

"Madeline Dupree? The true crimes writer?" Cynthia's brow wrinkled as if she were confronting the impossible. Then she shook her head and said, "No. Madeline is wrong."

Lucy was going to have to tell Maddie and watch her laugh her behind off. In fact, they would probably laugh themselves into comas, but at the moment there was nothing funny about it. She lifted a hand for the folder. "Thank you for your input, but I really need to get home." She smiled but was afraid it fell a little flat. She wanted to get the hell out of Cynthia's house, and at this point she didn't particularly care if it showed. "Gotta book to write."

"Ocular petechiae are not always present at a death by suffocation."

Lucy knew that and was sure Maddie did, too.

"And finding willing victims is incredibly easy." Cynthia finally stood. "Even when the police are on television warning men not to engage in bondage."

"Umm, yeah." Lucy glanced down at the folder in Cynthia's hand and wondered if she should just count to three, grab it, and run.

"They do it anyway. Every Friday and Saturday night, they come in and circle the aisle like sharks. After a few of them swim by, you can see they're just bottom feeders."

Lucy looked up as her brain skidded to a halt. "What?"

"You ruined it," Cynthia said. "You ruined everything."

Lucy felt her scalp get tight. She must have heard wrong. "What are you talking about?"

"In the beginning, I wrote to you because I wanted you to know how good I am at what I do. Just like you're good at what you do. Your books have always brought such joy to my life, and I wanted to give you something as a thank you," she said, looking for all the world as if they were discussing which brand of laundry soap worked best on stains. But they weren't, and there was no doubt in Lucy's mind that she was staring at a serial killer. "At first I thought I might send you some cookie recipes, but I didn't know if you liked to bake."

"Baking's good." Lucy took a few steps back and slid her hand into her purse. There was also no doubt in her mind that Cynthia wasn't going to allow her to leave. She felt her wallet and cell phone, her sunglasses and lipstick.

"After I sent you the first letters, and you didn't take them to the police, I thought you understood that dirty men had to be punished. I was so happy because I'd felt so alone for so long. I thought we were friends. Then I saw you with him and I knew it was all a lie. You lied to me."

"I'm sorry you felt lied to," Lucy reasoned as she edged toward the door. She felt her business card case and a pack of Breath Savers.

"No, you're not. I will not be pacified."

"I'm sorry." Anger welled up within Lucy, and she had to fight an inner battle to keep a calm head. Cynthia didn't look like she had a weapon, and Lucy was so mad that she thought she could probably beat her ass if it came to a fight.

"It's not that easy." Cynthia moved with her and slid sideways to block the door. "From reading your books, I knew to wear gloves and wigs and to set up false clues. I wore red and turquoise to the motel on Chinden, parading around as a member of the Peacock Society because I knew someone would see me." She stuck her chin up and set the folder on a shelf, scattering Snow White and her Seven Dwarfs. "I was brilliant."

Lucy felt a pen, but it wasn't her stun pen. She stared into Cynthia's eyes, still calm as could be, and forced herself to say, "That is brilliant."

"I walked into those houses and that motel room and left nothing of myself behind. As if I'd never been there. I learned it all from you."

"My books are fiction." Lucy felt the cool metal of her brass knuckles and slid them on her fingers. "They aren't how-to manuals."

"You told me to kill those men. You can't walk away from me now. I'm not going to let you."

"You're going to get caught," Lucy said and wrapped her hand around her stun pen. She would have preferred the mace. "You left your fingerprints in Robert Patterson's car."

Cynthia's nostrils flared and her eyes narrowed. "That's another lie. I was careful not to touch anything." She reached behind her and pulled a kitchen knife out of somewhere.

Shit. "The police know I'm here," Lucy bluffed as she took several steps back, keeping her gaze on the five-inch blade.

Cynthia shook her head and took a step toward Lucy. "You might be a good writer, but you're a bad liar. I'm too smart for them and I'm too smart for you."

"You left a fingerprint on the envelope you dropped in my mailbox."

That stopped Cynthia, and again her brow creased as if she were forced to confront an impossibility. "Stop lying!" She lunged forward, and Lucy pulled her hand out of her purse and swung. Her brass knuckles connected with Cynthia's forehead, and the other woman went down. Lucy sprang for the door without waiting to see if she'd knocked Cynthia out, but she only managed a few steps before Cynthia grabbed her ankle. Lucy fell on her side.

Cynthia was on top of Lucy before she could move. "I thought I'd feel bad killing you."

Lucy rolled onto her back, jammed the stun pen into Cynthia's boney thigh, and pressed the button. Nothing happened. "Shit!"

"I'm not going to feel bad at all." Cynthia raised the knife, and Lucy's mind raced. She wasn't going to die like this. No way. She kept her eyes on the five-inch blade, waiting for Cynthia to bring the knife down. When she did, Lucy knew what she would do. She'd knock Cynthia's arm with one hand and swing with the other. The only problem was that she'd have to let Cynthia get close enough so that she could punch her brass knuckles in the psychotic bitch's nose.

"You're just like the others," Cynthia said. "They underestimated me, too."

From outside the house, Lucy heard a shout a split second before the door burst open and sunlight flooded the living room. Within the path of golden rays, Cynthia looked up as a 9mm bullet drilled the pale flesh between her shocked eyes. Her head fell back, and Lucy pushed and scrambled from beneath her. She got to her feet and stumbled into a solid chest and waiting arms. She didn't have to look up to know it was Quinn who held her so tight she could hardly breathe. "She was trying to kill me," she gasped.

"I know."

"I hit her with my brass knuckles."

"Good girl."

"My stun pen didn't work." She turned her head to look behind her shoulder, but Quinn's hand brought her face back around.

"You don't want to see that," he said.

Kurt Weber brushed past, and Lucy glanced over Quinn's shoulder to the white car on the lawn and the red light swirling from the visor.

"Is she dead?" Lucy asked.

"Before she hit the floor," Kurt answered.

Lucy started to shake. "She's the one, Qu-Quinn."

"I know." He kept one arm around her as he re-holstered his gun. "Are you hurt?"

She shook her head as her knees began to knock.

Quinn took Lucy outside into the afternoon sunlight and moved with her to the driver side of the cruiser. The door was open, and he reached inside for a handheld microphone clipped to the radio. He stood, stringing the black cord along with him. Lucy grasped the top of the door frame as he called in the code. She lifted her face to the warm sun, felt the rays on her cheeks and forehead, and shook as if she were coming apart. She couldn't seem to get enough air into her lungs. Her mouth was dry and her throat hurt. She was afraid she just might hyperventilate.

Quinn tossed the mic onto the seat and got a blanket out of the trunk. He wrapped it around Lucy, then looked into her eyes. "Lucy, you're going to pass out if you don't try to take calm breaths." He ran his hands over the wool blanket on her shoulders. "We don't have much time before this place is crawling with cops, so I need you awake and coherent for what I'm going to tell you."

Concentrating on Quinn's face, she managed a deep breath. "Okay."

"An ambulance is on the way to check you out. If you're transported to the hospital, you'll be interviewed there. If you're okay and don't need to be transported, someone is going to take you to the office and interview you. I don't know who, but you'll be all right. Tell them everything you know."

"You won't b-be there?" she stuttered. If she concentrated, she could control her breathing, but no amount of willpower could stop the shakes.

"I'll be there, but I can't be there with you. I'm sorry."

Sirens cut through the sound in the distance. "I'll get through it. Do you have some wa-water?"

He shook his head. "I'm sorry I wasn't here sooner." He rubbed the side of his face with one hand. "I was en route when I got your voice mail. I think my heart stopped and hasn't started up again."

"It never even o-occurred to me that Cynthia Pool was Breath—less." She hugged herself inside the blanket. "She was so . . . bl-bland. Even when she was telling me who she w-was and all the horrible things she'd d-done. She was just so calm about it. Well, until the moment she came completely un-unhinged."

The sirens got closer, and Quinn hugged her to his chest. "You're safe now," he said next to her ear. "It's over and you're going to be okay."

Three police cruisers and an unmarked car screeched to a halt in the middle of the street, their sirens blaring and lights flashing. A moment later, an ambulance pulled in front of Quinn's Jeep parked at the curb.

Lucy was quickly hustled to the ambulance, and it wasn't until she was sitting in back with a blood pressure cuff on her arm and an oxygen mask on her face that she calmed down enough for everything to soak in. She could be the one dead right now. Not Cynthia. Stabbed to death by a deranged psycho.

No. She'd fought back and couldn't see herself going out like that. She was the type of woman to suck out the poison, after all. When push came to shove, she could punch a shark. Oddly, she felt more alive than she ever had before.

She glanced out the back of the ambulance, at the uniformed cops and plainclothes detectives, at the yards of crime scene tape that kept the public away. She didn't see Quinn.

She looked for him as she was escorted by a Detective Gonzalez to an unmarked car. She finally caught a glimpse of him while she was being driven away. He was standing by his car, talking to Kurt Weber. He glanced up, and his gaze met hers for a split second before he turned away. In that second she saw a sort of bleak sadness in his eyes, and her heart ached to be with him.

At the police station, the interview took a little over two hours, and by the time it was over, Lucy was exhausted and numb. She just wanted to go home. To her home and snuggle with her cat. Tomorrow she would call her family and friends and tell them what happened. Tonight she just wanted her flannel pj's, a cup of decaf tea, and a shower. If she was going to wait for Quinn, she preferred to be at home. She had the detective take her to her house instead of Quinn's.

As Detective Gonzalez pulled to a stop in front of her house, she looked across the car at him and asked the question she wanted to know most. "Where is Detective McIntyre?"

"Right about now, he's probably chatting with the guys from internal affairs."

"Thanks for the ride," she said and got out of the unmarked car. She let herself into her house and locked the door behind her. Mr. Snookums walked from the kitchen and let out a series of loud yowls, welcoming her home. She set her purse on the coffee table and scooped up her cat. Then for some reason she could not explain, she sank to her knees and burst into tears.

"I was so scared, Snook," she sobbed. She didn't know how long she knelt there on the floor, holding her cat while he purred. But once her tears subsided into mild hiccups, she filled Snookums's dish with food and made her way to the shower. She stepped beneath the warm water and closed her eyes. She was stiff and sore and didn't know if it was because of her fight with Cynthia or the result of all that shaking she'd done.

After her shower, she dressed in her flannel pajamas with the pink dogs on them. She made herself some chicken noodle soup and waited for Quinn. At ten o'clock, she watched the news. The film footage showed the front of Cynthia's house and the cops working the scene. Lucy spotted Quinn leaning his behind against the back of his car, looking as grim as she remembered when she'd been taken from the scene.

Pending notification of relatives, Cynthia's name was not released, but the news did report that the police believed her to be the person responsible for the deaths of four Boise men.

Lucy was reported as "a local woman," but Quinn was named as the officer who'd shot and killed the suspect.

After the news, Lucy took her cat and went to her bedroom. Maybe Quinn was planning to wait until morning to come and see her. An adrenalin overload had left her physically exhausted and emotionally spent—except where Quinn was concerned. She wasn't too tired to think about him.

She turned on the light on her nightstand and crawled into bed. Quinn had said they would continue to see each other after everything was over. The longer she sat in her bed waiting, the more she began to wonder if he'd meant it. He hadn't said he loved her. Their lives had been in such chaos lately that maybe he would want a break. She certainly didn't want a break, but if he did, she'd give it to him.

She picked Clare's latest romance novel off the nightstand, but after reading the same page three times, she gave it up. At 1:30 a.m., the telephone by her bed rang, and she picked up.

"I'm standing outside," he said. "I would have rung the doorbell, but I didn't want to frighten you."

She smiled, and her heart beat heavy in her chest. "I'll be right there." She didn't bother with a robe or looking through the peephole.

She opened the door, and there he stood, on her porch, beneath the soft glow of a sixty-watt bulb. The light shone in his hair and poured over the shirt she'd buttoned that morning. Had it really only been that morning?

His soft "Hello" filled the space between them.

"Hello, Quinn."

He stared at her for several long moments then cleared his throat. "How are you?" he asked.

"I'm doing okay. The interview wasn't bad."

"Good."

He continued to stare at her, looking a little uncertain, and she asked, "Do you want to come in?"

"Not yet." He shook his head. "I'm on paid suspension for a while. So I have some time on my hands." He was standing so still she was starting to feel a little uncertain herself.

"How long are you on suspension?"

"I'm not quite sure. We can talk about what happened later, but right now I want to ask you something important."

"What?"

He swallowed. "Would you go out with me?"

"Where?"

"On a date."

She smiled, and her stomach got a little spongy. "Right now?"

"I thought we should get started dating to-night."

"Okay." She moved aside, and he stepped into the house. Lucy closed the door and leaned her back against it. "Should I change?"

He shook his head. "What you're wearing is fine. I thought we'd grab your cat and I'd take you two to my house."

"Snookie's invited, too?"

"Yeah. Him too. I want to take you home and make sure you're really okay, and I think you'll relax more with your bag of fur around."

"Maybe *I* want to take care of *you*."

"Then let's go. I think it's time Mr. Snookums met Millie."

She bit the side of her lip. "You said 'Mr. Snookums.'"

A slow grin turned up the corners of his lips. "I must be in love with you," he said. "The name of your cat doesn't shrivel my sac any-more."

Her chest got all achy and she blinked away the sudden stinging in her eyes. "Well, I must be in love with you, because hearing you talk about your shriveling sac doesn't make me want to stab my ears."

He chuckled. "I guess that didn't sound very romantic."

She shook her head, and her eyes filled with tears. "No. You probably won't find it on a Hall-mark card."

He took a step forward as the first tear slipped over her lashes. He brushed beneath her eyes. "I love you. When I entered that house and saw that woman on top of you, I came apart inside."

She kissed his palm. "I love you, Quinn. I fell in love with you when I thought you were a plumber grieving for your dead wife. I tried not to love you when I found out you were a cop and Millie was your dog and you lied to me. I felt so foolish. I thought since I'd fallen for you so fast, I could get over you fast, too. That was truly foolish, because I'd fallen too hard."

He wrapped his arms around her waist and looked at her through those intense brown eyes she loved. "I wanted you when I thought you'd pull a bag over my head and snuff out my life. I wanted you more than I've wanted anything. I love you more than I've loved any-one. You burst into my life like sunshine and made me see how lonely I was. I don't want to live that way anymore." He pressed a kiss to her hairline. "I will love you with my last breath."

Lucy swallowed as another tear slid down her face. "This is the best date I've ever had."

"No. This is just the first date." He slipped his hand down her back to her behind. "The best date is yet to come."

Epilogue

The best date fell on August eighteenth. The bride wore a tea-length gown made of white satin and lace, while the groom wore the requisite black-and-white tuxedo. She promised to love Quinn McIntyre through sickness and in health, when he was trying to be good but especially when he was bad. Quinn vowed to love and honor and take care of Lucy Rothschild and Mr. Snookums as long as they lived.

The couple was surrounded by family and friends and thousands of white and pink roses. In the months leading up to the wedding, Lucy's mother and three friends had helped her plan the big event. Except for complaining and protesting the choice of attendance dresses, Maddie, Adele, and Clare had been great help. But no matter how much they'd protested, Lucy had turned a deaf ear on her friends and ordered matching pink satin and tulle fluff for the occasion.

After a fierce game of rock paper scissors, Clare won the position of maid of honor during cocktail night. Clare being Clare, she took the honor seriously and threw herself into the job. She arranged a beautiful bachelorette party and offered Lucy her great-grandmother's Tiffany pearls to wear as "something borrowed." On the day of the wedding, she forgot the pearls and had to race home to get them. She made it back fifteen minutes before preceding her friends down the aisle. Ever the thoughtful and responsible person, she stood stiff and attentive as Lucy said her vows.

The wedding reception took place at the Double Tree Hotel next to the Boise River. The guests gorged themselves on beef tips, chicken cordon bleu, and, of all things, weenie mac—which the McIntyre clan scarfed like manna from heaven. As the bride and groom took to the floor for their first dance, Clare took up a position by the bar. No one noticed her drinking more than her usual two glasses of wine until she threw off her shoes and attacked the dance floor like she'd come down with boogie fever.

After bumping and grinding her way through "Hot Legs," Maddie and Adele pulled her aside and asked if she was okay. She simply gave them her perfect Clare smile and said, "I'm fine."

But an hour later she disappeared, and Maddie and Adele were forced to leave the reception in search of her. They walked down the long hall, passed a Dale Carnegie dinner, and peeked into a large room stuffed with men of all shapes and stripes. The room had a cash bar next to a stage with a spotlight and karaoke machine.

Looking for all the world like an escapee from prom night, Clare Wingate stood center stage in front of an Idaho Steelheads hockey banner. The usually reserved, dignified, and obsessively self-contained romance writer held a wineglass in one hand and a microphone in the other while she belted out a song about a skinny lad.

Maddie and Adele looked at each other, twin expressions of shock rounding their mouths.

"What the hell is she singing?" Adele asked as they returned their attention to the stage. "Did she just say 'big fat fanny'? That sounds like Queen."

"Oh my God." Maddie gasped. "I think it's Fat Bottomed Girls."

The men watching the performance whooped and hollered and cheered Clare on as she went into the chorus and begged them to take her home tonight.

Together Maddie and Adele shoved their way through the crowd, two spots of pink froufrou among a throng of muscle-bound men. Something was wrong. Something terrible had happened in Clare's world. Whatever it was, was bad. Real bad. Bad enough to force the wheels off her perfect pony cart.

And now an excerpt from Rachel Gibson's deliciously hilarious next novel, coming soon from Avon Books . . .

The first time Clare Wingate found herself in a strange bed, she'd been twenty-one, the victim of a bad break-up and too many Jell-O shooters. The love of her life had dumped her for a blonde English major with an impressive rack, and Clare had spent the night at Humpin' Hannah's, holding down the bar and nursing her broken heart. The next morning she woke up in a bed smelling of patchouli and staring up at a poster of Bob Marley, the guy snoring beside her drowning out the pounding in her head. She hadn't known where she was or the snoring guy's name. She hadn't stuck around long enough to ask.

Instead, she'd grabbed her clothes and bolted. As she drove home in the cruel light of morning, she told herself there were worse things in life than random sexual encounters. Bad things like flunking out of college or getting caught in a burning building. Yeah, those were bad. Still, a one-night stand wasn't for her. It had left her feeling disgusted and disturbed, but by the time she reached her apartment, she'd chalked the whole thing up to a learning experience. Something a lot of young women experienced. Something that was good to know for the future. Something she vowed would never happen again.

Clare had not been raised to reach for a shot glass and a warm body to make herself feel better. No, she'd been taught to curb her impulses and contain her feelings behind a perfect facade of warm smiles, kind words, and cashmere sweater sets. Wingates did not drink too much, talk too loud, or wear white shoes before Memorial Day. Ever. And they certainly didn't jump into bed with total strangers.

Unfortunately for Clare, she was a romantic and destined for more heartache. In the pit of her soul she believed in love at first sight, instant attraction, and happily-ever-after. As a result, it took a few more years of painful relationships and drunken nights for Clare to keep her vow. But by her mid-twenties, she had learned to control her romantic impulses. In the process, she also learned two valuable lessons: Don't give your heart too easily and avoid alcohol when your heart gets broken.

For the next five years, she lived by those lessons. Then she met Lonny, the love of her life. The man she adored the moment she saw him at a Degas exhibit. Lonny was romantic and thoughtful, and she didn't have to control her impulses with him. He remembered birthdays and special occasions and was brilliant with floral arrangements. Clare's mother loved him because he knew how to use a tomato server. Clare loved him because he understood her work and left her alone when she was under a deadline.

Lonny, the perfect man. Or so she thought, right up to the moment she came home unexpectedly from a friend's wedding and found him *flagrante delicto* and her life spun out of control. . . .

Before Clare opened her eyes, the morning after the wedding, a feeling of déjà vu crept into her pounding head, a feeling she hadn't experienced in years. She peeked through scratchy eyelids at morning light falling through a wide crack in the heavy curtains and spilling onto the gold and brown quilt weighing her down. Panic tightened her chest and she sat straight up, the sound of her pulse beating in her ears. The quilt slid down her bare breasts and fell to her lap. Within the lighter shadows of the room, her gaze took in the king-sized bed, hotel desk, armoire, and wall lamps. The pillow beside hers was empty, but the heavy silver wristwatch on the bedside table and the sound of running water behind the closed bathroom door told her she was not alone.

She pushed the quilt aside and practically jumped out of bed. To her absolute dismay, she wore nothing from the day before but a spritz of Estée Lauder and a pink thong. She scooped up the pink bustier at her feet and quickly glanced about for her dress. It was thrown across a small couch along with a pair of man's Levi's.

No doubt about it, she'd done it again, and like those few times years before, she couldn't remember the important details. She recalled dancing at her friend Lucy's wedding the night before and had a vague memory of singing "Fat Bottomed Girls." Somewhere. After that, nothing.

Clare wrapped the bustier around her middle and endeavored to fasten the hooks between her breasts as she moved across the room toward the couch. Halfway, she tripped over one pink satin pump. The only clear memory in her head was that of Lonny.

Her heart pinched, but she didn't have time to dwell on the pain and utter astonishment of what she'd seen. She would deal with Lonny, but first she had to get out of that hotel room.

With the corset hooked partway between her breasts, she reached for her pink fluff of a bridesmaid dress. She threw it over her head and battled yards of tulle, twisting and turning, fighting and pushing, until she had it down around her waist. Out of breath, she shoved her arms through the spaghetti straps and reached behind her for the zipper and little buttons on the back of the dress.

The water shut off and Clare's attention flew to the closed bathroom door. She grabbed her clutch purse off the couch, and in a rustle of tulle and satin, raced across the room. She held up the front of her dress with one hand and scooped up her shoes with the other. There were worse things than waking up in a strange hotel room, she told herself. Once she got home, she'd think of something worse, too.

"Leaving so soon, Claresta?" spoke a rough male voice only a few feet behind her.

Clare came to an abrupt halt against the closed door. No one called her Claresta but her mother. Her head whipped around, and her purse and shoes fell to the floor with a muffled thud. The strap of her dress slipped down her arm as her gaze landed on a white towel wrapped around the bottom row of hard six-pack abs. Her eyes moved up the dark line of hair on his stomach to the defined chest muscles covered in short wet curls. Clare swallowed and her gaze continued up his neck and strong jaw, past a pair of lips pulled into a wicked smile. Then she looked into deep green eyes. She knew those eyes.

He shoved one shoulder against the bathroom door frame and his smile got even more wicked. "You've grown since the last time I saw you naked."